Praise for the Award-Winning

LOVE MEDICINE

"A dazzling series of family portraits.... This novel is simply about the power of love." —*Chicago Tribune*

"A wonderfully fresh and accomplished writer." —*Newsday*

"*Love Medicine* is a first novel of extraordinary promise and real achievement.... Louise Erdrich writes with sureness and grace." —*Saturday Review*

"Lyrical and funny, mystical and down-to-earth, *Love Medicine* entrances." —*Christian Science Monitor*

"Miss Erdrich [presents] a variety of voices: each forceful in its own way, each adding a different dimension—cruel, somber, humorous—to what is cumulatively a wondrous prose song.... *Love Medicine* is finally about the enduring verities of loving and surviving, and these truths are revealed in a narrative that is an invigorating mixture of the cosmic and the tragic." —*New York Times Book Review*

"A great Native American novel." —*Life* magazine

"*Love Medicine* is a remarkable first novel that stares more boldly at many of the truths of Native American life in this country than any fiction I've read.... It is a deeply if ironically spiritual novel." —*Chicago Sun-Times*

"*Love Medicine*, as no book before it has done, depicts the Native American experience as it truly is, full of humor, strength, beauty, and survival." —Susan Shown Harjo, Executive Director, Congress of American Indians

"Like some of the other spectacular debut works of the last few years—Marilynne Robinson's *Housekeeping* and Joan Chase's *During the Reign of the Queen of Persia*—there is nothing apprentice, nothing 'promising' about *Love Medicine*. It is a book that satisfies the expectations it creates and then some." —*San Francisco Chronicle*

LOVE MEDICINE

A NOVEL BY

LOUISE ERDRICH

HarperPerennial
A Division of HarperCollins*Publishers*

This is a work of fiction. All characters, events and details of the setting are imaginary. Any resemblance to persons living or dead is purely coincidental.

Grateful acknowledgment is made to the editors of the following magazines in which sections of this novel first appeared:

The Atlantic Monthly: "Saint Marie"; *Chicago* magazine: Another version of "The World's Greatest Fisherman" and "Crown of Thorns"; *Kenyon Review*: "Lulu's Boys"; *Mississippi Valley Review*: "The Red Convertible"; *Ms.* magazine: "Flesh and Blood"; *The North American Review*: "Scales," which also appeared in *The Best American Short Stories of 1983*.

Holt, Rinehart & Winston edition published October 1984.
Bantam Windstone Trade edition published December 1985.
Bantam Trade edition published September 1989.

HarperCollins books may be purchased for educational, business, or sales promotional use. For information please write: Special Markets Department, HarperCollins Publishers, Inc., 10 East 53rd Street, New York, NY 10022.

First HarperPerennial edition published 1993.

ISBN 0-06-097581-4

93 94 95 96 97 FG 10 9 8 7 6 5 4 3 2 1

*Grandma Mary Gourneau, Gertrude Crow Dog,
and my brothers Mark, Louis, Terry (Amikoos), and
Raoul were some people especially in my
thoughts as I wrote this book. I could
not have written it this way without
Michael Dorris, who gave his own ideas,
experiences, and devoted attention
to the writing. This book is
dedicated to him because he is
so much a part of it.*

CONTENTS

LOVE MEDICINE

THE WORLD'S GREATEST FISHERMEN

(1981)

1.

The morning before Easter Sunday, June Kashpaw was walking down the clogged main street of oil boomtown Williston, North Dakota, killing time before the noon bus arrived that would take her home. She was a long-legged Chippewa woman, aged hard in every way except how she moved. Probably it was the way she moved, easy as a young girl on slim hard legs, that caught the eye of the man who rapped at her from inside the window of the Rigger Bar. He looked familiar, like a lot of people looked familiar to her. She had seen so many come and go. He hooked his arm, inviting her to enter, and she did so without hesitation, thinking only that she might tip down one or two with him and then get her bags to meet the bus. She wanted, at least, to see if she actually knew him. Even through the watery glass she could see that he wasn't all that old and that his chest was thickly padded in dark red nylon and expensive down.

There were cartons of colored eggs on the bar, each glowing like a jewel in its wad of cellophane. He was peeling one, sky blue as a robin's, palming it while he thumbed the peel aside, when she walked through the door. Although the day was overcast, the snow itself reflected such light that she was momentarily blinded. It was like going underwater. What she walked toward more than anything else was that blue egg in the white hand, a beacon in the murky air.

He ordered a beer for her, a Blue Ribbon, saying she deserved a prize for being the best thing he'd seen for days. He peeled an egg for her, a pink one, saying it matched her turtleneck. She told him it was no turtleneck. You called these things shells. He said he would peel that for her, too, if she wanted, then he grinned at the bartender and handed her the naked egg.

June's hand was colder from the outdoors than the egg, and so she had to let it sit in her fingers for a minute before it stopped feeling rubbery warm. Eating it, she found out how hungry she was. The last of the money that the man before this one had given her was spent for the ticket. She didn't know exactly when she'd eaten last. This man seemed impressed, when her egg was finished, and peeled her another one just like it. She ate the egg. Then another egg. The bartender looked at her. She shrugged and tapped out a long menthol cigarette from a white plastic case inscribed with her initials in golden letters. She took a breath of smoke then leaned toward her companion through the broken shells.

"What's happening?" she said. "Where's the party?"

Her hair was rolled carefully, sprayed for the bus trip, and her eyes were deeply watchful in their sea-blue flumes of shadow. She was deciding.

"I don't got much time until my bus. . . ." she said.

"Forget the bus!" He stood up and grabbed her arm. "We're gonna party. Hear? Who's stopping us? We're having a good time!"

She couldn't help notice, when he paid up, that he had a good-sized wad of money in a red rubber band like the kind that holds bananas together in the supermarket. That roll helped. But what was more important, she had a feeling. The eggs were lucky. And he had a good-natured slowness about him that seemed different. He could be different, she thought. The bus ticket would stay good, maybe forever. They weren't expecting her up home on the reservation. She didn't even have a man there, except the one she'd divorced. Gordie. If she got desperate he would still send her money. So she went on to the next bar with this man in the dark red vest. They drove down the street in his Silverado pickup. He was a mud engineer. Andy. She didn't tell him she'd known any mud engineers before or about that one she'd heard was killed by a pressurized hose. The hose had shot up into his stomach from underground.

The thought of that death, although she'd only been half acquainted with the man, always put a panicky, dry lump in her throat. It was the hose, she thought, snaking up suddenly from its unseen nest, the idea of that hose striking like a live thing, that was fearful. With one blast it had taken out his insides. And that too made her throat ache, although she'd heard of worse things. It was that moment, that one moment, of realizing you were totally empty. He must have felt that. Sometimes, alone in her room in the dark, she thought she knew what it might be like.

Later on, the dark falling around them at a noisy bar, she closed her eyes for a moment against the smoke and saw that hose pop suddenly through black earth with its killing breath.

"Ahhhhh," she said, surprised, almost in pain, "you got to be."

"I got to be what, honeysuckle?" He tightened his arm around her slim shoulders. They were sitting in a booth with a few others, drinking Angel Wings. Her mouth, the lipstick darkly blurred now, tipped unevenly toward his.

"You got to be different," she breathed.

It was later still that she felt so fragile. Walking toward the Ladies she was afraid to bump against anything because her skin felt hard and brittle, and she knew it was possible, in this condition, to fall apart at the slightest touch. She locked herself in the bathroom stall and remembered his hand, thumbing back the transparent skin and crackling blue peel. Her clothing itched. The pink shell was sweaty and hitched up too far under her arms but she couldn't take off her jacket, the white vinyl her son King had given her, because the pink top was ripped across the stomach. But as she sat there, something happened. All of a sudden she seemed to drift out of her clothes and skin with no help from anyone. Sitting, she leaned down and rested her forehead on the top of the metal toilet-roll dispenser. She felt that underneath it all her body was pure and naked—only the skins were stiff and old. Even if he was no different, she would get through this again.

Her purse dropped out of her hand, spilling. She sat up straight. The doorknob rolled out of her open purse and beneath the stall. She had to take that doorknob with her every time she left her room. There was no other way of locking the battered door. Now she picked up the knob and held it by the metal shank. The round grip was porcelain, smooth and white. Hard as stone. She put it in the deep pocket of her jacket and, holding it, walked back to the booth through the gathering crowd. Her room was locked. And she was ready for him now.

It was a relief when they finally stopped, far out of town on a county road. Even in the dark, when he turned his headlights off, the snow reflected enough light to see by. She let him wrestle with her clothing, but he worked so clumsily that she had to help him along. She rolled her top up carefully, still hiding the rip, and arched her back to let him undo her slacks. They were made of a stretch fabric that crackled with electricity and shed blue sparks when he pushed them down around her ankles. He knocked his hand against the heater's controls. She felt it open at her shoulder like a pair of jaws, blasting heat, and had the momentary and voluptuous sensation that she was lying stretched out before a great wide mouth. The breath swept across her throat, tightening her nipples. Then his vest plunged down against her, so slick and plush that it was like being rubbed by an enormous tongue. She couldn't get a handhold anywhere. And she felt herself slipping along the smooth plastic seat, slipping away, until she wedged the crown of her head against the driver's door.

"Oh God," he was moaning. "Oh God, Mary. Oh God, it's good."

He wasn't doing anything, just moving his hips on top of her, and at last his head fell heavily.

"Say there," she said, shaking him. "Andy?" She shook him harder. He didn't move or miss a beat in his deep breathing. She knew there wasn't any rousing him now, so she lay still, under the weight of him. She stayed quiet until she felt herself getting frail again. Her skin felt smooth and strange. And then she knew that if she lay there any longer she would crack wide open, not in one place but in many pieces that he would crush by moving in his sleep. She thought to pull herself back together. So she hooked an arm over her head and brought her elbow down slowly on the handle, releasing it. The door suddenly sprang wide.

June had wedged herself so tight against the door that when she sprang the latch she fell out. Into the cold. It was a shock like being born. But somehow she landed with her pants halfway up, as though she'd hoisted them in midair, and then she quickly did her bra, pulled her shell down, and reached back into the truck. Without groping she found her jacket and purse. By now it was unclear whether she was more drunk or more sober than she'd ever been in her life. She left the door open. The heater, set to an automatic temperature, yawned hoarsely behind her, and she heard it, or thought she did, for about a half mile down the road. Then she heard nothing but her own boots crunching ice. The snow was bright, giving back starlight. She concentrated on her feet, on steering them strictly down the packed wheel ruts.

She had walked far enough to see the dull orange glow, the canopy of low, lit clouds over Williston, when she decided to walk home instead of going back there. The wind was mild and wet. A Chinook wind, she told herself. She made a right turn off the road, walked up a drift frozen over a snow fence, and began to pick her way through the swirls of dead grass and icy crust of open ranchland. Her boots were thin. So she stepped on dry ground where she could and avoided the slush and rotten, gray banks. It was exactly as if she were walking back from a fiddle dance or a friend's house to Uncle Eli's warm, man-smelling kitchen. She crossed the wide fields swinging her purse, stepping carefully to keep her feet dry.

Even when it started to snow she did not lose her sense of direction. Her feet grew numb, but she did not worry about the distance. The heavy winds couldn't blow her off course. She continued. Even when her heart clenched and her skin turned crackling cold it didn't matter, because the pure and naked part of her went on.

The snow fell deeper that Easter than it had in forty years, but June walked over it like water and came home.

2.
ALBERTINE JOHNSON

After that false spring, when the storm blew in covering the state, all the snow melted off and it was summer. It was almost hot by the week after Easter, when I found out, in Mama's letter, that

June was gone—not only dead but suddenly buried, vanished off the land like that sudden snow.

Far from home, living in a white woman's basement, that letter made me feel buried, too. I opened the envelope and read the words. I was sitting at my linoleum table with my textbook spread out to the section on "Patient Abuse." There were two ways you could think of that title. One was obvious to a nursing student, and the other was obvious to a Kashpaw. Between my mother and myself the abuse was slow and tedious, requiring long periods of dormancy, living in the blood like hepatitis. When it broke out it was almost a relief.

"We knew you probably couldn't get away from your studies for the funeral," said the letter, "so we never bothered to call and disturb you."

She always used the royal *we*, to multiply the censure of what she said by invisible others.

I put down the letter and just stared, the way you do when you are hit by a bad thing you can do nothing about. At first it made me so angry that Mama hadn't called me for the funeral that I couldn't even feel the proper way for Aunt June. Then after a while I saw where I was staring—through the window at the level of the earth—and I thought of her.

I thought of June sitting tense in Grandma's kitchen, flicking an ash, jiggling a foot back and forth in a pointed shoe. Or smartly cracking her purse to buy each of us children a dairy cone. I thought of her brushing my hair past my waist, when it was that long, and saying that I had princess hair. Princess hair! I wore it unbraided after she said that, until it tangled so badly that Mama cut precious inches off.

June was raised by Great-uncle Eli, the old bachelor in the family. He'd taken her in when Grandma's sister died and June's no-good Morrissey father ran off to high-time it in the Cities. After she had grown up and looked around for a while, June decided on my uncle, Gordie Kashpaw, and married him even though they had to run away to do it. They were cousins, but almost like brother and sister. Grandma wouldn't let them in the house for a year, she was so angry. As it turned out, it was an off-and-on marriage anyway. Being so much alike they both liked to have their fun. Then, too, June had no patience with children. She wasn't much as a mother; everyone in the family said so, even Eli who was crazy about his little girl.

Whatever she lacked as a mother, June was a good aunt to have—the kind that spoiled you. She always kept an extra stick of Doublemint in her coat pocket. Her neck smelled fresh and sweet. She talked to me the way she talked to grown-up people and never told me to play outside when I wanted to sit at the edge of a conversation. She had been pretty. "Miss Indian America," Grandpa called her. She had stayed pretty even when things got so bad with Gordie that she ran off alone, "like a no-good Morrissey," people said, leaving her son King. She always planned that she would make it somewhere else first, then send for the boy. But everything she tried fell through.

When she was studying to be a beautician, I remember, word came that she had purposely burned an unruly customer's hair stiff green with chemicals. Other secretaries did not like her. She reported drunk for work in dime stores and swaggered out of restaurants where she'd waitressed a week, at the first wisecrack. Sometimes she came back to Gordie and they made the marriage work for a while longer. Then she would leave again. As time went by she broke, little by little, into someone whose shoulders sagged when she thought no one was looking, a woman with long ragged nails and hair always growing from its beauty-parlor cut. Her clothes were full of safety pins and hidden tears. I thought now that her one last try had been Williston, a town full of rich, single cowboy-rigger oil trash.

One type I know is boom trash, the ones that bat around the

state in big pickups that are loaded with options. I know, because I worked with them, that to these types an Indian woman's nothing but an easy night. I saw it laid out clear, as I sat there at my table, how down to the limit that kind of life would have gotten June. But what did I know, in fact, about the thing that happened?

I saw her laughing, so sharp and determined, her purse clutched tight at the bar, her perfect legs crossed.

"Probably drank too much," Mama wrote. She naturally hadn't thought well of June. "Probably wandered off too intoxicated to realize about the storm."

But June grew up on the plains. Even drunk she'd have known a storm was coming. She'd have known by the heaviness in the air, the smell in the clouds. She'd have gotten that animal sinking in her bones.

I sat there at my table, thinking about June. From time to time, overhead, I heard my landlady's vacuum cleaner. Through my window there wasn't much to see—dirt and dead snow and wheels rolling by in the street. It was warm but the grass was brown, except in lush patches over the underground steam pipes on the campus. I did something that day. I put on my coat and went walking down the street until I came to a big stretch of university lawn that was crossed by a steam-pipe line of grass—so bright your eyes ached—and even some dandelions. I walked out there and lay down on that patch of grass, above the ground, and I thought of Aunt June until I felt the right way for her.

I was so mad at my mother, Zelda, that I didn't write or call for almost two months. She should have gone up the nun's hill to the convent, like she wanted, instead of having me. But she had married Swede Johnson from off-reservation, and I'd arrived premature. He'd had the grace, at least, to go AWOL from army boot camp and never let his face be seen again. All I knew of him was pictures, blond, bleak, and doomed to wander, perhaps as much by Mama's rage at her downfall as by the uniform. I'd been the one who'd really blocked my mother's plans for being pure. I'd forced her to work for money, keeping books, instead of pursuing tasks that would bring divine glory on her head. I'd caused her to live in a trailer near Grandma so that there would be someone to care for me. Later on, I'd provided her with years of grinding grief. I had gone through a long phase of wickedness and run away. Yet now that I was on the straight and narrow, things were even worse between us.

After two months were gone and my classes were done, and although I still had not forgiven my mother, I decided to go home. I wasn't crazy about the thought of seeing her, but our relationship was like a file we sharpened on, and necessary in that way. So I threw a few books and some clothes in the backseat of my Mustang. It was the first car I'd ever owned, a dull black hard-driven car with rusted wheel wells, a stick shift, and a windshield wiper only on the passenger side.

All along the highway that early summer the land was beautiful. The sky stretched bare. Tattered silver windbreaks bounded flat, plowed fields that the government had paid to lie fallow. Everything else was dull tan—the dry ditches, the dying crops, the buildings of farms and towns. Rain would come just in time that year. Driving north, I could see the earth lifting. The wind was hot and smelled of tar and the moving dust.

At the end of the big farms and the blowing fields was the reservation. I always knew it was coming a long way off. Even in the distance you sense hills from their opposites—pits, dried sloughs, ditches of cattails, potholes. And then the water. There would be water in the hills when there wasn't any on the plains, because the hollows saved it, collected runoff from the low slopes, and the dense trees held it, too. I thought of water in the roots of trees, brown and bark smelling, cold.

The highway narrowed off and tangled, then turned to gravel with ruts, holes, and tall blue alfalfa bunching in the ditches. Small hills reared up. Dogs leaped from nowhere and ran themselves out fiercely. The dust hung thick.

My mother lives just on the very edge of the reservation with her new husband, Bjornson, who owns a solid wheat farm. She's lived there about a year. I grew up with her in an aqua-and-silver trailer, set next to the old house on the land my great-grandparents were allotted when the government decided to turn Indians into farmers.

The policy of allotment was a joke. As I was driving toward the land, looking around, I saw as usual how much of the reservation was sold to whites and lost forever. Just three miles, and I was driving down the rutted dirt road, home.

The main house, where all of my aunts and uncles grew up, is one big square room with a cooking shack tacked onto it. The house is a light peeling lavender now, the color of a pale petunia, but it was never painted while I lived there. My mother had it painted for Grandma as an anniversary present one year. Soon after the paint job the two old ones moved into town where things were livelier and they didn't have to drive so far to church. Luckily, as it happened, the color suited my Aunt Aurelia, because she moved into the house and has taken care of it since.

Driving up to the house I saw that her brown car and my mother's creamy yellow one were parked in the yard. I got out. They were indoors, baking. I heard their voices from the steps and smelled the rich and browning piecrusts. But when I walked into the dim, warm kitchen they hardly acknowledged me, they were so involved in their talk.

"She sure *was* good-looking," Aurelia argued, hands buried in a dishpan of potato salad.

"Some people use spoons to mix." My mother held out a heavy tin one from the drawer and screwed her lips up like a coin purse to kiss me. She lit her eyes and widened them. "I was only saying she had seen a few hard times, and there was bruises. . . ."

"Wasn't either. You never saw her." Aurelia was plump, a "looker." She waved my mother's spoon off with a caked hand. "In fact, did anybody see her? Nobody saw her. Nobody knows for sure what happened, so who's to squawk about bruises and so on . . . nobody saw her."

"Well I heard," said Mama, "I heard she was with a man and he dumped her off."

I sat down, dipped a slice of apple in the bowl of sugar-cinnamon topping, and ate it. They were talking about June.

"Heard nothing," Aurelia snapped. "Don't trust nothing you don't see with your own eyes. June was all packed up and ready to come home. They found her bags when they busted in her room. She walked out there because"—Aurelia foundered, then her voice strengthened—"what did she have to come home to after all? Nothing!"

"Nothing?" said Mama piercingly. "Nothing to come home to?" She gave me a short glance full of meaning. I had, after all, come home, even if husbandless, childless, driving a fall-apart car. I looked away from her. She puffed her cheeks out in concentration, patting and crimping the edges of the pies. They were beautiful pies—rhubarb, wild Juneberry, apple, and gooseberry, all fruits preserved by Grandma Kashpaw or my mother or Aurelia.

"I suppose you washed your hands before you put them in that salad," she said to Aurelia.

Aurelia squeezed her face into crescents of patient exasperation. "Now Zelda," she said, "your girl's going to think you still treat me like your baby sister."

"Well you are aren't you? Can't change that."

"I'm back," I said.

They looked at me as if I had, at that very moment, walked in the door.

"Albertine's home," observed Aurelia. "My hands are full or I'd hug you."

"Here," said Mama, setting down a jar of pickles near me. "Aren't you dressed nice. Did you get your top in Fargo? Was the drive good?"

I said yes.

"Dice these pickles up." She handed me a bowl and knife.

"June went after Gordie like he didn't have no choice," my mother decided now. "She could at least have kept him happy once she got him in her clutch! It's just clear how Gordie loved her, only now he takes it out in liquor. He's always over at Eli's house trying to get Eli to join him for a toot. You know, after the way June treated him, I don't know why Gordie didn't just let her go to ruin."

"Well, she couldn't get much more ruined than dead," Aurelia said.

The odd thing about the two—Mama with her careful permanent and rough gray face, Aurelia with her flat blue-black ponytail, high rounded cheeks, tight jeans, and frilled rodeo shirts—was the differenter they acted the more alike they showed themselves. They clung to their rock-bottom opinions. They were so strong in their beliefs that there came a time when it hardly mattered what exactly those beliefs were; they all fused into a single stubbornness.

Mama gave up discussing June after Aurelia's observation and began on me.

"Have you met any marriageable boys in Fargo yet?" Her flat gray thumbs pursued each other around and around in circles, leaving perfect squeezed scallops. By marriageable I knew she meant Catholic. I shook my head no.

"At this rate I'll be too old and stiff to take care of my own grandchildren," Mama said. Then she smiled and shrugged her shoulders lightly. "My girl's choosy like me," she said. "Can't be too choosy."

Aurelia snorted, but contained her remark, which probably would have referred to Mama's first husband.

"Albertine's got time," Aurelia answered for me. "What's her rush? Believe me"—she addressed me now with mock serious vigor—"marriage is not the answer to it all. I tried it enough myself."

"I'm not interested anyway," I let them know. "I've got other things to do."

"Oh my," said Mama, "are you going to be a career girl?"

She froze with her hands in the air, seemingly paralyzed by the idea.

"*You* were a career girl," I accused her. I handed her the pickles, all diced into little cubes. Mama had kept books for the priests and nuns up at Sacred Heart since I could remember. She ignored me, however, and began to poke wheels of fork marks in the tops of the pies. Aurelia mixed. I watched my mother's hands precisely stabbing. After a while we heard the car from the main road as it slowed for the turn. It would be June's son, King, his wife, Lynette, and King Junior. They drove up to the front steps in their brand-new sportscar. King Junior was bundled in the front seat and both Grandma and Grandpa Kashpaw were stuffed, incredibly, into the tiny backseat.

"There's that white girl." Mama peeked out the window.

"Oh, for gosh sakes." Aurelia gave her heady snort again, and this time did not hold her tongue. "What about your Swedish boy?"

"Learnt my lesson," Mama wiped firmly around the edges of Aurelia's dishpan. "Never marry a Swedish is my rule."

Grandma Kashpaw's rolled-down nylons and brown support shoes appeared first, then her head in its iron-gray pageboy. Last of all the entire rest of her squeezed through the door, swathed in acres of tiny black sprigged flowers. When I was very young, she always seemed the same size to me as the rock cairns commemorating Indian defeats around here. But every time I saw her now I realized that she wasn't so large, it was just that her figure was weathered and massive as a statue roughed out in rock. She never changed much, at least not so much as Grandpa. Since I'd left home, gone to school, he'd turned into an old man. Age had come upon him suddenly, like a storm in fall, shaking yellow leaves down overnight, and now his winter, deep and quiet, was on him. As Grandma shook out her dress and pulled bundles through the back window, Grandpa sat quietly in the car. He hadn't noticed that it had stopped. "Why don't you tell him it stopped," Grandma called to Lynette.

Lynette was changing King Junior's diaper in the front seat. She generally used paper diapers with stick-'em tabs at her home in the Cities, but since she'd been here my mother had shamed her into using washable cloth diapers and sharp pins. The baby wiggled and fought her hands.

"You hear?" King, already out of the car and nervously examining his tires, stuck his head back in the driver's side window and barked at Lynette. "She was calling you. My father's mother. She just told you to do something."

Lynette's face, stained and swollen, bloomed over the wheel. She was a dirty blond, with little patches of hair that were bleached and torn. "Yes I heard," she hissed through the safety pins in her teeth. "You tell him."

Jerking the baby up, ankles pinned in the forks of her fingers, she repositioned the triangle of cloth under his bottom.

"Grandma told you to tell him." King leaned farther in. He had his mother's long slim legs, and I remembered all at once, seeing him bend all the way into the car, June bending that way too. Me behind her. She had pushed a rowboat off the gravel beach of some lake we'd all gone to visit together. I had jumped into the rowboat with her. She had one son at the time and didn't think that she would ever have another child. So she spoiled me and told me everything, believing I did not understand. She told me things you'd only tell another woman, full grown, and I had adored her wildly for these adult confidences, for her wreaths of blue smoke, for the figure she cut. I had adored her into telling me everything she needed to tell, and it was true, I hadn't understood the words at the time. But she hadn't counted on my memory. Those words stayed with me.

And even now, King was saying something to Lynette that had such an odd dreaming ring to it I almost heard it spoken out in June's voice.

June had said, "He used the flat of his hand. He hit me good." And now I heard her son say, " . . . flat of my hand . . . but good . . ."

Lynette rolled out the door, shedding cloth and pins, packing the bare-bottomed child on her hip, and I couldn't tell what had happened.

Grandpa hadn't noticed, whatever it was. He turned to the open door and stared at his house.

"This reminds me of something," he said.

"Well, it should. It's your house!" Mama barreled out the door, grabbed both of his hands, and pulled him out of the little backseat.

"You have your granddaughter here, Daddy!" Zelda shrieked carefully into Grandpa's face. "Zelda's daughter. She came all the way up here to visit from school."

"Zelda . . . born September fourteenth, nineteen forty-one . . ."

"No, Daddy. This here is my daughter, Albertine. Your granddaughter."

I took his hand.

Dates, numbers, figures stuck with Grandpa since he strayed, and not the tiring collection of his spawn, proliferating beyond those numbers into nowhere. He took my hand and went along, trusting me whoever I was.

Whenever he came out to the home place now, Grandpa had

to get reacquainted with the yard of stunted oaks, marigold beds, the rusted car that had been his children's playhouse and mine, the few hills of potatoes and stalks of rhubarb that Aurelia still grew. She worked nights, managing a bar called the So Long, and couldn't keep the place as nicely as Grandpa always had. Walking him slowly across the lawn, I sidestepped prickers. The hollyhocks were choked with pigweed, and the stones that lined the driveway, always painted white or blue, were flaking back to gray. So was the flat boulder under the clothesline—once my favorite cool place to sit doing nothing while the clothes dried, hiding me.

This land had been allotted to Grandpa's mother, old Rushes Bear, who had married the original Kashpaw. When allotments were handed out all of her eighteen children except the youngest—twins, Nector and Eli—had been old enough to register for their own. But because there was no room for them in the North Dakota wheatlands, most were deeded less-desirable parcels far off, in Montana, and had to move there or sell. The older children left, but the twin brothers still lived on opposite ends of Rushes Bear's land.

She had let the government put Nector in school, but hidden Eli, the one she couldn't part with, in the root cellar dug beneath her floor. In that way she gained a son on either side of the line. Nector came home from boarding school knowing white reading and writing, while Eli knew the woods. Now, these many years later, hard to tell why or how, my Great-uncle Eli was still sharp, while Grandpa's mind had left us, gone wary and wild. When I walked with him I could feel how strange it was. His thoughts swam between us, hidden under rocks, disappearing in weeds, and I was fishing for them, dangling my own words like baits and lures.

I wanted him to tell me about things that happened before my time, things I'd been too young to understand. The politics for instance. What had gone on? He'd been an astute political dealer, people said, horse-trading with the government for bits and shreds. Somehow he'd gotten a school built, a factory too, and he'd kept the land from losing its special Indian status under that policy called termination. I wanted to know it all. I kept asking questions as we walked along, as if he'd take the hook by miracle and blurt the memory out right there.

"Remember how you testified . . . ? What was it like . . . the old schools . . . Washington . . . ?"

Elusive, pregnant with history, his thoughts finned off and vanished. The same color as water. Grandpa shook his head, remembering dates with no events to go with them, names without faces, things that happened out of place and time. Or at least it seemed that way to me. Grandma and the others were always hushing up the wild things he said or talking loudly over them. Maybe they were bored with his craziness, and then again maybe his mind blurted secrets from the past. If the last was true, sometimes I thought I understood.

Perhaps his loss of memory was a protection from the past, absolving him of whatever had happened. He had lived hard in his time. But he smiled into the air and lived calmly now, without guilt or desolation. When he thought of June, for instance, she was a young girl who fed him black plums. That was the way she would always be for him. His great-grandson, King Junior, was happy because he hadn't yet acquired a memory, while perhaps Grandpa's happiness was in losing his.

We walked back down the driveway, along the flaking rocks. "He likes that busted lawn chair," Grandma hollered now, leaning out the door. "Set him there awhile."

"Want me to get you a plate from the kitchen?" I asked Grandpa. "Some bread and butter?"

But he was looking at the collapsed heap anxiously and did not answer.

I pulled the frayed, woven plastic and aluminum into the shape of a chair, he settled into it, and I left him counting something under his breath. Clouds. Trees. All the blades of grass.

I went inside. Grandma was unlocking her expensive canned ham. She patted it before putting it in the oven and closed the door carefully.

"She's not used to buying this much meat," Zelda said. "Remember we used to trade for it?"

"Or slaughter our own." Aurelia blew a round gray cloud of Winston smoke across the table.

"Pew," said Zelda. "Put the top on the butter." She flapped her hand in front of her nose. "You know, Mama, I bet this makes you wish it was like it used to be. All us kids in the kitchen again."

"Oh, I never had no trouble with kids," Grandma wiped each finger on a dishrag. "Except for once in a while."

"Except for when?" asked Aurelia.

"Well now . . ." Grandma lowered herself onto a long-legged stool, waving Zelda's more substantial chair away. Grandma liked to balance on that stool like an oracle on her tripod. "There was that time someone tried to hang their little cousin," she declared, and then stopped short.

The two aunts gave her quick, unbelieving looks. Then they were both uneasily silent, neither of them willing to take up the slack and tell the story I knew was about June. I'd heard Aurelia and my mother laughing and accusing each other of the hanging in times past, when it had been only a family story and not the private trigger of special guilts. They looked at me, wondering if I knew about the hanging, but neither would open her lips to ask. So I said I'd heard June herself tell it.

"That's right," Aurelia jumped in. "June told it herself. If she minded being hung, well she never let on!"

"Ha," Zelda said. "If she minded! You were playing cowboys.

You and Gordie had her up on a box, the rope looped over a branch, tied on her neck, very accurate. If she minded! I had to rescue her myself!"

"Oh, I know," Aurelia admitted. "But we saw it in the movies. Kids imitate them, you know. We got notorious after that, me and Gordie. Remember Zelda? How you came screaming in the house for Mama?"

"Mama! Mama!" Grandma yodeled an imitation of her daughter. "They're hanging June!"

"You came running out there, Mama!" Zelda was swept into the story. "I didn't know you could run so fast."

"We had that rope around her neck and looped over the tree, and poor June was shaking, she was so scared. But we *never* would have done it."

"Yes!" asserted Zelda. "You meant to!"

"Oh, I licked you two good," Grandma remembered. "Aurelia, you and Gordie both."

"And then you took little June in the house. . . ." Zelda broke down suddenly.

Aurelia put her hands to her face. Then, behind her fingers, she made a harsh sound in her throat. "Oh Mama, we could have killed her. . . ."

Zelda crushed her mouth behind a fist.

"But then she came in the house. You wiped her face off," Aurelia remembered. "That June. She yelled at me. 'I wasn't scared! You damn chicken!' "

And then Aurelia started giggling behind her hands. Zelda put her fist down on the table with surprising force.

"Damn chicken!" said Zelda.

"You had to lick her too." Aurelia laughed, wiping her eyes.

"For saying hell and damn . . ." Grandma nearly lost her balance.

"Then she got madder yet. . . ." I said.

"That's right!" Now Grandma's chin was pulled up to hold her laughter back. "She called me a damn old chicken. Right there! A damn old hen!"

Then they were laughing out loud in brays and whoops, sopping tears in their aprons and sleeves, waving their hands helplessly.

Outside, King's engine revved grandly, and a trickle of music started up.

"He's got a tape deck in that car," Mama said, patting her heart, her hair, composing herself quickly. "I suppose that costed extra money."

The sisters sniffed, fished Kleenex from their sleeves, glanced pensively at one another, and put the story to rest.

"King wants to go off after they eat and find Gordie," Zelda thought out loud. "He at Eli's place? It's way out in the bush."

"They expect to get Uncle Eli to ride in that new car," said Grandma in strictly measured, knowing tones.

"Eli won't ride in it." Aurelia lighted a cigarette. Her head shook back and forth in scarves of smoke. And for once Zelda's head shook, too, in agreement, and then Grandma's as well. She rose, pushing her soft wide arms down on the table.

"Why not?" I had to know. "Why won't Eli ride in that car?"

"Albertine don't know about that insurance." Aurelia pointed at me with her chin. So Zelda turned to me and spoke in her low, prim, explaining voice.

"It was natural causes, see. They had a ruling which decided that. So June's insurance came through, and all of that money went to King because he's oldest, legal. He took some insurance and first bought her a big pink gravestone that they put up on the hill." She paused. "Mama, we going up there to visit? I didn't see that gravestone yet."

Grandma was at the stove, bending laboriously to check the roast ham, and she ignored us.

"Just recently he bought this new car," Zelda went on, "with the rest of that money. It has a tape deck and all the furnishings. Eli doesn't like it, or so I heard. That car reminds him of his girl. You know Eli raised June like his own daughter when her mother passed away and nobody else would take her."

"King got that damn old money," Grandma said loud and sudden, "not because he was oldest. June named him for the money because he took after her the most."

So the insurance explained the car. More than that it explained why everyone treated the car with special care. Because it was new, I had thought. Still, I had noticed all along that nobody seemed proud of it except for King and Lynette. Nobody leaned against the shiny blue fenders, rested elbows on the hood, or set paper plates there while they ate. Aurelia didn't even want to hear King's tapes. It was as if the car was wired up to something. As if it might give off a shock when touched. Later, when Gordie came, he brushed the glazed chrome and gently tapped the tires with his toes. He would not go riding in it, either, even though King urged his father to experience how smooth it ran.

We heard the car move off, wheels crackling in the gravel and cinders. Then it was quiet for a long time again.

Grandma was dozing in the next room, and I had taken the last pie from the oven. Aurelia's new green Sears dryer was still huffing away in the tacked-on addition that held toilet, laundry, kitchen sink. The plumbing, only two years old, was hooked up to one side of the house. The top of the washer and dryer were covered with clean towels, and all the pies had been set there to cool.

"Well, where *are* they?" wondered Zelda now. "Joyriding?"

"That white girl," Mama went on, "she's built like a truck-driver. She won't keep King long. Lucky you're slim, Albertine."

"*Jeez,* Zelda!" Aurelia came in from the next room. "Why

can't you just leave it be? So she's white. What about the Swede? How do you think Albertine feels hearing you talk like this when her Dad was white?"

"I feel fine," I said. "I never knew him."

I understood what Aurelia meant though—I was light, clearly a breed.

"My girl's an *Indian*," Zelda emphasized. "I raised her an Indian, and that's what she is."

"Never said no different." Aurelia grinned, not the least put out, hitting me with her elbow. "She's lots better looking than most Kashpaws."

By the time King and Lynette finally came home it was near dusk and we had already moved Grandpa into the house and laid his supper out.

Lynette sat down next to Grandpa, with King Junior in her lap. She began to feed her son ground liver from a little jar. The baby tried to slap his hands together on the spoon each time it was lowered to his mouth. Every time he managed to grasp the spoon, it jerked out of his hands and came down with more liver. Lynette was weary, eyes watery and red. Her tan hair, caught in a stiff club, looked as though it had been used to drag her here.

"You don't got any children, do you Albertine," she said, holding the spoon away, licking it herself, making a disgusted face. "So you wouldn't know how they just can't leave anything alone!"

"She's not married yet," said Zelda, dangling a bright plastic bundle of keys down to the baby. "She thinks she'll wait for her baby until *after* she's married. Oochy koo," she crooned when King Junior focused and, in an effort of intense delight, pulled the keys down to himself.

Lynette bolted up, shook the keys roughly from his grasp, and snatched him into the next room. He gave a short outraged wail, then fell silent, and after a while Lynette emerged, pulling down her blouse. The cloth was a dark violet bruised color.

"Thought you wanted to see the gravestone," Aurelia quickly remembered, addressing Zelda. "You better get going before it's dark out. Tell King you want him to take you up there."

"I suppose," said Mama, turning to me, "Aurelia didn't see those two cases of stinking beer in their backseat. I'm not driving anywhere with a drunk."

"He's not a drunk!" Lynette wailed in sudden passion. "But I'd drink a few beers too if I had to be in this family."

Then she whirled and ran outside.

King was slumped morosely in the front seat of the car, a beer clenched between his thighs. He drummed his knuckles to the Oak Ridge Boys.

"I don't even let her drive it," he said when I asked. He nodded toward Lynette, who was strolling down the driveway ditch, adding to a straggly bunch of prairie roses. I saw her bend over, tearing at a tough branch.

"She's going to hurt her hands."

"Oh, she don't know nothing," said King. "She never been to school. I seen a little of the world when I was in the service. You get my picture?"

He'd sent a photo of himself in the uniform. I'd been surprised when I saw the picture because I'd realized then that my rough boy cousin had developed hard cheekbones and a movie-star gaze. Now, brooding under the bill of his blue hat, he turned that moody stare through the windshield and shook his head at his wife. "She don't fit in," he said.

"She's fine," I surprised myself by saying. "Just give her a chance."

"Chance." King tipped his beer up. "Chance. She took her chance when she married me. She knew which one I took after."

Then as if on cue, the one whom King did not take after drove into the yard with a squealing flourish, laying hard on his horn.

Uncle Gordie Kashpaw was considered good-looking, although not in the same way as his son King. Gordie had a dark, round, eager face, creased and puckered from being stitched up after an accident. There was always a compelling pleasantness about him. In some curious way all the stitches and folds had contributed to, rather than detracted from, his looks. His face was like something valuable that was broken and put carefully back together. And all the more lovable for the care taken. In the throes of drunken inspiration now, he drove twice around the yard before his old Chevy chugged to a halt. Uncle Eli got out.

"Well it's still standing up," Eli said to the house. "And so am I. But you," he addressed Gordie, "ain't."

It was true, Gordie's feet were giving him trouble. They caught on things as he groped on the hood and pulled himself out. The rubber foot mat, the fenders, then the little ruts and stones as he clambered toward the front steps.

"Zelda's in there," King shouted a warning, "and Grandma too!"

Gordie sat down on the steps to collect his wits before tangling with them.

Inside, Uncle Eli sat down next to his twin. They didn't look much alike anymore, for Eli had wizened and toughened while Grandpa was larger, softer, even paler than his brother. They happened to be dressed the same though, in work pants and jackets, except that Grandpa's outfit was navy blue and Eli's was olive green. Eli wore a stained, crumpled cap that seemed so much a part of his head not even Zelda thought of asking him to remove it. He nodded at Grandpa and grinned at the food; he had a huge toothless smile that took up his entire face.

"Here's my Uncle Eli," Aurelia said, putting down the plate of food for him. "Here's my favorite uncle. See, Daddy? Uncle Eli's here. Your brother."

"Oh Eli," said Grandpa, extending his hand. Grandpa grinned and nodded at his brother, but said nothing more until Eli started to eat.

"I don't eat very much anymore. I'm getting so old," Eli was telling us.

"You're eating a lot," Grandpa pointed out. "Is there going to be anything left?"

"You ate already," said Grandma. "Now sit still and visit with your brother." She fussed a little over Eli. "Don't mind him. Eat enough. You're getting thin."

"It's too late," said Grandpa. "He's eating everything."

He closely watched each bite his brother took. Eli wasn't bothered in the least. Indeed, he openly enjoyed his food for Grandpa.

"Oh, for heavensake." Zelda sighed. "Are we ever getting out of here? Aurelia. Why don't you take separate cars and drive us in? It's too late to see that gravestone now anyway, but I'm darned if I'm going to be here once they start on those cases in the back of June's car."

"Put the laundry out," said Grandma; "I'm ready enough. And you, Albertine"—she nodded at me as they walked out the door—"they can eat all they want. Just as long as they save the pies. Them pies are made special for tomorrow."

"Sure you don't want to come along with us now?" asked Mama.

"She's young," said Aurelia. "Besides, she's got to keep those drunken men from eating on those pies."

She bent close to me. Her breath was sweet with cake frosting, stale with cigarettes.

"I'll be back later on," she whispered. "I got to go see a friend."

Then she winked at me exactly the way June had winked about

her secret friends. One eye shut, the lips pushed into a small self-deprecating question mark.

Grandpa eased himself into the backseat and sat as instructed, arms spread to either side, holding down the piles of folded laundry.

"They can eat!" Grandma yelled once more. "But save them pies!"

She bucked forward when Aurelia's car lurched over the hole in the drive, and then they shot over the hill.

3.

"Say Albertine, did you know your Uncle Eli is the last man on the reservation that could snare himself a deer?"

Gordie unlatched a beer, pushed it across the kitchen table to me. We were still at that table, only now the plates, dishpans of salad, and pies were cleared away for ashtrays, beer, packs of cigarettes.

Although Aurelia kept the house now, it was like communal property for the Kashpaws. There was always someone camped out or sleeping on her fold-up cots.

One more of us had arrived by this time. That was Lipsha Morrissey, who had been taken in by Grandma and always lived with us. Lipsha sat down, with a beer in his hand like everyone, and looked at the floor. He was more a listener than a talker, a shy one with a wide, sweet, intelligent face. He had long eyelashes. "Girl-eyes," King used to tease him. King had beat up Lipsha so many times when we were young that Grandma wouldn't let them play on the same side of the yard. They still avoided each other. Even now, in the small kitchen, they never met each other's eyes or said hello.

I had to wonder, as I always did, how much they knew.

One secret I had learned from sitting quietly around the aunts, from gathering shreds of talk before they remembered me, was Lipsha's secret, or half of it at least. I knew who his mother was. And because I knew his mother I knew the reason he and King never got along. They were half brothers. Lipsha was June's boy, born in one of those years she left Gordie. Once you knew about her, and looked at him, it was easy to tell. He had her flat pretty features and slim grace, only on him these things had never even begun to harden.

Right now he looked anxious and bit his lips. The men were still talking about the animals they had killed.

"I had to save on my shells," said Eli thoughtfully; "they was dear."

"Only real old-time Indians know deer good enough to snare," Gordie said to us. "Your Uncle Eli's a real old-timer."

"You remember the first thing you ever got?" Eli asked King.

King looked down at his beer, then gave me a proud, sly, sideways glance. "A gook," he said. "I was in the Marines."

Lipsha kicked the leg of my chair. King made much of having been in combat but was always vague on exactly where and when he had seen action.

"Skunk," Gordie raised his voice. "King got himself a skunk when he was ten."

"Did you ever eat a skunk?" Eli asked me.

"It's like a piece of cold chicken," I ventured. Eli and Gordie agreed with solemn grins.

"How do you skin your skunk?" Eli asked King.

King tipped his hat down, shading his eyes from the fluorescent kitchen ring. A blue-and-white patch had been stitched on the front of his hat. "World's Greatest Fisherman," it said. King put his hands up in winning ignorance.

"How do *you* skin your skunk?" he asked Eli.

"You got to take the glands off first," Eli explained carefully, pointing at different parts of his body. "Here, here, here. Then you skin it just like anything else. You have to boil it in three waters."

"Then you honestly *eat* it?" said Lynette. She had come into the room with a fresh beer and was now biting contentedly on a frayed endstring of hair fallen from her ponytail.

Eli sat up straight and tilted his little green hat back.

"You picky too? Like Zelda! One time she came over to visit me with her first husband, that Swede Johnson. It was around dinnertime. I had a skunk dressed out, and so I fed it to them. Ooooooh when she found out what she ate she was mad at me, boy. 'Skunk!' she says. 'How disgusting! You old guys will eat anything!' "

Lipsha laughed.

"I'd eat it," Lynette declared to him, flipping her hair back with a chopping motion of her hand. "I'd eat it just like that."

"You'd eat shit," said King.

I stared at his clean profile. He was staring across the table at Lipsha, who suddenly got up from his chair and walked out the door. The screen door slammed. King's lip curled down in some imitation of soap-opera bravado, but his chin trembled. I saw him clench his jaw and then felt a kind of wet blanket sadness coming down over us all. I wanted to follow Lipsha. I knew where he had gone. But I didn't leave. Lynette shrugged brightly and brushed away King's remark. But it stayed at the table, as if it had opened a door on something—some sad, ugly scene we could not help but enter. I took a long drink and leaned toward Uncle Eli.

"A fox sleeps hard, eh?" said Eli after a few moments.

King leaned forward and pulled his hat still lower so it seemed to rest on his nose.

"I've shot a fox sleeping before," he said. "You know that little black hole underneath a fox's tail? I shot right through there. I was using a bow and my arrow went right through that fox. It got stiff. It went straight through the air. Flattened out like a flash and was gone down its hole. I never did get it out."

"Never shot a bow either," said Gordie.

"Hah, you're right. I never shot a bow either," admitted King with a strange, snarling little laugh. "But I heard of this guy once who put his arrow through a fox then left it thrash around in the bush until he thought it was dead. He went in there after it. You know what he found? That fox had chewed the arrow off either side of its body and it was gone."

"They don't got that name for nothing," Eli said.

"Fox," said Gordie, peering closely at the keyhole in his beer.

"Can you gimme a cigarette, Eli?" King asked.

"When you ask for a cigarette around here," said Gordie, "you don't say can I have a cigarette. You say *ciga swa*?"

"Them Michifs ask like that," Eli said. "You got to ask a real old Cree like me for the right words."

"Tell 'em Uncle Eli," Lynette said with a quick burst of drunken enthusiasm. "They've got to learn their own heritage! When you go it will all be gone!"

"What you saying there, woman. Hey!" King shouted, filling the kitchen with the jagged tear of his voice. "When you talk to my relatives have a little respect." He put his arms up and shoved at her breasts.

"You bet your life, Uncle Eli," he said more quietly, leaning back on the table. "You're the greatest hunter. But I'm the World's Greatest Fisherman."

"No you ain't," Eli said. His voice was effortless and happy. "I caught a fourteen-inch trout."

King looked at him carefully, focusing with difficulty. "You're the greatest then," he admitted. "Here."

He reached over and plucked away Eli's greasy olive-drab hat. Eli's head was brown, shiny through the white crew-cut stubble.

King took off his blue hat and pushed it down on Eli's head. The hat slipped over Eli's eyes.

"It's too big for him!" Lynette screamed in a tiny outraged voice.

King adjusted the hat's plastic tab.

"I gave you that hat, King! That's your best hat!" Her voice rose sharply in its trill. "You don't give that hat away!"

Eli sat calmly underneath the hat. It fit him perfectly. He seemed oblivious to King's sacrifice and just sat, his old cap perched on his knee, turning the can around and around in his hand without drinking.

King swayed to his feet, clutched the stuffed plastic backrest of the chair. His voice was ripped and swollen. "Uncle Eli." He bent over the old man. "Uncle Eli, you're my uncle."

"Damn right," Eli agreed.

"I always thought so much of you, my uncle!" cried King in a loud, unhappy wail.

"Damn right," said Eli. He turned to Gordie. "He's drunk on his behind. I got to agree with him."

"I think the fuckin' world of you, Uncle!"

"Damn right. I'm an old man," Eli said in a flat, soft voice.

King suddenly put his hands up around his ears and stumbled out the door.

"Fresh air be good for him," said Gordie, relieved. "Say there, Albertine. You ever hear this one joke about the Indian, the Frenchman, and the Norwegian in the French Revolution?"

"Issat a Norwegian joke?" Lynette asked. "Hey. I'm full-blooded Norwegian. I don't know nothing about my family, but I know I'm full-blooded Norwegian."

"No, it's not about the Norwegians really," Gordie went on. "So anyway . . ."

Nevertheless she followed King out the door.

"There were these three. An Indian. A Frenchman. A Norwegian. They were all in the French Revolution. And they were all set for the guillotine, right? But when they put the Indian in there the blade just came halfway down and got stuck."

"Fuckin' bitch! Gimme the keys!" King screamed just outside the door. Gordie paused a moment. There was silence. He continued the joke.

"So they said it was the judgment of God. You can go, they said to the Indian. So the Indian got up and went. Then it was the Frenchman's turn. They put his neck in the vise and were all set to execute him! But it happened the same. The blade stuck."

"Fuckin' bitch! Fuckin' bitch!" King shrieked again.

The car door slammed. Gordie's eyes darted to the door, back to me with questions.

"Should we go out?" I said.

But he continued the story. "And so the Frenchman went off and he was saved. But when it came to the Norwegian, see, the Norwegian looks up at the guillotine and says: 'You guys are sure dumb. If you put a little grease on it that thing would work fine!' "

"Bitch! Bitch! I'll kill you! Gimme the keys!" We heard a quick shattering sound, glass breaking, and left Eli sitting at the table.

Lynette was locked in the Firebird, crouched on the passenger's side. King screamed at her and threw his whole body against the car, thudded on the hood with hollow booms, banged his way across the roof, ripped at antennae and side-view mirrors with his fists, kicked into the broken sockets of headlights. Finally he ripped a mirror off the driver's side and began to beat the car rhythmically, gasping. But though he swung the mirror time after time into the windshield and side windows he couldn't smash them.

"King, baby!" Gordie jumped off the steps and hugged King to the ground with the solid drop of his weight. "It's her car. You're June's boy, King. Don't cry." For as they lay there, welded in shock, King's face was grinding deep into the cinders and his shoulders shook with heavy sobs. He screamed up through dirt at his father.

"It's awful to be dead. Oh my God, she's so cold."

They were up on their feet suddenly. King twisted out of Gordie's arms and balanced in a wrestler's stance. "It's your fault and you wanna take the car," he said wildly. He sprang at his father but Gordie stepped back, bracing himself, and once again he folded King violently into his arms, and again King sobbed and sagged against his father. Gordie lowered him back into the cinders. While they were clenched, Lynette slipped from the car and ran into the house. I followed her. She rushed through the kitchen, checked the baby, and then she came back.

"Sit down," I said. I had taken a chair beside Eli.

"Uh, uh."

She walked over to Eli. She couldn't be still.

"You got troubles out there," he stated.

"Yeah," she said. "His mom gave him the money!" She sneaked a cigarette from Eli's pack, giving him a coy smirk in return. "Because she wanted him to have responsibility. He never had responsibility. She wanted him to take care of his family."

Eli nodded and pushed the whole pack toward her when she stubbed out the cigarette half smoked. She lit another.

"You know he really must love his uncle," she cried in a small, hard voice. She plumped down next to Eli and steadily smiled at the blue hat. "That fishing hat. It's his number-one hat. I got that patch for him. King. They think the world of him down in the Cities. Everybody knows him. They know him by that hat. It's his number one. You better never take it off."

Eli took the hat off and turned it around in his hands. He squinted at the patch and read it aloud. Then he nodded, as if it had finally dawned on him what she was talking about, and he turned it back around.

"Let me wear it for a while," Lynette cajoled. Then she took it.

Put it on her head and adjusted the brim. "There it is."

Uncle Eli took his old cap off his knee and put it on his head. "This one fits me," he said.

In the next room King Junior began to cry.

"Oh, my baby!" Lynette shrieked as if he were in danger and darted out. I heard her murmuring King's name when the father and the son walked back inside. King sat down at the table and put his head in his folded arms, breathing hoarsely. Gordie got the keys from Lynette and told Eli they were going home now.

"He's okay," Gordie said, nodding at King. "Just as long as you let him alone."

So they drove off on that clear blue night. I put a blanket around Lynette's shoulders, and she sank onto the couch. I walked out, past King. He was still breathing hopelessly into his crossed arms. I walked down to where I knew Lipsha was, at the bottom of the hill below the house. Sure enough, he was sitting there, back against a log from the woodpile. He passed me a bottle of sweet rosé, I drank. I tipped the bottle, looked up at the sky, and nearly fell over, in amazement and too much beer, at the drenching beauty.

Northern lights. Something in the cold, wet atmosphere brought them out. I grabbed Lipsha's arm. We floated into the field and sank down, crushing green wheat. We chewed the sweet kernels and stared up and were lost. Everything seemed to be one piece. The air, our faces, all cool, moist, and dark, and the ghostly sky. Pale green licks of light pulsed and faded across it. Living lights. Their fires lobbed over, higher, higher, then died out in blackness. At times the whole sky was ringed in shooting points and puckers of light gathering and falling, pulsing, fading, rhythmical as breathing. All of a piece. As if the sky were a pattern of nerves and our thought and memories traveled across it. As if the sky were one gigantic memory for us all. Or a dance hall. And all the world's wandering souls were dancing there. I thought of June. She would be dancing if there was a dance hall in space. She would be dancing a two-step for wandering souls. Her long legs lifting and falling. Her laugh an ace. Her sweet perfume the way all grown-up women were supposed to smell. Her amusement at both the bad and the good. Her defeat. Her reckless victory. Her sons.

4.

I had to close my eyes after a while. The mix of beer and rosé made my head whirl. The lights, shooting high, made the ground rock underneath me. I waved away the bottle when Lipsha touched my hand with the cold end of it.

"Don't want no more?"

"Later on," I said. "Keep talking."

Lipsha's voice was a steady bridge over a deep black space of sickness I was crossing. If I just kept listening I knew I'd get past all right. He was talking about King. His voice was slurred and dreamy.

"I'll admit that," he said, "I'm scared of his mind. You can't never predict when he'll turn. Once, a long time ago, we went out hunting gophers. I let him get behind me. You know what he did? He hid in the bushes and took a potshot."

"Lucky."

"That's right. I steer clear of King. I never turn my back on him, either."

"Don't be scared of him," I said. I was managing to keep a slim hold on the conversation. I could do this as long as I only moved my lips and not the rest of me.

"Sure. King never took a potshot at you."

"He's scared underneath."

"Of what?" said Lipsha.

But I really didn't know. "Those vets," I said, "are really nuts."

"He's no vet," Lipsha began. But then blackness swung too hard, tipping me. For a while I heard nothing, saw nothing, and did not even dare move my lips to speak. That didn't matter. Lipsha went on talking.

"Energy," he said, "electromagnetic waves. It's because of the temperature, the difference sets them off." He was talking about the northern lights. Although he never did well in school, Lipsha knew surprising things. He read books about computers and volcanoes and the life cycles of salamanders. Sometimes he used words I had to ask him the meaning of, and other times he didn't make even the simplest sense. I loved him for being both ways. A wash of love swept me over the sickness. I sat up.

"I am going to talk to you about something particular. . . ." I began. My voice was serious, all of a sudden, and it scared him. He moved away from me, suspicious. I was going to tell him what I'd heard from hanging at the edge of the aunts' conversations. I was going to tell him that his mother was June. Since so many others knew, it was only right that he should, too.

"Your mother . . ." I began.

"I can never forgive what she done to a little child," he said. "They had to rescue me out of her grip."

I tried again.

"I want to talk about your mother. . . ."

Lipsha nodded, cutting me off. "I consider Grandma Kashpaw my mother, even though she just took me in like any old stray."

"She didn't do that," I said. "She wanted you."

"No," said Lipsha. "Albertine, you don't know what you're talking about."

Now I was the one who felt ignorant, confused.

"As for my mother," he went on, "even if she came back right now, this minute, and got down on her knees and said 'Son, I am sorry for what I done to you,' I would not relent on her."

I didn't know how to rescue my intentions and go on. I thought for a while, or tried to, but sitting up and talking had been too much.

"What if your mother never meant to?" I lay down again, lowering myself carefully into the wheat. The dew was condensing. I was cold, damp, and sick. "What if it was just a kind of mistake?" I asked.

"It wasn't no mistake," said Lipsha firmly. "She would have drowned me."

Laying still, confused by my sickness and his certainty, I almost believed him. I thought he would hate June if he knew, and anyway it was too late. I justified my silence. I didn't tell him.

"What about your father?" I asked instead. "Do you wish you knew him?"

Lipsha was quiet, considering, before he answered.

"I wouldn't mind."

Then I was falling, and he was talking again. I hung on and listened.

"Did you ever dream you flew through the air?" he asked. "Did you ever dream you landed on a planet or star?

"I dreamed I flew up there once," he said, going on. "It was all lighted up. Man, it was beautiful! I landed on the moon, but once I stood there at last, I didn't dare take a breath."

I moved closer. He had a light nylon jacket. He took it off and laid it over me. I was suddenly comfortable, very comfortable, and warm.

"No," he said. "No, I was scared to breathe."

I woke up. I had fallen asleep in the arms of Lipsha's jacket, in the cold wet wheat under the flashing sky. I heard the clanging sound of struck metal, pots tumbling in the house. Gordie was gone. Eli was gone. "Come on," I said, jumping straight up at the noise. "They're fighting." I ran up the hill, Lipsha pounding behind me. I stumbled straight into the lighted kitchen and saw at once that King was trying to drown Lynette. He was pushing her face in the sink of cold dishwater. Holding her by the nape and the ears. Her arms were whirling, knocking spoons and knives and bowls out of the drainer. She struggled powerfully, but he had her. I grabbed a block of birch out of the woodbox and hit King on the back of the neck. The wood bounced out of my fists. He pushed her lower, and her throat caught and gurgled.

I grabbed his shoulders. I expected that Lipsha was behind me. King hardly noticed my weight. He pushed her lower. So I had no choice then. I jumped on his back and bit his ear. My teeth met and blood filled my mouth. He reeled backward, bucking me off, and I flew across the room, hit the refrigerator solidly, and got back on my feet.

His hands were cocked in boxer's fists. He was deciding who to hit first, I thought, me or Lipsha. I glanced around. I was alone. I stared back at King, scared for the first time. Then the fear left and I was mad, just mad, at Lipsha, at King, at Lynette, at June. . . . I looked past King and I saw what they had done.

All the pies were smashed. Torn open. Black juice bleeding through the crusts. Bits of jagged shells were stuck to the wall and some were turned completely upside down. Chunks of rhubarb were scraped across the floor. Meringue dripped from the towels.

"The pies!" I shrieked. "You goddamn sonofabitch, you broke the pies!"

His eyes widened. When he glanced around at the destruction, Lynette scuttled under the table. He took in what he could, and then his fists lowered and a look at least resembling shame, confusion, swept over his face, and he rushed past me. He stepped down flat on his fisherman hat as he ran, and after he was gone I picked it up.

I went into the next room and stuffed the hat under King Junior's mattress. Then I sat for a long time, listening to his light breathing. He was always a good baby, or more likely a wise soul. He slept through everything he could possibly sleep through.

Lynette had turned the lights out in the kitchen as she left the house, and now I heard her outside the window begging King to take her away in the car.

"Let's go off before they all get back," she said. "It's them. You always get so crazy when you're home. We'll get the baby. We'll go off. We'll go back to the Cities, go home."

And then she cried out once, but clearly it was a cry like pleasure. I thought I heard their bodies creak together, or perhaps it was just the wood steps beneath them, the old worn boards bearing their weight.

They got into the car soon after that. Doors slammed. But they traveled just a few yards and then stopped. The horn blared softly. I suppose they knocked against it in passion. The heater roared on from time to time. It was a cold, spare dawn.

Sometime that hour I got up, leaving the baby, and went into the kitchen. I spooned the fillings back into the crusts, married slabs of dough, smoothed over edges of crusts with a wetted finger, fit crimps to crimps and even fluff to fluff on top of berries or pudding. I worked carefully for over an hour. But once they smash there is no way to put them right.

SAINT MARIE

(1934)

MARIE LAZARRE

So when I went there, I knew the dark fish must rise. Plumes of radiance had soldered on me. No reservation girl had ever prayed so hard. There was no use in trying to ignore me any longer. I was going up there on the hill with the black robe women. They were not any lighter than me. I was going up there to pray as good as they could. Because I don't have that much Indian blood. And they never thought they'd have a girl from this reservation as a saint they'd have to kneel to. But they'd have me. And I'd be carved in pure gold. With ruby lips. And my toenails would be little pink ocean shells, which they would have to stoop down off their high horse to kiss.

I was ignorant. I was near age fourteen. The length of sky is just about the size of my ignorance. Pure and wide. And it was just that—the pure and wideness of my ignorance—that got me up the hill to Sacred Heart Convent and brought me back down alive. For maybe Jesus did not take my bait, but them Sisters tried to cram me right down whole.

You ever see a walleye strike so bad the lure is practically out its back end before you reel it in? That is what they done with me. I don't like to make that low comparison, but I have seen a walleye do that once. And it's the same attempt as Sister Leopolda made to get me in her clutch.

I had the mail-order Catholic soul you get in a girl raised out in the bush, whose only thought is getting into town. For Sunday Mass is the only time my father brought his children in except for school, when we were harnessed. Our soul went cheap. We were so anxious to get there we would have walked in on our hands and knees. We just craved going to the store, slinging bottle caps in the dust, making fool eyes at each other. And of course we went to church.

Where they have the convent is on top of the highest hill, so that from its windows the Sisters can be looking into the marrow of the town. Recently a windbreak was planted before the bar "for the purposes of tornado insurance." Don't tell me that. That poplar stand was put up to hide the drinkers as they get the transformation. As they are served into the beast of their burden. While they're drinking, that body comes upon them, and then they stagger or crawl out the bar door, pulling a weight they can't move past the poplars. They don't want no holy witness to their fall.

Anyway, I climbed. That was a long-ago day. There was a road then for wagons that wound in ruts to the top of the hill where they had their buildings of painted brick. Gleaming white. So white the sun glanced off in dazzling display to set forms whirling behind your eyelids. The face of God you could hardly look at. But that day it drizzled, so I could look all I wanted. I saw the homelier side. The cracked whitewash and swallows nesting in the busted ends of eaves. I saw the boards sawed the size of broken windowpanes and the fruit trees, stripped. Only the tough wild rhubarb flourished. Goldenrod rubbed up their walls. It was a poor convent. I didn't see that then but I know that now. Compared to others it was humble, ragtag, out in the middle of no place. It was the end of the world to some. Where the maps stopped. Where God had only half a hand in the creation. Where the Dark One had put in thick bush, liquor, wild dogs, and Indians.

I heard later that the Sacred Heart Convent was a catchall place for nuns that don't get along elsewhere. Nuns that complain too much or lose their mind. I'll always wonder now, after hearing that, where they picked up Sister Leopolda. Perhaps she had scarred someone else, the way she left a mark on me. Perhaps she was just sent around to test her Sisters' faith, here and there, like the spot-checker in a factory. For she was the definite most-hard trial to anyone's endurance, even when they started out with veils of wretched love upon their eyes.

I was that girl who thought the black hem of her garment would help me rise. Veils of love which was only hate petrified by longing—that was me. I was like those bush Indians who stole the holy black hat of a Jesuit and swallowed little scraps of it to cure their fevers. But the hat itself carried smallpox and was killing them with belief. Veils of faith! I had this confidence in Leopolda. She was different. The other Sisters had long ago gone blank and given up on Satan. He slept for them. They never noticed his comings and goings. But Leopolda kept track of him and knew his habits, minds he burrowed in, deep spaces where he hid. She knew as much about him as my grandma, who called him by other names and was not afraid.

In her class, Sister Leopolda carried a long oak pole for opening high windows. It had a hook made of iron on one end that could jerk a patch of your hair out or throttle you by the collar—

all from a distance. She used this deadly hook-pole for catching Satan by surprise. He could have entered without your knowing it—through your lips or your nose or any one of your seven openings—and gained your mind. But she would see him. That pole would brain you from behind. And he would gasp, dazzled, and take the first thing she offered, which was pain.

She had a stringer of children who could only breathe if she said the word. I was the worst of them. She always said the Dark One wanted me most of all, and I believed this. I stood out. Evil was a common thing I trusted. Before sleep sometimes he came and whispered conversation in the old language of the bush. I listened. He told me things he never told anyone but Indians. I was privy to both worlds of his knowledge. I listened to him, but I had confidence in Leopolda. She was the only one of the bunch he even noticed.

There came a day, though, when Leopolda turned the tide with her hook-pole.

It was a quiet day with everyone working at their desks, when I heard him. He had sneaked into the closets in the back of the room. He was scratching around, tasting crumbs in our pockets, stealing buttons, squirting his dark juice in the linings and the boots. I was the only one who heard him, and I got bold. I smiled. I glanced back and smiled and looked up at her sly to see if she had noticed. My heart jumped. For she was looking straight at me. And she sniffed. She had a big stark bony nose stuck to the front of her face for smelling out brimstone and evil thoughts. She had smelled him on me. She stood up. Tall, pale, a blackness leading into the deeper blackness of the slate wall behind her. Her oak pole had flown into her grip. She had seen me glance at the closet. Oh, she knew. She knew just where he was. I watched her watch him in her mind's eye. The whole class was watching now. She was staring, sizing, following his scuffle. And all of a sudden she tensed down, posed on her bent kneesprings, cocked her arm back. She threw the oak pole singing over my head, through my braincloud. It cracked through the thin wood door of the back closet, and the heavy pointed hook drove through his heart. I turned. She'd speared her own black rubber overboot where he'd taken refuge in the tip of her darkest toe.

Something howled in my mind. Loss and darkness. I understood. I was to suffer for my smile.

He rose up hard in my heart. I didn't blink when the pole cracked. My skull was tough. I didn't flinch when she shrieked in my ear. I only shrugged at the flowers of hell. He wanted me. More than anything he craved me. But then she did the worst. She did what broke my mind to her. She grabbed me by the collar and dragged me, feet flying, through the room and threw me in the closet with her dead black overboot. And I was there. The only light was a crack beneath the door. I asked the Dark One to enter into me and boost my mind. I asked him to restrain my tears, for they was pushing behind my eyes. But he was afraid to come back there. He was afraid of her sharp pole. And I was afraid of Leopolda's pole for the first time, too. I felt the cold hook in my heart. How it could crack through the door at any minute and drag me out, like a dead fish on a gaff, drop me on the floor like a gutshot squirrel.

I was nothing. I edged back to the wall as far as I could. I breathed the chalk dust. The hem of her full black cloak cut against my cheek. He had left me. Her spear could find me any time. Her keen ears would aim the hook into the beat of my heart.

What was that sound?

It filled the closet, filled it up until it spilled over, but I did not recognize the crying wailing voice as mine until the door cracked open, brightness, and she hoisted me to her camphor-smelling lips.

"He *wants* you," she said. "That's the difference. I give you love."

Love. The black hook. The spear singing through the mind. I saw that she had tracked the Dark One to my heart and flushed him out into the open. So now my heart was an empty nest where she could lurk.

Well, I was weak. I was weak when I let her in, but she got a foothold there. Hard to dislodge as the year passed. Sometimes I felt him—the brush of dim wings—but only rarely did his voice compel. It was between Marie and Leopolda now, and the struggle changed. I began to realize I had been on the wrong track with the fruits of hell. The real way to overcome Leopolda was this: I'd get to heaven first. And then, when I saw her coming, I'd shut the gate. She'd be out! That is why, besides the bowing and the scraping I'd be dealt, I wanted to sit on the altar as a saint.

To this end, I went up on the hill. Sister Leopolda was the consecrated nun who had sponsored me to come there.

"You're not vain," she said. "You're too honest, looking into the mirror, for that. You're not smart. You don't have the ambition to get clear. You have two choices. One, you can marry a no-good Indian, bear his brats, die like a dog. Or two, you can give yourself to God."

"I'll come up there," I said, "but not because of what you think."

I could have had any damn man on the reservation at the time. And I could have made him treat me like his own life. I looked good. And I looked white. But I wanted Sister Leopolda's heart. And here was the thing: sometimes I wanted her heart in love and admiration. Sometimes. And sometimes I wanted her heart to roast on a black stick.

She answered the back door where they had instructed me to call. I stood there with my bundle. She looked me up and down.

"All right," she said finally. "Come in."

She took my hand. Her fingers were like a bundle of broom

straws, so thin and dry, but the strength of them was unnatural. I couldn't have tugged loose if she was leading me into rooms of white-hot coal. Her strength was a kind of perverse miracle, for she got it from fasting herself thin. Because of this hunger practice her lips were a wounded brown and her skin deadly pale. Her eye sockets were two deep lashless hollows in a taut skull. I told you about the nose already. It stuck out far and made the place her eyes moved even deeper, as if she stared out the wrong end of a gun barrel. She took the bundle from my hands and threw it in the corner.

"You'll be sleeping behind the stove, child."

It was immense, like a great furnace. There was a small cot close behind it.

"Looks like it could get warm there," I said.

"Hot. It does."

"Do I get a habit?"

I wanted something like the thing she wore. Flowing black cotton. Her face was strapped in white bandages, and a sharp crest of starched white cardboard hung over her forehead like a glaring beak. If possible, I wanted a bigger, longer, whiter beak than hers.

"No," she said, grinning her great skull grin. "You don't get one yet. Who knows, you might not like us. Or we might not like you."

But she had loved me, or offered me love. And she had tried to hunt the Dark One down. So I had this confidence.

"I'll inherit your keys from you," I said.

She looked at me sharply, and her grin turned strange. She hissed, taking in her breath. Then she turned to the door and took a key from her belt. It was a giant key, and it unlocked the larder where the food was stored.

Inside there was all kinds of good stuff. Things I'd tasted only once or twice in my life. I saw sticks of dried fruit, jars of orange peel, spice like cinnamon. I saw tins of crackers with ships painted on the side. I saw pickles. Jars of herring and the rind of pigs. There was cheese, a big brown block of it from the thick milk of goats. And besides that there was the everyday stuff, in great quantities, the flour and the coffee.

It was the cheese that got to me. When I saw it my stomach hollowed. My tongue dripped. I loved that goat-milk cheese better than anything I'd ever ate. I stared at it. The rich curve in the buttery cloth.

"When you inherit my keys," she said sourly, slamming the door in my face, "you can eat all you want of the priest's cheese."

Then she seemed to consider what she'd done. She looked at me. She took the key from her belt and went back, sliced a hunk off, and put it in my hand.

"If you're good you'll taste this cheese again. When I'm dead and gone," she said.

Then she dragged out the big sack of flour. When I finished that heaven stuff she told me to roll my sleeves up and begin doing God's labor. For a while we worked in silence, mixing up the dough and pounding it out on stone slabs.

"God's work," I said after a while. "If this is God's work, then I've done it all my life."

"Well, you've done it with the Devil in your heart then," she said. "Not God."

"How do you know?" I asked. But I knew she did. And I wished I had not brought up the subject.

"I see right into you like a clear glass," she said. "I always did."

"You don't know it," she continued after a while, "but he's come around here sulking. He's come around here brooding. You brought him in. He knows the smell of me, and he's going to make a last ditch try to get you back. Don't let him." She glared over at me. Her eyes were cold and lighted. "Don't let him touch you. We'll be a long time getting rid of him."

So I was careful. I was careful not to give him an inch. I said a rosary, two rosaries, three, underneath my breath. I said the Creed. I said every scrap of Latin I knew while we punched the dough with our fists. And still, I dropped the cup. It rolled under that monstrous iron stove, which was getting fired up for baking.

And she was on me. She saw he'd entered my distraction.

"Our good cup," she said. "Get it out of there, Marie."

I reached for the poker to snag it out from beneath the stove. But I had a sinking feel in my stomach as I did this. Sure enough, her long arm darted past me like a whip. The poker lighted in her hand.

"Reach," she said. "Reach with your arm for that cup. And when your flesh is hot, remember that the flames you feel are only one fraction of the heat you will feel in his hellish embrace."

She always did things this way, to teach you lessons. So I wasn't surprised. It was playacting, anyway, because a stove isn't very hot underneath right along the floor. They aren't made that way. Otherwise a wood floor would burn. So I said yes and got down on my stomach and reached under. I meant to grab it quick and jump up again, before she could think up another lesson, but here it happened. Although I groped for the cup, my hand closed on nothing. That cup was nowhere to be found. I heard her step toward me, a slow step. I heard the creak of thick shoe leather, the little *plat* as the folds of her heavy skirts met, a trickle of fine sand sifting, somewhere, perhaps in the bowels of her, and I was afraid. I tried to scramble up, but her foot came down lightly behind my ear, and I was lowered. The foot came down more firmly at the base of my neck, and I was held.

"You're like I was," she said. "He wants you very much."

"He doesn't want me no more," I said. "He had his fill. I got the cup!"

I heard the valve opening, the hissed intake of breath, and knew that I should not have spoke.

"You lie," she said. "You're cold. There is a wicked ice forming in your blood. You don't have a shred of devotion for God. Only wild cold dark lust. I know it. I know how you feel. I see the beast . . . the beast watches me out of your eyes sometimes. Cold."

The urgent scrape of metal. It took a moment to know from where. Top of the stove. Kettle. Lessons. She was steadying herself with the iron poker. I could feel it like pure certainty, driving into the wood floor. I would not remind her of pokers. I heard the water as it came, tipped from the spout, cooling as it fell but still scalding as it struck. I must have twitched beneath her foot, because she steadied me, and then the poker nudged up beside my arm as if to guide. "To warm your cold ash heart," she said. I felt how patient she would be. The water came. My mind went dead blank. Again. I could only think the kettle would be cooling slowly in her hand. I could not stand it. I bit my lip so as not to satisfy her with a sound. She gave me more reason to keep still.

"I will boil him from your mind if you make a peep," she said, "by filling up your ear."

Any sensible fool would have run back down the hill the minute Leopolda let them up from under her heel. But I was snared in her black intelligence by then. I could not think straight. I had prayed so hard I think I broke a cog in my mind. I prayed while her foot squeezed my throat. While my skin burst. I prayed even when I heard the wind come through, shrieking in the busted bird nests. I didn't stop when pure light fell, turning slowly behind my eyelids. God's face. Even that did not disrupt my continued praise. Words came. Words came from nowhere and flooded my mind.

Now I could pray much better than any one of them. Than all of them full force. This was proved. I turned to her in a daze when she let me up. My thoughts were gone, and yet I remember how surprised I was. Tears glittered in her eyes, deep down, like the sinking reflection in a well.

"It was so hard, Marie," she gasped. Her hands were shaking. The kettle clattered against the stove. "But I have used all the water up now. I think he is gone."

"I prayed," I said foolishly. "I prayed very hard."

"Yes," she said. "My dear one, I know."

We sat together quietly because we had no more words. We let the dough rise and punched it down once. She gave me a bowl of mush, unlocked the sausage from a special cupboard, and took that in to the Sisters. They sat down the hall, chewing their sausage, and I could hear them. I could hear their teeth bite through their bread and meat. I couldn't move. My shirt was dry but the cloth stuck to my back, and I couldn't think straight. I was losing the sense to understand how her mind worked. She'd gotten past me with her poker and I would never be a saint. I despaired. I felt I had no inside voice, nothing to direct me, no darkness, no Marie. I was about to throw that cornmeal mush out to the birds and make a run for it, when the vision rose up blazing in my mind.

I was rippling gold. My breasts were bare and my nipples flashed and winked. Diamonds tipped them. I could walk through panes of glass. I could walk through windows. She was at my feet, swallowing the glass after each step I took. I broke through another and another. The glass she swallowed ground and cut until her starved insides were only a subtle dust. She coughed. She coughed a cloud of dust. And then she was only a black rag that flapped off, snagged in bob wire, hung there for an age, and finally rotted into the breeze.

I saw this, mouth hanging open, gazing off into the flagged boughs of trees.

"Get up!" she cried. "Stop dreaming. It is time to bake."

Two other Sisters had come in with her, wide women with hands like paddles. They were evening and smoothing out the firebox beneath the great jaws of the oven.

"Who is this one?" they asked Leopolda. "Is she yours?"

"She is mine," said Leopolda. "A very good girl."

"What is your name?" one asked me.

"Marie."

"Marie. Star of the Sea."

"She will shine," said Leopolda, "when we have burned off the dark corrosion."

The others laughed, but uncertainly. They were mild and sturdy French, who did not understand Leopolda's twisted jokes, although they muttered respectfully at things she said. I knew they wouldn't believe what she had done with the kettle. There was no question. So I kept quiet.

"*Elle est docile,*" they said approvingly as they left to starch the linens.

"Does it pain?" Leopolda asked me as soon as they were out the door.

I did not answer. I felt sick with the hurt.

"Come along," she said.

The building was wholly quiet now. I followed her up the narrow staircase into a hall of little rooms, many doors. Her cell was the quietest, at the very end. Inside, the air smelled stale, as if the door had not been opened for years. There was a crude straw mattress, a tiny bookcase with a picture of Saint Francis hanging over it, a ragged palm, a stool for sitting on, a crucifix. She told me to remove my blouse and sit on the stool. I did so. She took a pot of salve from the bookcase and began to smooth it upon my burns. Her hands made slow, wide circles, stopping the pain. I closed my eyes. I expected to see blackness. Peace. But instead the vision reared up again. My chest was still tipped with diamonds. I was walking through windows. She was chewing up the broken litter I left behind.

"I am going," I said. "Let me go."

But she held me down.

"Don't go," she said quickly. "Don't. We have just begun."

I was weakening. My thoughts were whirling pitifully. The pain had kept me strong, and as it left me I began to forget it; I couldn't hold on. I began to wonder if she'd really scalded me with the kettle. I could not remember. To remember this seemed the most important thing in the world. But I was losing the memory. The scalding. The pouring. It began to vanish. I felt like my mind was coming off its hinge, flapping in the breeze, hanging by the hair of my own pain. I wrenched out of her grip.

"He was always in you," I said. "Even more than in me. He wanted you even more. And now he's got you. Get thee behind me!"

I shouted that, grabbed my shirt, and ran through the door throwing it on my body. I got down the stairs and into the kitchen, even, but no matter what I told myself, I couldn't get out the door. It wasn't finished. And she knew I would not leave. Her quiet step was immediately behind me.

"We must take the bread from the oven now," she said.

She was pretending nothing happened. But for the first time I had gotten through some chink she'd left in her darkness. Touched some doubt. Her voice was so low and brittle it cracked off at the end of her sentence.

"Help me, Marie," she said slowly.

But I was not going to help her, even though she had calmly buttoned the back of my shirt up and put the big cloth mittens in my hands for taking out the loaves. I could have bolted for it then. But I didn't. I knew that something was nearing completion. Something was about to happen. My back was a wall of singing flame. I was turning. I watched her take the long fork in one hand, to tap the loaves. In the other hand she gripped the black poker to hook the pans.

"Help me," she said again, and I thought, Yes, this is part of it. I put the mittens on my hands and swung the door open on its hinges. The oven gaped. She stood back a moment, letting the first blast of heat rush by. I moved behind her. I could feel the heat at my front and at my back. Before, behind. My skin was turning to beaten gold. It was coming quicker than I thought. The oven was like the gate of a personal hell. Just big enough and hot enough for one person, and that was her. One kick and Leopolda would fly in headfirst. And that would be one-millionth of the heat she would feel when she finally collapsed in his hellish embrace.

Saints know these numbers.

She bent forward with her fork held out. I kicked her with all my might. She flew in. But the outstretched poker hit the back wall first, so she rebounded. The oven was not so deep as I had thought.

There was a moment when I felt a sort of thin, hot disappointment, as when a fish slips off the line. Only I was the one going to be lost. She was fearfully silent. She whirled. Her veil had cutting edges. She had the poker in one hand. In the other she held that long sharp fork she used to tap the delicate crusts of loaves. Her face turned upside down on her shoulders. Her face turned blue. But saints are used to miracles. I felt no trace of fear.

If I was going to be lost, let the diamonds cut! Let her eat ground glass!

"Bitch of Jesus Christ!" I shouted. "Kneel and beg! Lick the floor!"

That was when she stabbed me through the hand with the fork, then took the poker up alongside my head, and knocked me out.

It must have been a half an hour later when I came around. Things were so strange. So strange I can hardly tell it for delight at the remembrance. For when I came around this was actually taking place. I was being worshiped. I had somehow gained the altar of a saint.

I was laying back on the stiff couch in the Mother Superior's office. I looked around me. It was as though my deepest dream had come to life. The Sisters of the convent were kneeling to me. Sister Bonaventure. Sister Dympna. Sister Cecilia Saint-Claire. The two French with hands like paddles. They were down on their knees. Black capes were slung over some of their heads. My name was buzzing up and down the room, like a fat autumn fly lighting on the tips of their tongues between Latin, humming up the heavy blood-dark curtains, circling their little cosseted heads. Marie! Marie! A girl thrown in a closet. Who was afraid of a rubber overboot. Who was half overcome. A girl who came in the back door where they threw their garbage. Marie! Who never found the cup. Who had to eat their cold mush. Marie! Leopolda had her face buried in her knuckles. Saint Marie of the Holy Slops! Saint Marie of the Bread Fork! Saint Marie of the Burnt Back and Scalded Butt!

I broke out and laughed.

They looked up. All holy hell burst loose when they saw I'd woke. I still did not understand what was happening. They were watching, talking, but not to me.

"The marks . . ."

"She has her hand closed."

"*Je ne peux pas voir.*"

I was not stupid enough to ask what they were talking about. I couldn't tell why I was laying in white sheets. I couldn't tell why they were praying to me. But I'll tell you this: it seemed entirely natural. It was me. I lifted up my hand as in my dream. It was completely limp with sacredness.

"Peace be with you."

My arm was dried blood from the wrist down to the elbow. And it hurt. Their faces turned like flat flowers of adoration to follow that hand's movements. I let it swing through the air, imparting a saint's blessing. I had practiced. I knew exactly how to act.

They murmured. I heaved a sigh, and a golden beam of light suddenly broke through the clouded window and flooded down directly on my face. A stroke of perfect luck! They had to be convinced.

Leopolda still knelt in the back of the room. Her knuckles were crammed halfway down her throat. Let me tell you, a saint has senses honed keen as a wolf. I knew that she was over my barrel now. How it happened did not matter. The last thing I remembered was how she flew from the oven and stabbed me. That one thing was most certainly true.

"Come forward, Sister Leopolda." I gestured with my heavenly wound. Oh, it hurt. It bled when I reopened the slight heal. "Kneel beside me," I said.

She kneeled, but her voice box evidently did not work, for her mouth opened, shut, opened, but no sound came out. My throat clenched in noble delight I had read of as befitting a saint. She could not speak. But she was beaten. It was in her eyes. She stared at me now with all the deep hate of the wheel of devilish dust that rolled wild within her emptiness.

"What is it you want to tell me?" I asked. And at last she spoke.

"I have told my Sisters of your passion," she managed to choke out. "How the stigmata . . . the marks of the nails . . . appeared in your palm and you swooned at the holy vision. . . ."

"Yes," I said curiously.

And then, after a moment, I understood.

Leopolda had saved herself with her quick brain. She had witnessed a miracle. She had hid the fork and told this to the others. And of course they believed her, because they never knew how Satan came and went or where he took refuge.

"I saw it from the first," said the large one who put the bread in the oven. "Humility of the spirit. So rare in these girls."

"I saw it too," said the other one with great satisfaction. She sighed quietly. "If only it was me."

Leopolda was kneeling bolt upright, face blazing and twitching, a barely held fountain of blasting poison.

"Christ has marked me," I agreed.

I smiled the saint's smirk into her face. And then I looked at her. That was my mistake.

For I saw her kneeling there. Leopolda with her soul like a rubber overboot. With her face of a starved rat. With the desperate eyes drowning in the deep wells of her wrongness. There would be no one else after me. And I would leave. I saw Leopolda kneeling within the shambles of her love.

My heart had been about to surge from my chest with the blackness of my joyous heat. Now it dropped. I pitied her. I pitied her. Pity twisted in my stomach like that hook-pole was driven through me. I was caught. It was a feeling more terrible than any amount of boiling water and worse than being forked. Still, still, I could not help what I did. I had already smiled in a saint's mealy forgiveness. I heard myself speaking gently.

"Receive the dispensation of my sacred blood," I whispered.

But there was no heart in it. No joy when she bent to touch the floor. No dark leaping. I fell back into the white pillows. Blank dust was whirling through the light shafts. My skin was dust. Dust my lips. Dust the dirty spoons on the ends of my feet.

Rise up! I thought. Rise up and walk! There is no limit to this dust!

WILD GEESE

(1934)

NECTOR KASHPAW

On Friday mornings, I go down to the sloughs with my brother Eli and wait for the birds to land. We have built ourselves a little blind. Eli has second sense and an aim I cannot match, but he is shy and doesn't like to talk. In this way it is a good partnership. Because I got sent to school, I am the one who always walks into town and sells what we shoot. I get the price from the Sisters, who cook for the priests, and then I come home and split the money in half. Eli usually takes his bottle off into the woods, while I go into town, to the fiddle dance, and spark the girls.

So there is a Friday near sundown, the summer I am out of school, that finds me walking up the hill with two geese slung from either wrist, tied with leather bands. Just to set the record clear, I am a good-looking boy, tall and slim, without my father's belly hanging in the way. I can have the pick of girls, is what I'm saying. But that doesn't matter anyhow, because I have already decided that Lulu Nanapush is the one. She is the only one of them I want.

I am thinking of her while I walk—those damn eyes of hers, sharp as ice picks, and the curl of her lips. Her figure is round and plush, yet just at the edge of slim. She is small, yet she will never be an armful or an eyeful because I'll never get a bead on her. I know that even now. She never stops moving long enough for me to see her all in a piece. I catch the gleam on her hair, the flash of her arm, a sly turn of hip. Then she is gone. I think of her little wet tongue and I have to stop then and there, in my tracks, at the taste that floods into my mouth. She is a tart berry full of juice, and I know she is mine. I cannot wait for the night to start. She will be waiting in the bush.

Because I am standing there, lost on the empty road, half drowned in the charms of Lulu, I never see Marie Lazarre barrel down. In fact, I never even hear her until it is too late. She comes straight down like a wagon unbraked, like a damn train. Her eye is on me, glaring under a stained strip of sheet. Her hand is wound tight in a pillowcase like a boxer's fist.

"Whoa," I say, "slow down girl."

"Move aside," she says.

She tries to pass. Out of reflex I grab her arm, and then I see the initialed pillowcase. *SHC* is written on it in letters red as wine. Sacred Heart Convent. What is it doing on her arm? They say I am smart as a whip around here, but this time I am too smart for my own good. Marie Lazarre is the youngest daughter of a family of horse-thieving drunks. Stealing sacred linen fits what I know of that blood, so I assume she is running off with the Sisters' pillowcase and other valuables. Who knows? I think a chalice might be hidden beneath her skirt. It occurs to me, next moment, I may get a money bonus if I bring her back.

And so, because I am saving for the French-style wedding

band I intend to put on the finger of Lulu Nanapush, I do not let Marie Lazarre go down the hill.

Not that holding on to her is easy.

"Lemme go, you damn Indian," she hisses. Her teeth are strong looking, large and white. "You stink to hell!"

I have to laugh. She is just a skinny white girl from a family so low you cannot even think they are in the same class as Kashpaws. I shake her arm. The dead geese tied to my wrist swing against her hip. I never move her. She is planted solid as a tree. She begins to struggle to get loose, and I look up the hill. No one coming from that direction, or down the road, so I let her try. I am playing with her. Then she kicks me with her hard-sole shoe.

"Little girl," I growl, "don't play with fire!"

Maybe I shouldn't do this, but I twist her arm and screw it up tight. Then I am ashamed of myself because tears come, suddenly, from her eyes and hang bitter and gleaming from her lashes. So I let up for a moment. She moves away from me. But it is just to take aim. Her brown eyes glaze over like a wounded mink's, hurt but still fighting vicious. She launches herself forward and rams her knee in my stomach.

I lose my balance and pitch over. The geese pull me down. Somehow in falling I grip the puffed sleeve of her blouse and tear it from her shoulder.

There I am, on the ground, sprawled and burdened by the geese, clutching that sky-color bit of cloth. I think at first she will do me more damage with her shoes. But she just stands glaring down on me, rail-tough and pale as birch, her face loose and raging beneath the white cloth. I think that now the tears will spurt out. She will sob. But Marie is the kind of tree that doubles back and springs up, whips singing.

She bends over lightly and snatches the sleeve from my grip.

"Lay there you ugly sonofabitch," she says.

I never answer, never say one word, just surge forward, knock her over, and roll on top of her and hold her pinned down underneath my whole length.

"Now we'll talk, skinny white girl, dirty Lazarre!" I yell in her face.

The geese are to my advantage now; their weight on my arms helps pin her; their dead wings flap around us; their necks loll, and their black eyes stare, frozen. But Marie is not the kind of girl to act frightened of a few dead geese.

She stares into my eyes, furious and silent, her lips clenched white.

"Just give me that pillowcase," I say, "and I'll let you go. I'm gonna bring that cloth back to the nuns."

She burns up at me with such fierceness, then, that I think she hasn't understood what a little thing I am asking. Her eyes are tense and wild, animal eyes. My neck chills.

"There now," I say in a more reasonable voice, "quit clutching it and I'll let you up and go. You shouldn't have stole it."

"Stole it!" she spits. "Stole!"

Her mouth drops wide open. If I want I could look all the way down her throat. Then she makes an odd raspfile noise, cawing like a crow.

She is laughing! It is too much. The Lazarre is laughing in my face!

"Stop that." I put my hand across her mouth. Her slick white teeth click, harmless, against my palm, but I am not satisfied.

"Lemme up," she mumbles.

"No," I say.

She lays still, then goes stiller. I look into her eyes and see the hard tears have frozen in the corners. She moves her legs. I keep her down. Something happens. The bones of her hips lock to either side of my hips, and I am held in a light vise. I stiffen like I am shocked. It hits me then I am lying full length across a woman, not a girl. Her breasts graze my chest, soft and pointed. I cannot help but lower myself the slightest bit to feel them better. And then I am caught. I give way. I cannot help myself, because, to my everlasting wonder, Marie is all tight plush acceptance, graceful movements, little jabs that lead me underneath her skirt where she is slick, warm, silk.

When I come back, and when I look down on her, I know how badly I have been weakened. Her tongue flattens against my palm. I know that when I take my hand away the girl will smile, because somehow I have been beaten at what I started on this hill. And sure enough, when I take my hand away she speaks.

"I've had better."

I know that isn't true, that I was just now the first, and I can even hear the shake in her voice, but that makes no difference. She scares me. I scramble away from her, holding the geese in front. Although she is just a little girl knocked down in the dirt, she sits up, smooth as you please, fixes the black skirt over her knees, rearranges the pillowcase tied around her hand.

We are unsheltered by bushes. Anyone could have seen us. I glance around. On the hill, the windows dark in the whitewashed brick seem to harbor a thousand holy eyes widening and narrowing.

How could I? It is then I panic, mouth hanging open, all but certain. They saw! I can hardly believe what I have done.

Marie is watching me. She sees me swing blind to the white face of the convent. She knows exactly what is going through my mind.

"I hope they saw it," she says in the crow's rasp.

I shut my mouth, then open it, then shut my mouth again. Who is this girl? I feel my breath failing like a stupid fish in the airless space around her. I lose control.

"I never did!" I shout, breaking my voice. I whirl to her. She is looking at the geese I hold in front to hide my shame. I speak wildly.

"You made me! You forced me!"

"I made you!" She laughs and shakes her hand, letting the pillowcase drop clear so that I can see the ugly wound.

"I didn't make you do anything," she says.

Her hand looks bad, cut and swollen, and it has not been washed. Even afraid as I am, I cannot help but feel how bad her hand must hurt and throb. Thinking this causes a small pain to shoot through my own hand. The girl's hand must have hurt when I threw her on the ground, and yet she didn't cry out. Her head, too. I have to wonder what is under the bandage. Did the nuns catch her and beat her when she tried to steal their linen?

The dead birds feel impossibly heavy. I untie them from my wrists and let them fall in the dirt. I sit down beside her.

"You can take these birds home. You can roast them," I say. "I am giving them to you."

Her mouth twists. She tosses her head and looks away.

I'm not ashamed, but there are some times this happens: alone in the woods, checking the trapline, I find a wounded animal that hasn't died well, or, worse, it's still living, so that I have to put it out of its misery. Sometimes it's just a big bird I only winged. When I do what I have to do, my throat swells closed sometimes. I touch the suffering bodies like they were killed saints I should handle with gentle reverence.

This is how I take Marie's hand. This is how I hold her wounded hand in my hand.

She never looks at me. I don't think she dares let me see her face. We sit alone. The sun falls down the side of the world and the hill goes dark. Her hand grows thick and fevered, heavy in my own, and I don't want her, but I want her, and I cannot let go.

THE BEADS

(1948)

MARIE KASHPAW

I didn't want June Morrissey when they first brought her to my house. But I ended up keeping her the way I would later end up keeping her son, Lipsha, when they brought him up the steps. I didn't want her because I had so many mouths I couldn't feed. I didn't want her because I had to pile the children in a cot at night. One of the babies slept in a drawer to the dresser. I didn't want June. Sometimes we had nothing to eat but grease on bread. But then the two drunk ones told me how the girl had survived—by eating pine sap in the woods. Her mother was my sister, Lucille. She died alone with the girl out in the bush.

"We don't know how the girl done it," said the old drunk woman who I didn't claim as my mother anymore.

"Lucille was coughing blood," offered the Morrissey, the whining no-good who had not church-married my sister.

"You dog," I said. "Where were you when she died?"

"He was working in the potato fields," the old drunk one wheedled. Her eyes had squeezed back into her face. Her nose had spread and her cheeks were shot with black veins.

"He was rolling in his own filth more like it," I said.

They were standing on my steps because I would not ask them onto my washed floor.

"I can't take in another wild cat," I said. Maybe it scared me, the feeling I might have for this one. I knew how it was to lose a child that got too special. I'd lost a boy. I had also lost a girl who would have almost been the age this poor stray was.

Those Lazarres just stood there, yawning and picking their gray teeth, with the girl between them most likely drunk too. Not older than nine years. She could hardly stand upright. I looked at her. What I saw was starved bones, a shank of black strings, a piece of rag on her I wouldn't have used to wipe a pig. There were beads around her neck. Black beads on a silver chain.

"What's that, a rosary on her neck?"

They started laughing, seesawing against the rail, whooping when they tried to tell the joke out.

"It was them bug eyes," said the old one, "them ignoret bush Crees who found her and couldn't figure out how she was raised, except the spirits."

"They slung them beads around her neck."

"To protect themselves."

"Get out of here"—I grabbed the girl—"before I sic the dogs on you."

"Too good," the old drunk flapped, "too damn good to wipe your own crap, ain't you. Storing money in your jar. What about your mother! Ignatius!" she shrieked. That was the name of my father.

The Morrissey had enough sense to be dragging her down the steps.

"Prince!" I yelled. "Dukie! Rex!"

The dogs came bounding up. The two went stumbling off, holding each other's sagging weighted arms, and that was all I had to see of those Lazarres for a long time.

So I took the girl. I kept her. It wasn't long before I would want to hold her against me tighter than any of the others. She was like me, and she was not like me. Sometimes I thought she was more like Eli. The woods were in June, after all, just like in him, and maybe more. She had sucked on pine sap and grazed grass and nipped buds like a deer.

The only Lazarre I had any use for was Lucille, so from the first I tried to find my sister's looks in the girl. I took her down behind the shack, where we kept the washtub in the summer, lugging a kettle of boiling water and a can of fuel. I put the kerosene in her hair, wiped the nits out with a rag and comb. I knew how much the fuel on her scalp must have burned. But she never moved, just kept her eyes screwed shut and plainly endured. That was the only likeness I saw to Lucille.

Otherwise, as I scrubbed the pitiful scraps of her and wiped ointment over the sores, I saw nothing, no feature that belonged to either one, Lazarre or Morrissey, and I was glad. It was as if she really was the child of what the old people called Manitous, invisible ones who live in the woods. I could tell, even as I washed, that the Devil had no business with June. There was no mark on her. When the sores healed she would be perfect. As I clipped her hair away from her face I even saw that she might be pretty looking. Really not like Lucille, I thought, or anyone else I was related to. It was no wonder, but this made me like the girl still better.

She was dark, but even so her looks started to gleam and shine once I had her eating like a human. I cut down a dress of Zelda's, a pair of Gordie's pants, a blouse I had owned myself. The one thing she kept on wearing was the beads. Trying to explain to her they were holy beads, not mere regular jewelry, did no good. She just backed away and clutched them in her fist. She wore them constant, even though the others teased her and jerked them lightly from behind when I was not looking. There was no Devil in her. If there was I would have seen. She hardly spoke two words to anyone and never fought back when Aurelia pinched her arm or Gordie sneaked a bun off her plate.

That is why, as things went on, I found myself talking for her. "Gordie," I'd say, "stop. She hates you to pull her hair."

It was as though I took over and became the voice that wouldn't come from her lips but could be seen, very plain, in the wide upslanted black eyes. At first, because I liked her so, I thought I knew what she was thinking, but as it turned out I did not know what went through her mind at all.

They used to like playing in the woods, and I liked them to play there, too. They could run and scream all day, as loud as they wanted. I liked the house to myself, afternoons. The babies fell asleep, and Nector worked off in the fields for someone else. Then I could think. I didn't have to sit still to think; all I needed was the quiet. I worked hard but I let my thoughts run out like water from a dam. I was churning and thinking that day. With each stroke of my dasher I progressed in thinking what to make of Nector. I had plans, and there was no use him trying to get out of them. I'd known from the beginning I had married a man with brains. But the brains wouldn't matter unless I kept him from the bottle. He would pour them down the drain, where his liquor went, unless I stopped the holes, wore him out, dragged him back each time he drank, and tied him to the bed with strong ropes.

I had decided I was going to make him into something big on this reservation. I didn't know what, not yet; I only knew when he got there they would not whisper "dirty Lazarre" when I walked down from church. They would wish they were the woman I was. Marie Kashpaw. I thought of my mother, strip of old blanket for her belt, and I dashed so hard the cream stuck to the wood.

I heard yells, Zelda's high, strained voice, the note she used when something she could tell on had happened. She flopped in the door.

"What's it now?" I asked, expecting Gordie had put a burr in her hair.

"It's June," she gasped. "Mama, they're hanging June out in the woods!"

I jumped. It was like a string snapped me from my chair. I ran out like a mad thing, over the field, right on Zelda's heels. When I got to the place, I saw Gordie was standing there with one end of the rope that was looped high around a branch. The other end was tied in a loose loop around June's neck.

"You got to tighten it," I heard June say clearly, "before you hoist me up."

I rushed forward. I flung off the noose. I grabbed Gordie's ear and I rapped his hind end. For good measure I grabbed Aurelia and licked her good, too. When I'd finished I threw them down and stood staring at them, panting and furious.

"Do you know what you almost did?" I screamed.

"She *wanted* us to hang her," Gordie said. "We were playing. She stole the horse."

"She told us to," Aurelia said. "She said where to put the rope."

Their lies maddened me.

"I'll show you where to put the rope," I yelled. I was going to knot it and use it again on them, when I heard a dry little sound, a tearless weeping sound, from June, and I turned.

She was standing upright, tall and bone-thin and hopeless, with the rosary wrapped around her hand as it is wrapped around the hands of the dead.

"You ruined it." Her eyes blinked at me, dry, as she choked it out. "I stole their horse. So I was supposed to be hanged."

I gaped at her.

"Child," I said, "you don't know how to play. It's a game, but if they hang you they would hang you for real."

She put her head down. I could almost have sworn she knew what was real and what was not real, and that I'd still ruined it.

"You damn old bitch." I heard, unbelievably, those words muttered under her breath.

"What?"

"You damn old bitch," she said, aloud, again.

I grabbed the back of her shirt and yanked her flying across the field. She was light as a leaf. I tossed her in the house. Then I grabbed the jaw and packed a handful of soap flakes in her mouth. None of my children ever called me a bad name before. She spat and bubbled.

"Damn old chicken!" she gasped again. Looking at her face, strained and wild, sick and greening on the soap, I had to wonder if she knew what she was saying. Was her mind shot? The other children were gaping at the door, satisfied with horror, thrilled with her punishment.

"Chores!" I said. They vanished in a whirl of clothes and flying hair. Then I set June down in front of me and closely watched her.

Brave as me, that was June. The soap flakes surely gagged her. But she spat them carefully into the dishcloth I put in her hands. She wouldn't look at me.

"Look at me," I said.

I turned her head toward me and looked in her sorrowful black eyes. I looked a long time, as if I was falling down a hill. She blinked gravely and returned my stare. There was a sadness I couldn't touch there. It was a hurt place, it was deep, it was with her all the time like a broke rib that stabbed when she breathed. I took her hand.

"June Morrissey," I said, "your mama was my sister."

She looked at me, still not speaking.

"Your mama died," I said.

There was a flicker of a lash.

"You can be my girl and live here."

She spoke to me, finally, with no expression. "I don't care."

Maybe she cared and maybe she did not. She stayed shut. Nector had no time for any of them then, not him with his slim wages and his chips at the pool hall and home-brewed wine. If I wasn't feeding children I was chasing Nector down. I knew all the back rooms. I'd take money from his hand that was lighting on the bar. I'd leave him nothing. He'd have to come home and beg when he needed more. So I didn't have much time for any one of the children about then, and I was glad, that summer, when Eli came around.

Spring and summer, when the furs were thin, we'd see more of Eli around home. He lived in a mud-chink bachelor shack on the other end of the land. He was a nothing-and-nowhere person, not a husband match for any woman, but I had to like him. Eli drank but he never lost his head. He rarely spoke. Sometimes we sat in a room all evening, hardly talking, although he spoke easy with the children. I'd overhear. He had a soft hushed voice, like he was stalking something very near. He showed them how to carve, how to listen for the proper birdcall, how to whistle on their own fingers like a flute. He taught June.

Or she taught him. They went into the woods with their snares and never came home empty-handed. They went to the sloughs to shoot mud hens and brought home a bag of the tiny, black, greasy birds. Nector was rarely home then. He worked late or sneaked to gamble. We'd roast the birds and make a high pile of their twig bones in the middle of the table. Eli would sing his songs. Wild unholy songs. Cree songs that made you lonely. Hunting songs used to attract deer or women. He wasn't shy when he sang them. I had to keep to my mending.

I was seeing how the girl spoke more often once he started

coming. She'd picked an old scrap of billed hat from a dump and wore it just like him, soft and squashed in on her hair. I began to understand what she was doing as time went on. It was a mother she couldn't trust after what had happened in the woods. But Eli was different. He could chew pine sap too.

The old hens were starting to cackle.

Seven senses. Seven senses for scandal was what they had in those days. They came around to my door just to pass the time away. I let them in for brewed coffee. They were the ones I knew the smell of, who made novenas and holy days and nosed up to the priests. They were eager to sniff what was happening in my house.

"Where's Nector?" Old Lady Blue, innocent as day, wonders. She thinks she saw him passed out around back of the agency pump house. But certainly that could not be him!

"Does Eli, your brother-in-law, live here now instead?" Sly and shriveled old bean pod!

"How about that girl," says old, fat LaRue. "Do you trust him alone with her all the time like that? I see them coming out of the woods, down the road. What do they got in their bag?"

I just laugh, don't let them get a wedge in. Then I turn the table on them, because they don't know how many goods I have collected in town.

"How's your son? Too bad he crossed the border. I heard he had to go. Are you taking in his newborn?"

"I tell you for your own good. Your man goes to Lamartine's house with a bagged bottle, Mrs. Blue."

"How's your heart? It's a shame your daughter left you."

I didn't like to be the one to remind these old cows of their own bad lives. But I had to protect my plans. There was just a temporary hitch in them—Nector having a last fling.

One night and then another night he didn't come home. The second night Eli sang late until the children hung asleep in their chairs. They had to be carried off and fit together on the rollaway, neat puzzles of arms and legs. When they were all arranged we went back in the kitchen. This was usually the time Eli walked back to his place. But instead of taking leave, he sat down at the table again and rolled a stub of tobacco from his pouch.

It was nothing. I sewed a long rip. A longer seam. It was nothing. But I felt his eyes resting upon me and I couldn't look up at him. The cloth turned in my hands. The lamp burned. I thought of lake-shore pebbles, naked as eyes and smooth, and I thought of his lean hands, and I did not dare move. Something dark and wavering, fringed like a flower's mouth, was collecting in the room between us. I felt him standing up. I felt the rustle of his soft, stained clothes. He stepped once. The board creaked. I went helpless at the sound, and my hands locked.

"Marie?" he asked, very quiet.

I did not look up.

When I didn't answer, he stepped to the door quickly, all of a sudden, and walked out.

My head snapped up. I looked directly into the face of June. Soundless as air she had unwound herself from all the others and stood in the doorway, waiting and watching for what she felt in the air. She didn't know what she felt. I put the needle down.

"Come here," I said.

She came, walking as in a dream, and I held her in my lap for the first and only time. I held her and I stroked her hair and hummed in her ear. She pretended to sleep, breathing evenly and pure. I stroked the beads around her neck. Then sleep took her for real. The strain went out of her. The breath came deep. She sagged like an empty sack. I held her until my legs went numb under her weight, until the lampwick smoked, until the board creaked again and it was Nector, come home.

I had fallen asleep in the chair. I don't know how long he'd stood there, staring at me with the child in my arms. I saw that he had gone through the wringer. He was red-eyed, gaunt, and he was drunk. When I opened my eyes he began to reach into his pockets with both hands.

He pulled out bills, coins, and crumpled dollars. He laid them in the mending. He took the money from his hatband. He emptied his shoes. He had a small roll in his sock. He had a bill clipped to his belt.

"C'mere now," he said. The money was a rumpled, winking pile. I never moved. He bent over and took June from my arms. He laid her in the small space of bed where she belonged, and then he came back to the kitchen for me.

I didn't ask him where he got all that money.

I went down beneath his hands and lay quiet. I rolled with his current like a stone in the lake. He fell on me like a wave. But like a wave he washed away, leaving no sign he'd been there. I was smooth as before. I slept hard, and when I woke he was gone.

All day with the children, I felt a low grief I couldn't name yet. Something inside me had shrunk and hardened in the deep. One thing more. He had not left behind even a trace of coin. When I went out to the kitchen, I saw that the table was bare. He might not have even come home. It so discouraged me I could not go out this time and drag him back. I was so deeply sunk that I was not surprised when the girl came to me, anxious and still. I was not surprised that she would speak to me.

I was peeling potatoes in the same chair we sat in the night before. But she'd slept through that, of course, and would not remember.

"I want to live with Eli," she said in a voice clear as the voice she used giving directions to be hung. "I'm going to Eli's house."

"Go ahead, then," I said.

I kept peeling the potato. One long spiral and it's finished. I never even looked when she walked out the door, and only later in the season, when everything was bare and the rain slashed down without the mercy to turn to clean snow, did I reach my hand deep in the lard can where I kept my spools, scraps, and papers of pins. I knew before I even touched them. Her beads in a black heap.

I don't pray. When I was young, I vowed I never would be caught begging God. If I want something I get it for myself. I go to church only to show the old hens they don't get me down.

I don't pray, but sometimes I do touch the beads.

It has become a secret. I never look at them, just let my fingers roam to them when no one is in the house. It's a rare time when I do this. I touch them, and every time I do I think of small stones. At the bottom of the lake, rolled aimless by the waves, I think of them polished. To many people it would be a kindness. But I see no kindness in how the waves are grinding them smaller and smaller until they finally disappear.

LULU'S BOYS

(1957)

On the last day that Lulu Lamartine spent as Henry's widow, her boys were outside drinking beers and shooting plastic jugs. Her deceased husband's brother, Beverly, was sitting across from her at the kitchen table. Having a name some people thought of as feminine had turned Beverly Lamartine to building up his muscles in his youth, and they still bulged, hard as ingots in some places, now lost in others. His plush belly strained open the bottom buttons of his black shirt, and Lulu saw his warm skin peeking through. She also saw how the tattoos he and Henry had acquired on their arms, and which Lulu had always admired, were now deep black and so fuzzy around the edges that she could hardly tell what they were.

Beverly saw her looking at the old tattoos and pushed his sleeves up over his biceps. "Get an eyeful." He grinned. As of old, he stretched his arms across the table, and she gazed at the figures commemorating the two brothers' drunken travels outside her life.

There was a doll, a skull with a knife stuck in it, an eagle, a swallow, and Beverly's name, rank, and serial number. Looking at the arm made Lulu remember her husband's tattoos. Henry's arms had been imprinted with a banner bearing some other woman's name, a rose with a bleeding thorn, two lizards, and like his brother's, with his name, rank, and serial number.

Sometimes Lulu could not help it. She thought of everything so hard that her mind felt warped and sodden as a door that swells up in spring. It would not close properly to keep the troublesome thoughts out.

Right now she thought of those two lizards on either one of Henry's arms. She imagined them clenching together when he put his arms around her. Then she thought of them coupling the same way she and Henry did. She thought of this while looking at Beverly's lone swallow, a bird with outstretched wings deep as ink and bleeding into his flesh. She remembered Beverly's trick: the wings were carefully tattooed on certain muscles, so that when he flexed his arm the bird almost seemed to hover in a dive or swoop.

Lulu hadn't seen her husband's brother since the funeral in 1950, with the casket closed because of how badly Henry had suffered in the car wreck. Drunk, he had started driving the old Northern Pacific tracks and either fallen asleep or passed out, his car straddling the rails. As he'd left the bar that night everyone who had been there remembered his words.

"She comes barreling through, you'll never see me again."

At first they had thought he was talking about Lulu. But even at the time they knew she didn't lose her temper over drinking. It was the train Henry had been talking about. They realized that later when the news came and his casket was sealed.

Beverly Lamartine had shown up from the Twin Cities one

hour before his brother's service was held. He had brought along the trophy flag—a black swastika on torn red cloth—that he had captured to revenge the oldest Lamartine, a quiet boy, hardly spoken of now, who was killed early on while still in boot camp.

When the men from the veteran's post had lowered Henry's casket into the grave on ropes, there was a U.S. flag draped across it already. Beverly had shaken out the trophy flag. He'd let it go in the air, and the wind seemed to suck it down, the black arms of the insignia whirling like a spider.

Watching it, Lulu had gone faint. The sudden spokes of the black wheel flashed before her eyes and she'd toppled dizzily, then stumbled over the edge of the grave.

The men were still lowering Henry on ropes. Lulu plunged heavily down with the trophy flag, and the ropes burned out of the pallbearers' hands. The box hit bottom. People screamed and there was a great deal of commotion, during which Beverly jumped down to revive Lulu. All together, the pallbearers tugged and hoisted her out. The black garments seemed to make her even denser than she was. Her round face and chubby hands were a pale dough color, cold and wet with shock. For hours afterward she trembled, uttered senseless vowels, jumped at sounds and touches. Some people, assuming that she had jumped in the grave to be buried along with Henry, thought much better of her for a while.

But most of her life Lulu had been known as a flirt. And that was putting it mildly. Tongues less kind had more indicting things to say.

For instance, besides the fact of Lulu Lamartine's first husband, why did each of the boys currently shooting milk jugs out front of Henry's house look so different? There were eight of them. Some of them even had her maiden name. The three oldest were Nanapushes. The next oldest were Morrisseys who took the name Lamartine, and then there were more assorted younger Lamartines who didn't look like one another, either. Red hair and blond abounded; there was some brown. The black hair on the seven-year-old at least matched his mother's. This boy was named Henry Junior, and he had been born approximately nine months after Henry Senior's death.

Give or take a week, Beverly thought, looking from Henry Junior out the window back to the woman across the table. Beverly was quite certain that he, and not his brother, was the father of that boy. In fact, Beverly had come back to the reservation with a hidden purpose.

Beverly Lamartine wanted to claim Henry Junior and take him home.

In the Twin Cities there were great relocation opportunities for Indians with a certain amount of natural stick-to-it-iveness and pride. That's how Beverly saw it. He was darker than most, but his parents had always called themselves French or Black Irish and considered those who thought of themselves as Indians quite backward. They had put the need to get ahead in Beverly. He worked devilishly hard.

Door to door, he'd sold children's after-school home workbooks for the past eighteen years. The wonder of it was that he had sold any workbook sets at all, for he was not an educated man and if the customers had, as they might naturally do, considered him an example of his product's efficiency they might not have entrusted their own children to those pages of sums and reading exercises. But they did buy the workbook sets regularly, for Bev's ploy was to use his humble appearance and faulty grammar to ease into conversation with his hardworking get-ahead customers. They looked forward to seeing the higher qualities, which they could not afford, inculcated in their own children. Beverly's territory was a small-town world of earnest dreamers. Part of Bev's pitch, and the one that usually sold the books, was to show the wife or husband a wallet-sized school photo of his son.

That was Henry Junior. The back of the photo was inscribed

"To Uncle Bev," but the customer never saw that, because the precious relic was encased in a cardboard-backed sheet of clear plastic. This covering preserved it from thousands of mill-toughened thumbs in the working-class sections of Minneapolis and small towns within its one-hundred-mile radius. Every year or so Beverly wrote to Lulu, requesting another picture. It was sent to him in perfect goodwill. With every picture Beverly grew more familiar with his son and more inspired in the invention of tales he embroidered, day after day, on front porches that were to him the innocent stages for his routine.

His son played baseball in a sparkling-white uniform stained across the knees with grass. He pitched no-hitters every few weeks. Teachers loved the boy for getting so far ahead of the other students on his own initiative. They sent him on to various higher grades, and he was invited to the parties of children in the wealthy suburb of Edina. Henry Junior cleared the hurdles of class and intellect with an ease astonishing to Beverly, who noted to his wistful customers how swiftly the young surpass the older generation.

"Give them wings!" he would urge, flipping softly through the cheap pulp-flecked pages. The sound of the ruffled paper was like the panic of fledglings before they learn how to glide. People usually bought, and only later, when they found themselves rolling up a work-skills book to slaughter a fly or scribbling phone numbers down on the back of *Math Enrichment*, would they realize that their children had absolutely no interest in taking the world by storm through self-enlightenment.

Some days, after many hours of stories, the son became so real in Bev's mind that when he came home to the apartment, he half expected the boy to pounce on him before he put his key in the door. But when the lock turned his son vanished, for Elsa would be there, and she was not particularly interested in children, real or not. She was a typist who changed jobs incessantly. Groomed with exquisite tawdriness, she'd fashioned for Bev the image of a modern woman living the ideal career life. Her salary only fluctuated by pennies from firm to firm, but her importance and value as a knower-of-ropes swelled. She believed herself indispensable, but she heartlessly left employers hanging in their times of worst need to go on to something better.

Beverly adored her.

She was a natural blond with birdlike legs and, true, no chin, but great blue snapping eyes. She smoked exotically, rolling smoke off her tongue, and often told Bev that two weeks from now he might not be seeing her again. Then she would soften toward him. The possibilities she gave up to be with him impressed Bev so much, every time, that it ceased to bother him that Elsa only showed him off to her family in Saint Cloud at the height of summer, when they admired his perfect tan.

The boy, though, who was everywhere in his life and yet nowhere, fit less easily into Bev's fantasy of how he lived. The boy made him ache in hidden, surprising places sometimes at night when he lay next to Elsa, his knuckles resting lightly against her emphatic spine. That was the limit of touching she would tolerate in slumber. She even took her sleeping breath with a certain rigid meanness, holding it stubbornly and releasing it with small explosive sighs. Bev hardly noticed, though, for beside her his mind raced through the ceilings and walls.

One night he saw himself traveling. He was driving his sober green car westward, past the boundaries of his salesman's territory, then over the state line and on across to the casual and lonely fields, the rich, dry violet hills of the reservation. Then he was home where his son really lived. Lulu came to the door. He habitually blotted away her face and body, so that in his thoughts she was a doll of flour sacking with a curly black mop on her head. She was simply glad that he had come at last to take the son she had such trouble providing for off her hands. She was glad

Henry Junior would be wafted into a new and better metropolitan existence.

This scenario became so real through the quiet hours he lay beside Elsa that Bev even convinced himself that his wife would take to Henry Junior, in spite of the way she shuddered at children in the streets and whispered "Monkeys!" And then, by the time the next workday was half over, he'd arranged for a vacation and made an appointment to have a once-over done on his car.

Of course, Lulu was not made of flour sacking and yarn. Beverly had realized that in the immediacy of her arms. She grabbed him for a hug when he got out of his car, and, tired by the long trip, his head whirled for a moment in a haze of yellow spots. When she released him, the boys sauntered up, poker-faced and mildly suspicious, to stand in a group around him and await their introductions. There seemed to be so many that at first he was speechless. Each of them was Henry Junior in a different daydream, at a different age, and so alike were their flat expressions he couldn't even pick out the one whose picture sold the record number of home workbooks in the Upper Midwestern Regional Division.

Henry Junior, of course, was perfectly recognizable after Lulu introduced him. After all, he did look exactly like the picture in Bev's wallet. He put his hand out and shook manfully like his older brothers, which pleased Bev, although he had trouble containing a moment of confusion at the utter indifference in the boy's eyes. He had to remember the boy was meeting him for the first time. In a child's world strange grown-ups are indistinguishable as trees in a forest. Even the writing on the back of those photographs was probably, now that he thought of it, Lulu's.

They went away, started shooting their guns, and then Bev was left with the unexpected problem of the mother of his son, the woman he would just as soon forget. During a moment of adjustment, however, he decided to go through whatever set of manipulations were necessary. He wanted to handle the situation in the ideal, firm, but diplomatic manner. And then, after he'd recovered from the strength of her hug, he had absolutely no doubt that things would go on according to his plan.

"My my my," he said to Lulu now. She was buttering a piece of bread soft as the plump undersides of her arms. "Lot of water under the dam."

She agreed, taking alert nips of her perfectly covered slice. She had sprinkled a teaspoon of sugar over it, carefully distributing the grains. That was how she was. Even with eight boys her house was neat as a pin. The candy bowl on the table sat precisely on its doily. All her furniture was brushed and straightened. Her coffee table held a neat stack of *Fate* and *True Adventure* magazines. On her walls she'd hung matching framed portraits of poodles, kittens, and an elaborate embroidered portrait of Chief Joseph. Her windowsills were decorated with pincushions in the shapes of plump little hats and shoes.

"I make these." She cupped a tiny blue sequined pump in her hand. "You have a girl friend? I'll give it to you. Here."

She pushed the little shoe across the table. It skittered over the edge, fell into his lap, and Beverly retrieved it quickly, for he saw that her hand was following. He set the blue slipper between them without addressing her implicit question on his status—girl friend, married, or just looking around. He was intent on bringing up the subject of Henry Junior.

"Remember that time . . ." he started. Then he didn't know what he was going to say. What did come out surprised him. "You and me and Henry were playing cards before you got married and the boys were sleeping?"

He could have kicked himself for having blurted that out. Even after all these years he couldn't touch on the memory without running a hand across his face or whistling tunelessly to drive it from his mind. It didn't seem to have bothered her all these years though. She picked up the story smoothly and went on.

"Oh, you men," she laughed chidingly. Her face was so little like Beverly's flour sacking doll he wondered how he had stood imagining her that way all these years. Her mouth was small, mobile, like a puckering flower, and her teeth were unusually tiny and white. He remembered having the urge to lick their smoothness once. But now she was talking.

"I suppose you thought you could take advantage of a poor young woman. I don't know who it was, you or Henry, that suggested after several too many beers that we change our penny-ante poker game to strip. Well I still have to laugh. I had you men right down to your boxer shorts in no time flat, and I was sitting there, warm and cozy as you please. I was still in my dress with my shoes on my feet."

"You had them beads on, clip earrings, bangle bracelets, silk stockings," Beverly pouted.

"Garters and other numerous foundation garments. Of course I did. I am a woman of detachable parts. You should know by now. You simply weren't playing in your league with strip poker."

She had the grace to put a hand to her lips as they uncurved, hiding the little gap-toothed smile he'd doted over at the time of that game.

"Want to know something I never told before?" she said. "It was after I won your shorts with my pair of deuces and Henry's with my eights, and you were naked, that I decided which one to marry."

Beverly was shocked at this statement, bold even for Lulu. His wind felt knocked out of him for a moment, because her words called up the old times so clearly, the way he felt when she decided to marry his brother. He'd buried the feelings eventually in the knowledge that she wasn't right for him, man of the world that he was becoming. He congratulated himself for years after on getting free of her slack, ambitionless, but mindlessly powerful female clutches. Right now his reasoning had ripped wide open, however, and jealousy kicked him in the stomach.

Lulu cooed. Her voice was like a wind chime rattling. Cheap, sweet, maddening. "Some men react in that situation and some don't," she told him. "It was reaction I looked for, if you know what I mean."

Beverly was silent.

Lulu winked at him with her bold, gleaming blackberry eyes. She had smooth tight skin, wrinkled only where she laughed, always fragrantly powdered. At the time her hair was still dark and thickly curled. Later she would burn it off when her house caught fire, and it would never grow back. Because her face was soft and yet alert, vigilant as some small cat's, plump and tame but with a wildness in its breast, Beverly had always felt exposed, preyed on, undressed around her, even before the game in which she'd stripped him naked and now, as he found, appraised him in his shame.

You got your reaction when you needed it, he wanted to say.

Yet, even in his mounting exasperation, he did not lose control and stoop to discussing what had happened after Henry's wake, when they both went outside to get some air. He rolled his sleeves down and fished a soft pack of Marlboros from her side of the table. She watched his hand as he struck the match, and her eyes narrowed. They were so black the iris sometimes showed within like blue flames. He thought her heartless, suddenly, and wondered if she even remembered the two of them in the shed after Henry's wake. But there was no good way he could think of to ask without getting back down to her level.

Henry Junior came to the window, hungry, and Lulu made a sandwich for him with baloney and hot-dog relish. The boy was seven years old, sturdy, with Lulu's delicate skin and the almost Asian-looking eyes of all the Lamartines. Beverly watched the boy with electrified attention. He couldn't really say if anything about the child reminded him of himself, unless it was the gaze. Beverly had tried to train his gaze like a hawk to use in barroom stare-downs during his tour of duty. It came in handy, as well, when he made a sale, although civilian life had long ago taken the edge off his intensity, as it had his muscles, his hero's stubborn, sagging flesh that he could still muster in a crisis. There was a crisis now. The boy seemed to have acquired the stare-down technique naturally. Beverly was the first to look away.

"Uncle Bev," Henry Junior said. "I always heard about the bird on your arm. Could you make it fly?"

So Beverly rolled up shirt sleeve once more and forced his blood up. He flexed powerfully, over and over, until the boy was bored, satisfied, and fled back to his brothers. Beverly let his arm down carefully. It was numb. The sound of the .22 reports came thick and fast for a while, then all the boys paused to reload and set the jugs in a line against the fence and argue over whose shot went where.

"They're teaching him to shoot," explained Lulu. "We had two bucks brought down last fall. And pheasants? Those boys will always put meat on my table."

She rambled on about them all, and Bev listened with relief, gathering his strength to pull the conversation back his way again.

One of the oldest boys was going down to Haskell Junior College, while another, Gerry, was testing the limits of the mission school system, at twelve. Lulu pointed Gerry out among the others. Bev could see Lulu most clearly in this boy. He laughed at everything, or seemed barely to be keeping amusement in. His eyes were black, sly, snapping with sparks. He led the rest in play without a hint of effort, just like Lulu, whose gestures worked as subtle magnets. He was a big boy, a born leader, light on his feet and powerful. His mind seemed quick. It would not surprise Bev to hear, after many years passed on, that this Gerry grew up to be both a natural criminal and a hero whose face appeared on the six-o'clock news.

Lulu managed to make the younger boys obey perfectly, Bev noticed, while the older ones adored her to the point that they did not tolerate anything less from anyone else. As her voice swirled on, Bev thought of some Tarzan book he had read. In that book there was a queen protected by bloodthirsty warriors who smoothly dispatched all of her enemies. Lulu's boys had grown into a kind of pack. They always hung together. When a shot went true, their gangling legs, encased alike in faded denim, shifted as if a ripple went through them collectively. They moved in dance steps too intricate for the noninitiated eye to imitate or understand. Clearly they were of one soul. Handsome, rangy, wildly various, they were bound in total loyalty, not by oath but by the simple, unquestioning belongingness of part of one organism.

Lulu had gone silent, suddenly, to fetch something from her icebox. In that quiet moment something about the boys outside struck Beverly as almost dangerous.

He watched them close around Henry Junior in an impenetrable mass of black-and-white sneakers, sweatshirts, baseball hats, and butts of Marlin rifles. Through the chinks between their bodies Beverly saw Gerry, dark and electric as his mother, kneel behind Henry Junior and arm-over-arm instruct him how to cradle, aim, and squeeze-fire the .22. When Henry Junior stumbled, kicked backward by the recoil, missing the jug, the boys dusted him clean and set him back behind the rifle again. Slowly, as he watched, Beverly's uneasy sense of menace gave way to some sweet apprehension of their kinship. He was remembering the way he and Henry and Slick, the oldest of his brothers, used to put themselves on the line for each other in high school. People used to say you couldn't drive a knife edge between the

Lamartines. Nothing ever came between them. Nothing ever did or would.

Even while he was thinking that, Beverly knew it wasn't true.

What had come between them was a who, and she was standing across from him now at the kitchen counter. Lulu licked some unseen sweetness from her fingers, having finished her sugared bread. Her tongue was small, flat, and pale as a little cat's. Her eyes had shut in mystery. He wondered if she knew his thoughts.

She padded easily toward him, and he stood up in an odd panic as she approached. He felt his heart knock urgently as a stranger in trouble, and then she touched him through his pants. He was helpless. His mouth fell on hers and kept traveling, through the walls and ceilings, down the levels, through the broad, warm reaches of the years.

The boys came back very late in the afternoon. By then, Beverly had drastically revised his plans for Henry Junior to the point where he had no plans at all. In a dazed, immediate, unhappy bewilderment he sat on the doily-bedecked couch opening and closing his hands in his lap. Lulu was bustling about the kitchen in a calm, automatic frenzy. She seemed to fill pots with food by pointing at them and take things from the oven that she'd never put in. The table jumped to set itself. The pop foamed into glasses, and the milk sighed to the lip. The youngest boy, Lyman, crushed in a high chair, watched eagerly while things placed themselves around him. Everyone sat down. Then the boys began to stuff themselves with a savage and astonishing efficiency. Before Bev had cleaned his plate once, they'd had thirds, and by the time he looked up from dessert, they had melted through the walls. The youngest had levitated from his high chair and was sleeping out of sight. The room was empty except for Lulu and himself.

He looked at her. She turned to the sinkful of dishes and disappeared in a cloud of steam. Only the round rear of her blue flowered housedress was visible, so he watched that. It was too late now. He had fallen. He could not help but remember their one night together.

They had gone into the shed while the earth was still damp and the cut flowers in their foam balls still exuded scent over Henry's grave. Beverly had kissed the small cries back onto Lulu's lips. He remembered. Then passion overtook them. She hung on to him like they were riding the tossing ground, her teeth grinding in his ear. He wasn't man or woman. None of that mattered. Yet he was more of a man than he'd ever been. The grief of loss for the beloved made their tiny flames of life so sad and precious it hardly mattered who was what. The flesh was only given so that the flame could touch in a union however less than perfect. Afterward they lay together, breathing the dark in and out. He had wept the one other time in his life besides post combat, and after a while he came into her again, tasting his own miraculous continuance.

Lulu left him sitting on the couch and went back into the sacred domain of her femininity. That was the bedroom with the locking door that she left open just a crack. She pulled down the blue-and-white-checked bedspread, put the pillows aside, and lay down carefully with her hands folded on her stomach. She closed her eyes and breathed deep. She went into herself, sinking through her body as if on a raft of darkness, until she reached the very bottom of her soul where there was nothing to do but wait.

Things had gotten by Beverly. Night came down. His sad dazzlement abated and he tried to avoid thinking of Elsa. But she was there filing her orange nails whichever way he ducked. And then there was the way he was proud of living his life. He wanted to go back and sell word-enrichment books. No one on the reservation would buy them, he knew, and the thought panicked him. He realized that the depth and danger of his situation was great if he had forgotten that basic fact. The moon went black. The bushes seemed to close around the house.

Retrench, he told himself, as the boys turned heavily and mumbled in their invisible cots and all along the floors around him. Retreat if you have to and forget about Henry Junior. He finally faced surrender and knew it was the only thing he could possibly have the strength for.

He planned to get into his car while it was still dark, before dawn, and drive back to Minneapolis without Henry Junior. He would simply have to bolt without saying good-bye to Lulu. But when he rose from the couch, he walked down the hall to her bedroom door. He didn't pause but walked right through. It was like routine he'd built up over time in marriage. The close dark was scented with bath lilac. Glowing green spears told the hour in her side-table clock. The bedclothes rustled. He stood holding the lathed wooden post. And then his veins were full of warm ash and his tongue swelled in his throat.

He lay down in her arms.

Whirling blackness swept through him, and there was nothing else to do.

The wings didn't beat as hard as they used to, but the bird still flew.

THE PLUNGE OF THE BRAVE

(1957)

NECTOR KASHPAW

I never wanted much, and I needed even less, but what happened was that I got everything handed to me on a plate. It came from being a Kashpaw, I used to think. Our family was respected as the last hereditary leaders of this tribe. But Kashpaws died out around here, people forgot, and I still kept getting offers.

What kind of offers? Just ask . . .

Jobs for one. I got out of Flandreau with my ears rung from playing football, and the first thing they said was "Nector Kashpaw, go West! Hollywood wants *you*!" They made a lot of westerns in those days. I never talk about this often, but they were hiring for a scene in South Dakota and this talent scout picked me out from the graduating class. His company was pulling in extras for the wagon-train scenes. Because of my height, I got hired on for the biggest Indian part. But they didn't know I was a Kashpaw, because right off I had to die.

"Clutch your chest. Fall off that horse," they directed. That was it. Death was the extent of Indian acting in the movie theater.

So I thought it was quite enough to be killed the once you have to die in this life, and I quit. I hopped a train down the wheat belt and threshed. I got offers there too. Jobs came easy. I worked a year. I was thinking of staying on, but then I got a proposition that discouraged me out of Kansas for good.

Down in the city I met this old rich woman. She had her car stopped when she saw me pass by.

"Ask the chief if he'd like to work for me," she said to her man up front. So her man, a buffalo soldier, did.

"Doing what?" I asked.

"I want him to model for my masterpiece. Tell him all he has to do is stand still and let me paint his picture."

"Sounds easy enough." I agreed.

The pay was fifty dollars. I went to her house. They fed me, and later on they sent me over to her barn. I went in. When I saw her dressed in a white coat with a hat like a little black pancake on her head, I felt pity. She was an old wreck of a thing. Snaggle-toothed. She put me on a block of wood and then said to me, "Disrobe."

No one had ever told me to take off my clothes just like that. So I pretended not to understand her. "What robe?" I asked.

"Disrobe," she repeated. I stood there and looked confused. Pitiful! I thought. Then she started to demonstrate by clawing at her buttons. I was just about to go and help her when she said in a near holler, "Take off your clothes!"

She wanted to paint me without a stitch on, of course. There were lots of naked pictures in her barn. I wouldn't do it. She offered money, more money, until she offered me so much that I had to forget my dignity. So I was paid by this woman a round two hundred dollars for standing stock still in a diaper.

I could not believe it, later, when she showed me the picture. *Plunge of the Brave,* was the title of it. Later on, that picture would become famous. It would hang in the Bismarck state capitol. There I was, jumping off a cliff, naked of course, down into a rocky river. Certain death. Remember Custer's saying? The only good Indian is a dead Indian? Well from my dealings with whites I would add to that quote: "The only interesting Indian is dead, or dying by falling backwards off a horse."

When I saw that the greater world was only interested in my doom, I went home on the back of a train. Riding the rails one night the moon was in the boxcar. A nip was in the air. I remembered that picture, and I knew that Nector Kashpaw would fool the pitiful rich woman that painted him and survive the raging water. I'd hold my breath when I hit and let the current pull me toward the surface, around jagged rocks. I wouldn't fight it, and in that way I'd get to shore.

Back home, it seemed like that was happening for a while. Things were quiet. I lived with my mother and Eli in the old place, hunting or roaming or chopping a little wood. I kept thinking about the one book I read in high school. For some reason this priest in Flandreau would teach no other book all four years but *Moby Dick*, the story of the great white whale. I knew that book inside and out. I'd even stolen a copy from school and taken it home in my suitcase.

This led to another famous misunderstanding.

"You're always reading that book," my mother said once. "What's in it?"

"The story of the great white whale."

She could not believe it. After a while, she said, "What do they got to wail about, those whites?"

I told her the whale was a fish as big as the church. She did not believe this either. Who would?

"Call me Ishmael," I said sometimes, only to myself. For he survived the great white monster like I got out of the rich lady's picture. He let the water bounce his coffin to the top. In my life so far I'd gone easy and come out on top, like him. But the river wasn't done with me yet. I floated through the calm sweet spots, but somewhere the river branched.

So far I haven't mentioned the other offers I had been getting. These offers were for candy, sweet candy between the bedcovers. There was girls like new taffy, hardened sourballs of married ladies, rich marshmallow widows, and even a man, rock salt and barley sugar in a jungle of weeds. I never did anything to bring these offers on. They just happened. I never thought twice. Then I fell in love for real.

Lulu Nanapush was the one who made me greedy.

At boarding school, as children, I treated her as my sister and shared out peanut-butter-syrup sandwiches on the bus to stop her crying. I let her tag with me to town. At the movies I bought her licorice. Then we grew up apart from each other, I came home, and saw her dancing in the Friday-night crowd. She was doing the butterfly with two other men. For the first time, on seeing her, I knew exactly what I wanted. We sparked each other. We met behind the dance house and kissed. I knew I wanted more of that sweet taste on her mouth. I got selfish. We were flowing easily toward each other's arms.

Then Marie appeared, and here is what I do not understand: how instantly the course of your life can be changed.

I only know that I went up the convent hill intending to sell geese and came down the hill with the geese still on my arm. Beside me walked a young girl with a mouth on her like a flophouse, although she was innocent. She grudged me to hold her hand. And yet I would not drop the hand and let her walk alone.

Her taste was bitter. I craved the difference after all those years of easy sweetness. But I still had a taste for candy. I could never have enough of both, and that was my problem and the reason that long past the branch in my life I continued to think of Lulu.

Not that I had much time to think once married years set in. I liked each of our babies, but sometimes I was juggling them from both arms and losing hold. Both Marie and I lost hold. In one year, two died, a boy and a girl baby. There was a long spell of quiet, awful quiet, before the babies showed up everywhere again. They were all over in the house once they started. In the bottoms of cupboards, in the dresser, in trundles. Lift a blanket and a bundle would howl beneath it. I lost track of which were ours and which Marie had taken in. It had helped her to take them in after our two others were gone. This went on. The youngest slept between us, in the bed of our bliss, so I was crawling over them to make more of them. It seemed like there was no end.

Sometimes I escaped. I had to have relief. I went drinking and caught holy hell from Marie. After a few years the babies started walking around, but that only meant they needed shoes for their feet. I gave in. I put my nose against the wheel. I kept it there for many years and barely looked up to realize the world was going by, full of wonders and creatures, while I was getting old baling hay for white farmers.

So much time went by in that flash it surprises me yet. What they call a lot of water under the bridge. Maybe it was rapids, a swirl that carried me so swift that I could not look to either side but had to keep my eyes trained on what was coming. Seventeen years of married life and come-and-go children.

And then it was like the river pooled.

Maybe I took my eyes off the current too quick. Maybe the fast movement of time had made me dizzy. I was shocked. I remember the day it happened. I was sitting on the steps, wiring a pot of Marie's that had broken, when everything went still. The children stopped shouting. Marie stopped scolding. The babies slept. The cows chewed. The dogs stretched full out in the heat. Nothing moved. Not a leaf or a bell or a human. No sound. It was like the air itself had caved in.

In that stillness, I lifted my head and looked around.

What I saw was time passing, each minute collecting behind me before I had squeezed from it any life. It went so fast, is what I'm saying, that I myself sat still in the center of it. Time was rushing around me like water around a big wet rock. The only difference is, I was not so durable as stones. Very quickly I would be smoothed away. It was happening already.

I put my hand to my face. There was less of me. Less muscle, less hair, less of a hard jaw, less of what used to go on below. Fewer offers. It was 1952, and I had done what was expected—fathered babies, served as chairman of the tribe. That was the extent of it. Don't let the last fool you, either. Getting into the big-time local politics was all low pay and no thanks. I never even ran for the office. Someone put my name down on the ballots, and the night I accepted the job I became somebody less, almost instantly. I grew gray hairs in my sleep. The next morning they were hanging in the comb teeth.

Less and less, until I was sitting on my steps in 1952 thinking I should hang on to whatever I still had.

That is the state of mind I was in when I began to think of Lulu. The truth is I had never gotten over her. I thought back to how swiftly we had been moving toward each other's soft embrace before everything got tangled and swept me on past. In my mind's eye I saw her arms stretched out in longing while I shrank into the blue distance of marriage. Although it had happened with no effort on my part, to ever get back I'd have to swim against the movement of time.

I shook my head to clear it. The children started to shout. Marie scolded, the babies blubbered, the cow stamped, and the dogs complained. The moment of stillness was over; it was brief, but the fact is when I got up from the front steps I was changed.

I put the fixed pot on the table, took my hat off the hook, went out and drove my pickup into town. My brain was sending me the kind of low ache that used to signal a lengthy drunk, and yet that was not what I felt like doing.

Anyway, once I got to town and stopped by the tribal offices, a drunk was out of the question. An emergency was happening.

And here is where events loop around and tangle again.

It is July. The sun is a fierce white ball. Two big semis from the Polar Bear Refrigerated Trucking Company are pulled up in the yard of the agency offices, and what do you think they're loaded with? Butter. That's right. Seventeen tons of surplus butter on the hottest day in '52. That is what it takes to get me together with Lulu.

Coincidence. I am standing there wrangling with the drivers, who want to dump the butter, when Lulu drives by. I see her, riding slow and smooth on the luxury springs of her Nash Ambassador Custom.

"Hey Lulu," I shout, waving her into the bare, hot yard. "Could you spare a couple hours?"

She rolls down her window and says perhaps. She is high and distant ever since the days of our youth. I'm not thinking, I swear, of anything but delivering the butter. And yet when she alights I cannot help notice an interesting feature of her dress. She turns sideways. I see how it is buttoned all the way down the back. The buttons are small, square, plump, like the mints they serve next to the cashbox in a fancy restaurant.

I have been to the nation's capital. I have learned there that spitting tobacco is frowned on. To cure myself of chewing I've took to rolling my own. So I have the makings in my pocket, and I quick roll one up to distract myself from wondering if those buttons hurt her where she sits.

"Your car's air-cooled?" I ask. She says it is. Then I make a request, polite and natural, for her to help me deliver these fifty-pound boxes of surplus butter, which will surely melt and run if they are left off in the heat.

She sighs. She looks annoyed. The hair is frizzled behind her neck. To her, Nector Kashpaw is a nuisance. She sees nothing of their youth. He's gone dull. Stiff. Hard to believe, she thinks, how he once cut the rug! Even his eyebrows have a little gray in them now. Hard to believe the girls once followed him around!

But he is, after all, in need of her air conditioning, so what the heck? I read this in the shrug she gives me.

"Load them in," she says.

So the car is loaded up, I slip in the passenger's side, and we begin delivering the butter. There is no set way we do it, since this is an unexpected shipment. She pulls into a yard and I drag out a box, or two, if they've got a place for it. Between deliveries we do not speak.

Each time we drive into the agency yard to reload, less butter is in the semis. People have heard about it and come to pick up the boxes themselves. It seems surprising, but all of that tonnage is going fast, too fast, because there still hasn't been a word exchanged between Lulu and myself in the car. The afternoon is heated up to its worst, where it will stay several hours. The car is soft inside, deep cushioned and cool. I hate getting out when we drive into the yards. Lulu smiles and talks to the people who come out of their houses. As soon as we are alone, though, she clams up and hums some tune she heard on the radio. I try to get through several times.

"I'm sorry about Henry," I say. Her husband was killed on the railroad tracks. I never had a chance to say I was sorry.

"He was a good man." That is all the answer I get.

"How are your boys?" I ask later. I know she has a lot of them, but you would never guess it. She seems so young.

"Fine."

In desperation, I say she has a border of petunias that is the envy of many far-flung neighbors. Marie has often mentioned it.

"My petunias," she tells me in a flat voice, "are none of your business."

I am shut up for a time, then. I understand that this is useless. Whatever I am doing it is not what she wants. And the truth is, I do not know what I want from it either. Perhaps just a mention that I, Nector Kashpaw, middle-aged butter mover, was the young hard-muscled man who thrilled and sparked her so long ago.

As it turns out, however, I receive so much more. Not because of anything I do or say. It's more mysterious than that.

We are driving back to the agency after the last load, with just two boxes left in the backseat, my box and hers. Since the petunias, she has not even hummed to herself. So I am more than surprised, when, in a sudden burst, she says how nice it would be to drive up to the lookout and take in the view.

Now I'm the shy one.

"I've got to get home," I say, "with this butter."

But she simply takes the turn up the hill. Her skin is glowing, as if she were brightly golden beneath the brown. Her hair is dry and electric. I heard her tell somebody, where we stopped, that she didn't have time to curl it. The permanent fuzz shorts out here and there above her forehead. On some women this might look strange, but on Lulu it seems stylish, like her tiny crystal earrings and the French rouge on her cheeks.

I do not compare her with Marie. I would not do that. But the way I ache for Lulu, suddenly, is terrible and sad.

"I don't think we should," I say to her when we stop. The shadows are stretching, smooth and blue, out of the trees.

"Should what?"

Turning to me, her mouth a tight gleaming triangle, her cheekbones high and pointed, her chin a little cup, her eyes lit, she watches.

"Sit here," I say, "alone like this."

"For heavensake," she says, "I'm not going to bite. I just wanted to look at the view."

Then she does just that. She settles back. She puts her arm out the window. The air is mild. She looks down on the spread of trees and sloughs. Then she shuts her eyes.

"It's a damn pretty place," she says. Her voice is blurred and contented. She does not seem angry with me anymore, and because of this, I can ask her what I didn't know I wanted to ask all along. It surprises me by falling off my lips.

"Will you forgive me?"

She doesn't answer right away, which is fine, because I have to get used to the fact that I said it.

"Maybe," she says at last, "but I'm not the same girl."

I'm about to say she hasn't changed, and then I realize how much she has changed. She has gotten smarter than I am by a long shot, to understand she is different.

"I'm different now, too," I am able to admit.

She looks at me, and then something wonderful happens to her face. It opens, as if a flower bloomed all at once or the moon rode out from behind a cloud. She is smiling.

"So your butter's going to melt," she says, then she is laughing outright. She reaches into the backseat and grabs a block. It is wrapped in waxed paper, squashed and soft, but still fresh. She smears some on my face. I'm so surprised that I just sit there for a moment, feeling stupid. Then I wipe the butter off my cheek. I take the block from her and I put it on the dash. When we grab each other and kiss there is butter on our hands. It wears off as we touch, then undo, each other's clothes. All those buttons! I make her turn around so I won't rip any off, then I carefully unfasten them.

"You're different," she agrees now, "better."

I do not want her to say anything else. I tell her to lay quiet. Be still. I get the backrest down with levers. I know how to do this because I thought of it, offhand, as we were driving. I did not plan what happened, though. How could I have planned? How could I have known that I would take the butter from the dash? I rub a handful along her collarbone, then circle her breasts, then let it slide down between them and over the rough little tips. I rub the butter in a circle on her stomach.

"You look pretty like that," I say. "All greased up."

She laughs, laying there, and touches the place I should put more. I do. Then she guides me forward into her body with her hands.

Midnight found me in my pickup, that night in July. I was surprised, worn out, more than a little frightened of what we'd done, and I felt so good. I felt loose limbed and strong in the dark breeze, roaring home, the cold air sucking the sweat through my clothes and my veins full of warm, sweet water.

As I turned down our road I saw the lamp, still glowing. That meant Marie was probably sitting up to make sure I slept out in the shack if I was drunk.

I walked in, letting the screen whine softly shut behind me.

"Hello," I whispered, hoping to get on into the next dark room and hide myself in bed. She was sitting at the kitchen table, reading an old catalog. She did not look up from the pictures.

"Hungry?"

"No," I said.

Already she knew, from my walk or the sound of my voice, that I had not been drinking. She flipped some pages.

"Look at this washer," she said. I bent close to study it. She said I smelled like a churn. I told her about the seventeen tons of melting butter and how I'd been hauling it since first thing that afternoon.

"Swam in it too," she said, glancing at my clothes. "Where's ours?"

"What?"

"Our butter."

I'd forgotten it in Lulu's car. My tongue was stuck. I was speechless to realize my sudden guilt.

"You forgot."

She slammed down the catalog and doused the lamp.

I had a job as night watchman at a trailer-hitch plant. Five times a week I went and sat in the janitor's office. Half the night I pushed a broom or meddled with odd repairs. The other half I drowsed, wrote my chairman's reports, made occasional rounds. On the sixth night of the week I left home, as usual, but as soon as I got to the road Lulu Lamartine lived on I turned. I hid the truck in a cove of brush. Then I walked up the road to her house in the dark.

On that sixth night it was as though I left my body at the still wheel of the pickup and inhabited another more youthful one. I moved, witching water. I was full of sinkholes, shot with rapids. Climbing in her bedroom window, I rose. I was a flood that strained bridges. Uncontainable. I rushed into Lulu, and the miracle was she could hold me. She could contain me without giving way. Or she could run with me, unfolding in sheets and snaky waves.

I could twist like a rope. I could disappear beneath the surface. I could run to a halt and Lulu would have been there every moment, just her, and no babies to be careful of tangled somewhere in the covers.

And so this continued five years.

How I managed two lives was a feat of drastic proportions. Most of the time I was moving in a dim fog of pure tiredness. I never got one full morning of sleep those years, because there were babies holed up everywhere set to let loose their squawls at the very moment I started to doze. Oh yes, Marie kept taking in babies right along. Like the butter, there was a surplus of babies on the reservation, and we seemed to get unexpected shipments from time to time.

I got nervous, and no wonder, with demands weighing me down. And as for Lulu, what started off carefree and irregular became a clockwork precision of timing. I had to get there prompt on night number six, leave just before dawn broke, give and take all the pleasure I could muster myself to stand in between. The more I saw of Lulu the more I realized she was not from the secret land of the Nash Ambassador, but real, a woman like Marie, with a long list of things she needed done or said to please her.

I had to run down the lists of both of them, Lulu and Marie. I had much trouble to keep what they each wanted, when, straight.

In that time, one thing that happened was that Lulu gave birth.

It was when she was carrying the child I began to realize this woman was not only earthly, she had a mind like a wedge of iron. For instance, she never did admit that she was carrying.

"I'm putting on the hog." She clicked her tongue, patting her belly, which was high and round while the rest of her stayed slim.

One night, holding Lulu very close, I felt the baby jump. She said nothing, only smiled. Her white teeth glared in the dark. She snapped at me in play like an animal. In that way she frightened me from asking if the baby was mine. I was jealous of Lulu, and she knew this for a fact. I was jealous because I could not control her or count on her whereabouts. I knew what a lively, sweet-fleshed figure she cut.

And yet I couldn't ask her to be true, since I wasn't. I was two-timing Lulu in being married to Marie, and vice versa of course. Lulu held me tight by that string while she spun off on her own. Who she saw, what she did, I have no way to ever know. But I do think the boy looked like a Kashpaw.

Every so often I would try to stop time again by finding a still place and sitting there. But the moment I was getting the feel of quietness, leaning up a tree, parked in the truck, sitting with the cows, or just smoking on a rock, so many details of love and politics would flood me. It would be like I had dried my mind out only to receive the fresh dousing of, say, more tribal news.

Chippewa politics was thorns in my jeans. I never asked for the chairmanship, or for that matter, anything, and yet I was in the thick and boil of policy. I went to Washington about it. I talked to the governor. I had to fight like a weasel, but I was fighting with one paw tied behind my back because of wrangling over buying a washer for Marie.

For a time there, Marie only wanted one thing that I could give her. Not love, not sex, just a wringer washer. I didn't blame her, with all the diapers and the overhalls and shirts. But our little stockpile of money kept getting used up before it came anywhere near a down payment on the price.

This wrangling and tearing went on with no letup. It was worse than before I'd stopped or took the butter from the dash. Lulu aged me while at the same time she brought back my youth. I was living fast and furious, swept so rapidly from job to home to work to Lulu's arms, and back again, that I could hardly keep my mind on straight at any time. I could not fight this, either. I had to speed where I was took. I only trusted that I would be tossed up on land when everyone who wanted something from Nector Kashpaw had wrung him dry.

So I was ready for the two things that happened in '57. They were almost a relief, to tell the truth, because they had to change my course.

Number one was a slick, flat-faced Cree salesman out of Minneapolis that came and parked his car in Lulu's yard. He was Henry's brother, Beverly Lamartine, a made-good, shifty type who would hang Lulu for a dollar. I told her that. She just laughed.

"There's no harm in him," she said.

"I'll kill him if he puts a hand on you."

She gave me a look that said she wouldn't call a bluff that stupid or mention the obvious except to say, blasting holes in me, "If it wasn't for Marie . . ."

"What?" I said.

She bit her lip and eyed me. I went cold. It entered my mind that she was thinking to marry this urban Indian, this grease-haired vet with tattoos up his arms.

"Oh no," I said, "you wouldn't."

I got desperate with the thought, but I was helpless to sway her anvil mind. I laid her down. I pinned her arms back. I pulled her hair so her chin tipped up. Then I tried my best to make her into my own private puppet that I could dance up and down any way I moved her. That's what I did. Her body sweat and twisted. I made her take my pleasure. But when I fell back there was still no way I could have Lulu but one—to leave Marie—which was not possible.

Or so I thought.

That night I left Lulu right after she fell back in the pillows. I got in my truck and drove to the lake. I parked alone. I turned the lights off. And then, because even in the stillest of hours, by the side of the water, I was not still, I took off my clothes and walked naked to the shore.

I swam until I felt a clean tug in my soul to go home and forget about Lulu. I told myself I had seen her for the last time that night. I gave her up and dived down to the bottom of the lake where it was cold, dark, still, like the pit bottom of a grave. Perhaps I should have stayed there and never fought. Perhaps I should have taken a breath. But I didn't. The water bounced me up. I had to get back in the thick of my life.

The next day, I was glad of my conclusion to leave Lulu forever. The area redevelopment went through. I was glad, because if I hadn't betrayed Lulu before, I had to do it now, over the very land she lived on. It was not hers. Even though she planted petunias and put the birdbath beneath her window, she didn't own the land, because the Lamartines had squatted there. That land had always belonged to the tribe, I was sorry to find, for now the tribal council had decided that Lulu's land was the one perfect place to locate a factory.

Oh, I argued. I did as much as I could. But government money was dangling before their noses. In the end, as tribal chairman, I was presented with a typed letter I should sign that would formally give notice that Lulu was kicked off the land.

My hand descended like in a dream. I wrote my name on the dotted line. The secretary licked it in an envelope and then someone delivered it to Lulu's door. I tried to let things go, but I was trapped behind the wheel. Whether I liked it or not I was steering something out of control.

That night, I tried to visit Lulu's window out of turn. It was not the sixth night of the week, but I know she expected me. I know because she turned me away.

And that is where the suffering and burning set in to me with fierceness beyond myself. No sooner had I given her up than I wanted Lulu back.

It is a hot night in August. I am sitting in the pool of lamplight at my kitchen table. It is night six, but I am home with Marie and the children. They are all around me, breathing deep or mumbling in a dream. Aurelia and Zelda are hunched in the roll-cot beside the stove. Zelda moans in the dim light and says "Oh, quick!" Her legs move and twitch like she is chasing something. Her head is full of crossed black pins.

I have my brown cowhide briefcase beside me, open, spilling neat-packed folders and brochures and notes. I take out a blue-lined tablet and a pencil that has never been sharpened. I shave the pencil to a point with my pocketknife. Then I clean the knife and close it up and wonder if I'm really going to write what some part of my mind has decided.

I lick my thumb. The pencil strokes. *August 7, 1957*. My hand moves to the left. *Dear Marie*. I skip down two lines as I was taught in the government school. *I am leaving you*. I press so hard the lead snaps on the pencil.

Zelda sits bolt upright, sniffing the air. She was always a restless sleeper. She would walk through the house as a little girl, to come and visit her parents. Often I would wake to find her standing at the end of our bed, holding the post with both hands as if it was dragging her someplace.

Now, almost full-grown, Zelda frowns at something in her dream and then slowly sinks back beneath her covers and disappears but for one smudge of forehead. I give up. I take the pencil in my hand and begin to write.

> Dear Marie,
> Can't see going on with this when every day I'm going down even worse. Sure I loved you once, but all this time I am seeing Lulu also. Now she pressured me and the day has come I must get up and go. I apologize. I found true love with her. I don't have a choice. But that doesn't mean Nector Kashpaw will ever forget his own.

After I write this letter, I fold it up very quickly and lay it in the briefcase. Then I tear off a fresh piece of paper and begin another.

> Dear Lulu,
> You wanted me for so long. Well you've got me now! Here I am for the taking, girl, all one hundred percent yours. This is my official proposal put down in writing.
>
> Yours till hell freezes over,
> Nector

And then, because maybe I don't mean it, maybe I just need to get it off my mind, I lock the letters in the briefcase, blow out the lamp, and make my way around sleeping children to Marie. I hang my shirt and pants on the bedpost and slip in next to her. She always sleeps on her side, back toward me, curved around the baby, which is next to the wall so it won't tumble off. She sleeps like this ever since I rolled over on one of them. I fit around her and crook my arm at her waist.

She smells of milk and wood ash and sun-dried cloth. Marie has never used a bottle of perfume. Her hands are big, nicked from sharp knives, roughed by bleach. Her back is hard as a plank. Still she warms me. I feel like pleading with her but I don't know what for. I lay behind her, listening to her breath sigh in and out, and the ache gets worse. It fills my throat like a lump of raw metal. I want to clutch her and never let go, to cry to her and tell her what I've done.

I make a sound between my teeth and she moves, still in her dream. She pulls my arm down tighter, mumbles into her pillow. I take a breath with her breath. I take another. And then my body becomes her body. We are breathing as one, and I am falling gently into sleep still not knowing what will happen.

I sleep like I've been clubbed, all night, very hard. When I wake she has already gone into town with Zelda. They were up early, canning apples. The jars are stacked upside down at one end of the table, reddish gold, pretty with the sun shining through them. I brew my morning coffee and chew the cold galette she has left for me. I am still wondering what I am going to do. It seems as though, all my life up till now, I have not had to make a decision. I just did what came along, went wherever I was taken, accepted when I was called on. I never said no. But now it is one or the other, and my mind can't stretch far enough to understand this.

I go outside and for a long time I occupy myself chopping

wood. The children know how to take care of themselves. I pitch and strain at the wood, splitting with a wedge and laying hard into the ax, as if, when the pile gets big enough, it will tell me what to do.

As I am working I suddenly think of Lulu. I get a clear mental picture of her sitting on the lap of her brother-in-law. I see Beverly's big ham reach out and wrap around her shoulder. Lulu's head tips to the side, and her eyes gleam like a bird's. He is nodding at her. Then his mouth is falling onto hers.

I throw the ax. The two lovebirds propel me into the house. I am like a wildman, clutching through my briefcase. I find the letter to Marie and I take it out, read it once, then anchor it on the table with the jar of sugar. I cram the letter to Lulu in my pocket, and then I go.

All I can see, as I gallop down the steps and off into the woods, is Lulu's small red tongue moving across her teeth. My mind quivers, but I cannot stop myself from seeing more. I see his big face nuzzle underneath her chin. I see her hands fly up to clutch his head. She rolls her body expertly beneath his, and then I am crashing through the brush, swatting leaves, almost too blind to see the old deerpath that twists through the woods.

I creep up on her house, as though I will catch them together, even though I have heard he is back in the Cities. I crouch behind some bushes up the hill, expecting her dogs to scent me any moment. I watch. Her house is fresh painted, yellow with black trim, cheerful as a bee. Her petunias are set out front in two old tractor tires painted white. After a time, when the dogs don't find me, I realize they have gone off somewhere. And then I see how foolish I am. The house is quiet. No Beverly. No boys in the yard, either, fixing cars or target practicing. They are gone, leaving Lulu alone.

I put my hands to my forehead. It is burning as if I have a fever. Since the Nash I have never taken off Lulu's clothes in the daylight, and it enters my head, now, that I could do this if I went down to her house. So I make my way out of the dense bush.

For the first time ever, I go up to her front door and knock. This feels so normal, I am almost frightened. Something in me is about to burst. I need Lulu to show me what this fearful thing is. I need her hand to pull me in and lead me back into her bedroom, and her voice to tell me how we were meant for each other by fate. I need her to tell me I am doing right.

But no one comes to the door. There is no sound. It is a hot, still afternoon, and nothing stirs in Lulu's dull grass, though deep in the trees, to all sides, I have the sense now of something moving slowly forward. An animal that is large, dense furred, nameless. These thoughts are crazy, I know, and I try to cast them from my mind. I round the house. The backyard is the one place where Lulu's tidiness has been defeated. The ground is cluttered with car parts, oil pans, pieces of cement block, and other useful junk.

No one answers at the back door either, so I sit down on the porch. I tell myself that no matter how long it takes Lulu to get here, I will wait. I am not good at waiting, like my brother Eli, who can sit without moving a muscle for an hour while deer approach him. I am not good at waiting, but I try. I roll a cigarette and smoke it as slow as possible. I roll another. I try to think of anything but Lulu or Marie or my children. I think back to the mad captain in *Moby Dick* and how his leg was bit off. Perhaps I was wrong, about Ishmael I mean, for now I see signs of the captain in myself. I bend over and pick up a tin can and crush it flat. For no reason! A bit later I bang the side of her house until my fist hurts. I drop my head in my hands. I tell her, out loud, to get back quick. I do not know what I will do if she doesn't.

I am tired. I have started to shake. That is when I take out the letter I have crumpled in my pocket. I decide that I will read it a hundred times, very slowly, before I do anything else. So I read it, word by word, until the words make no sense. I go on reading it. I am keeping careful, concentrated count, when suddenly I think of Marie.

I see her finding the other letter now. Sugar spills across the table as she sits, crying out in her shock. A jar of apples explodes. The children shout, frightened. Grease bubbles over on the stove. The dogs howl. She clutches the letter and tears it up.

I lose count. I try reading Lulu's letter once more, but I cannot finish it. I crumple it in a ball, throw it down, then I light up another cigarette and begin to smoke it very quick while I am rolling a second to keep my hands distracted.

This is, in fact, how the terrible thing happens.

I am so eager to smoke the next cigarette that I do not notice I have thrown down my half-smoked one still lit on the end. I throw it right into the ball of Lulu's letter. The letter smokes. I do not notice right off what is happening, and then the paper flares.

Curious and dazed, I watch the letter burn.

I swear that I do nothing to help the fire along.

Weeds scorch in a tiny circle, and then a bundle of greasy rags puffs out in flames. It burns quickly. I leave the steps. An old strip of rug curls and catches onto some hidden oil slick in the grass. The brown blades spurt and crackle until the flame hits a pile of wood chips. Behind that are cans of gasoline that the boys have removed from dead cars. I step back. The sun is setting in the windows, black and red. I duck. The gas cans roar, burst. Blue lights flash on behind my eyelids, and now long oily flames are licking up the side of the house, moving snakelike along the windows of the porch, finding their way into the kitchen where the kerosene is stored and where Lulu keeps her neatly twine-tied bundles of old newspapers.

The fire is unstoppable. The windows are a furnace. They pop out, raining glass, but I merely close my eyes and am untouched.

I have done nothing.

I feel the heat rise up my legs and collect, burning for Lulu, but burning her out of me.

I don't know how long I stand there, moving back inch by inch as fire rolls through the boards, but I have nearly reached the woods before the heat on my face causes me to abandon the sight, finally, and turn.

That is when I see that I have not been alone.

I see Marie standing in the bush. She is fourteen and slim again. I can do nothing but stare, rooted to the ground. She stands tall, straight and stern as an angel. She watches me. Red flames from the burning house glare and flicker in her eyes. Her skin sheds light. We are face to face, and then she begins to lift on waves of heat. Her breast is a glowing shield. Her arm is a white-hot spear. When she raises it the bush behind her spreads, blazing open like wings.

I go down on my knees, a man of rags and tinder. I am ready to be burned in the fire, too, but she reaches down and lifts me up.

"Daddy," she says, "let's get out of here. Let's go."

FLESH AND BLOOD

(1957)

MARIE KASHPAW

There was surely no reason I should go up that hill again. For days, for weeks after I heard Sister Leopolda was dying, I told myself I was glad. I told myself good riddance to her puckered mind. Boiling jars that morning, pouring syrup, I told myself what she deserved. The jars were hot. She deserved to be packed in one alive. But as soon as I imagined that, I pitied her in the jar, balled up in her black rag, staring through the glass. It was always that way. Through the years I had thought up many various punishments I would like to commit on the nun who'd cracked my head and left a scar that was tight and cold in my palm, a scar that ached on Good Friday and throbbed in the rain. But every time I thought of her damned, I relented. I saw her kneeling, dead faced, without love.

I stood in my kitchen packing apples in jars, pouring the boiling syrup and cinnamon over them. I knew what I knew. She had gone steadily downhill. In the past years of her life it was canes, chairs, confinement. They said she prayed to herself twenty-four hours at a stretch. There were some who touched the hem of her garment to get blessed. As if she were the saint. Bag of bones! I knew the truth. She had to pray harder than the others because the Devil still loved her far better than any on that hill. She walked the sorrowful mysteries one year with bloody feet. There were those who kept the gravel stones she bled on. I wouldn't. I knew the Devil drove her toward grace with his persistence. She got famous. Like Saint Theresa, she lived for many weeks on Sacred Hosts.

But I hadn't seen her visiting the sick nor raising the sad ones up. No everyday miracles for her. Her talent was the relishment of pain, foaming at the mouth, and it was no surprise to me that lately there had been a drastic disarrangement of her mind.

I heard that she was kept in her little closet now. Confined. I heard she had an iron spoon that she banged on the bedstead to drive away spirits. Sparks flew up her walls. They had to keep her room very clean, I heard, otherwise she licked dust off the window-sills. She made meals of lint. They didn't dare let a dust ball collect beneath her bed. I knew why this had happened. I knew it was the heat. The prolonged heat of praying had caused her brain to boil. I also knew what they did not know about her appetite for dust.

She ate dust for one reason: to introduce herself to death. So now she was inhabited by the blowing and the nameless.

Packing apples in my jars, I came to the last. I was thinking of her with such concentration that I poured the syrup on my hand.

"Damn buzzard!" I screamed, as if she'd done it. And she might have. Who knew how far the influence spread?

I slipped my apron off and hung it on a chair. A sign perhaps. My hand was scalded. I hardly noticed. I was going up the hill.

"I'll visit her," I said, to hear it said out loud. "I'll bring Zelda."

That was one thing I had not expected of myself. Deciding that I'd bring the girl along with me, I realized another reason. I would visit Leopolda not just to see her, but to let her see me. I would let her see I had not been living on wafers of God's flesh but the fruit of a man. Long ago she had tried for my devotion. Now I'd let her see where my devotion had gone and where it had got me. For by now I was solid class. Nector was tribal chairman. My children were well behaved, and they were educated too.

I went to the wardrobe and pulled out the good wool dress I would wear up the hill, even on a day this hot. Royal plum, they called the color of it in the Grand Forks clothing shop. I had paid down twenty dollars for it and worn it the day they swore Nector to the chair with me beside him.

It was a good dress, manufactured, of a classic material. It was the kind of solid dress no Lazarre ever wore.

Zelda was sixteen, older than I was when I took on the nun and pulled the demon from her sleeve. Zelda was older in age but not in mind; that is, she did not know what she wanted yet, whereas my mind had made itself up once I walked down the hill. Fourteen years, that was all the older I was at that time, yet I was a woman enough to snare Nector Kashpaw. But Zelda still floundered, even with her advantages, and sometimes I found her staring in a quiet mood across the field.

This morning, however, she had been working in the garden as supervisor of the younger ones. As always, she had kept clean.

"Where are you going?" she asked, coming in the door. "You're wearing your dress."

"I'm wearing it," I said, "to visit the nuns. I want you to come along with me, so hurry up and change."

"All right!" She was glad to go up there anytime. She was friendly with a few of them, and could be found at Holy Mass any day of the week. Yet she had not decided to go any special route.

It did not take her long. She wore a pressed white blouse and plaid skirt. With her money from the potato fields she had bought herself anklets. Her saddle shoes were polished clean white. I would never have believed this was the granddaughter of Ignatius Lazarre, that sack of brew. There was even a ribbon in her hair, which she put up every night in pinned coils to get the curl.

So we went. It was a long enough walk, and the road was hot when we came out of the woods. I had my dress on, so I did not let myself sweat. The hill was covered with dust. Dust hung gray, in shifting bands, around the white convent walls. There had been no rain that fall, and the fields were blowing through the town. But we walked. We passed the place on the road where Nector had tried to throw me. We had passed this place many times before without me thinking of Nector, but today I was remembering everything.

"This is where I met your father," I told Zelda. For all I knew, it was the place we made Gordon as well, but I never exactly said that.

"Your father could not keep away from me," I suddenly bragged. I suppose I said that to put some other expression on my daughter's face. She was getting that serious glazed-over stare, as if she had to look down the well of her soul. But now she started, and went red.

"Don't give me that cow look," I said to her shocked face. "Maybe you're a little backwards about men, but your time will come."

She wouldn't look at me after that.

"How come we're visiting?" she asked, after we walked a bit farther.

"Take them some apples," I said. In my hand I held a jar of fresh canned crabs. I had planted the tree myself twelve years before, and for a long time it was the only apple tree on the reservation. Then the nuns had planted two on their hill. But those trees hardly bore yet. Mine was established.

"And also," I told Zelda, "to see the old nun who was my teacher. That's Leopolda."

"I never knew she was your teacher," said Zelda. "She's pretty old."

"Well she's sick now, too," I said. "That's why we're going to see her."

We came to the door. The lawn had shrunk back, to make room for a parking lot. Large square hedges went off to either side. The walls still blazed with cheap whitewash as before, but now most of the cracks were filled and the birds' nests were knocked down. The old convent had got a few fresh nuns and come up in the world.

I rang the bell. It made a deep and costly sound in the hall. I heard the knock of thick black shoes, the rustle of heavy cloth, and a slight wind caught me. I had imagined coming back here many times to this door, and always it was the carved bone of Leopolda's face that met me, not Dympna, who opened the door and plumply smiled. She had only three teeth left, now, in her wide pale face. Two were on the top and one was on the bottom. That, and her eyes so red and blank, gave her the look of a great rabbit.

I realized the strangeness of what was happening. Over twenty years had passed since I'd set foot in this place and been worshiped on the couch of the Superior as a saint. Twenty years since Leopolda had speared me with her bread poker. Twenty years while I also came up in the world.

"We are here to see Sister Leopolda," I said.

"Come in! Come in!" The rabbit seemed pleased and eyed my jar. "Are these apples from your tree?"

"Yes." I offered them.

"This must be your mother," Dympna decided. Zelda nodded. The nun did not recognize me. "Please come upstairs."

She took the apples from my hands and led us down the hall. We went up a flight of brown tile stairs that I remembered. We went down a shorter hall and stopped at the very end. All her grown life, Leopolda had lived in the same room.

Dympna tapped. There was silence.

"Maybe she's asleep," said Zelda.

"I am not asleep," the voice said, very low, so we hardly heard it from our side.

"Please go in," said Dympna, "she'll be expecting you now."

So Dympna left us, and we stood by the door as it fell, opening slowly into the dim camphor-ball air of Leopolda's room. I stepped in first, Zelda following. I saw nothing but the bed sheets, so white they almost glowed. Leopolda was among them. As my eyes grew accustomed to the light I made her out, a small pile of sticks wrapped in a white gown.

Not even the kindling to start a fire, I thought.

"It's dark in here," I said.

She did not answer.

"I came to visit you."

Still, silence.

"I brought my daughter. Zelda Kashpaw."

"I don't know who you are," she finally said.

"Marie."

I opened the curtains a crack. A beam of light came through. I saw her clearly, wrapped in sheets and shawls, and I was so surprised at what I saw that I let the curtain fall back. She had shriveled on the stick bones. Her arms were thin as ropes. And her hair. The hair shocked me first, because I never thought of nuns as having any, and then for the strangeness of it. Her hair was pure white and sprang out straight and thin from her skull like the floss of dandelions. I was almost afraid to breathe, as if the hair would float off. The rest of her, too, was frail as a dead plant.

"Marie!" she said suddenly. Her voice went deep and hoarse. "Star of the Sea! You'll shine when we burn off the salt!"

"At least you have not forgot me." I groped for a chair and sat. Zelda stood at the foot of the bed watching the two of us. At first I was relieved. I was expecting that the nun would rave at us or have taken complete absence of her senses. But it seemed that her mind was still clear. Just her body was affected. I started feeling sorry for her, so dried up and shriveled. That was always my mistake. For I grasped her hand like a common consoling friend and felt, immediately, the grim forbidding strength of her, undiminished all these years.

"Oh no, I never forgot you," she said, and squeezed my hand still tighter. "I knew you would come back."

I was not going to let her get a hold on me, especially as I knew she had her mind now. I pulled away.

"I felt sorry for you," I said.

But this only made her laugh, a dry crackle like leaves crushed underfoot.

"I feel sorry for you too, now that I see."

It was dim. She saw nothing, unless she had the vision of a night thing, which I doubted even with the miracle of her strength.

"Why?" I asked. Solid in my good dress, I was proud and could ask. But the dress was what she picked up and threw in my face.

"So poor that you had to cut an old Easter shroud up and sew it," she said, pointing. Her finger was a stick of glass.

"You're blind," I said. "It's no shroud, it's good wool."

"It's purple."

How she noticed the color of it I don't know. I guess she took me all in like I did her when the light came through the crack in the curtains.

"I suppose you had brats with the Indian," she went on, ignoring Zelda, "sickly and mean. It turns out that way with them."

"Look here," I said, "this is my daughter."

Anyone could see Zelda wasn't sick, or mean, and she was perfectly dressed. The nun did seem to take a certain interest. She turned to Zelda, who stood quietly at her feet in a soft shadow. She looked at Zelda standing there. Moments passed. Then Leopolda suddenly shifted and turned back to me.

"Yes," she whispered. "Similar. Very much the same."

"Of course," I said, settling myself, although I knew Zelda and me were not the same at all. "And I have four more at home, just about full-grown like Zelda here."

"How do you feed them?" The nun looked down the long spear of her nose.

"I don't have a problem with that," I said. "My husband is chairman of this tribe."

I paused to let that sink inside her skull.

"Sometimes they bring him to Washington," I said.

The nun just watched me. Her eyes were two steady lightless beams.

"Once a senator came to our house," I went on. "They went hunting in the woods, but they never got anything. Another time . . ."

But she had already started making her dry noise, her laughter, and her mouth gaped black and wide.

". . . he ate supper with the governor," I said.

"So you've come up in the world," she mocked, using my thoughts against me. "Or your husband has, it sounds like, not you, Marie Lazarre."

"Marie Kashpaw," I said. "He is what he is because I made him."

I felt my daughter's gaze train on me, but what I said was true, and Zelda knew it. She had seen me drag him back from the bootlegger's house. She had seen me sitting all night by the door with an ax handle so he would not wander off in search of liquor. She had seen me ration him down, mixing his brandy with water, until he came clean. So she knew the truth of what I said.

"No doubt," said the nun. "You had a certain talent." Her breath was like a small wind stirring the dust, and I remembered her hands on my back, rubbing a buttery ointment into the scalding burns that she herself had put there. The scar in my hand began to itch. I'd had a talent, it was true.

"I got out of here alive," I said. "I had to have a talent to do that."

I could feel Zelda stiffen in bewilderment at what I said.

This time when the nun laughed it was deep and harsh, like dry twigs breaking in her chest, and it ended in a coughing fit that turned her face bright blue as any time I'd seen her in a rage.

"You're sick," I said, pouring the pity in my voice, "sicker than a dog. I'm sorry for you."

"I'm sorry for you," she said immediately, again, "now that I see you're going to suffer in hell."

But I had my answer on the tip of my tongue.

"Why should I go there?" I said. "I've been good to my neighbors. I fed my children from my own mouth. I kept Nector from hurting himself."

"Ah—" she began. I cut her off.

"You're the one. So proud of shredding your feet! Getting worshiped as a saint! While all the time you're measly and stingy to the sick at your door. I heard!"

Again her face was darkening. Zelda reached forward in alarm. But I wasn't finished.

"I quit that when I walked down the hill. Dust, it was dust. I saw that clear. The meek will inherit the earth!"

The nun drew a racking breath.

"I don't want the earth," she said.

Then she did something that showed me that, for all the conversation we had, she wasn't right in the head after all. She pulled the bed sheet over her and dived beneath the covers. She surfaced quickly with the heavy black spoon in her fist. And then she began to beat on the spools of the iron bedstead, knocking flakes of white paint off, making an unholy racket. She beat and she beat. Zelda put her hands over her ears. I did also. We hollered at her to stop, but she beat the louder. No one came. I'd had enough. I reached over and grabbed the end of the spoon.

Again, I'd forgotten she had the strength of the grave. She snatched it easily back to herself.

"They all try that," she said.

"Oh yes?"

And then I knew what I had come there for. It came to me with the touch of iron. I wanted that spoon.

I wanted that spoon because it was a hell-claw welded smooth. It was the iron poker that she'd marked me with, flattened. It had power. It was like her soul boiled down and poured in a mold and hardened. That was the shape of it. If I had that spoon I'd have her to stir in my pot. I'd have her to whack the bannock, fry the fish, lift out the smoking meat. Every time I held the spoon handle I'd know that she was nothing but a ghost, a black wind. I'd have her helpless in the scar of my palm.

I would get that spoon.

I watched it. The spoon was large, black, seasoned, but I could still see myself turned upside down in its face, as if it was made of shining silver.

"I came here to get your blessing," I told her.

Leopolda glared at me, the spoon tight in her claw. She looked suspiciously at Zelda, who smiled in her ignorance.

"Bless my girl too," I said. "She might have a vocation."

There was interest. I was certain. She was hooked by the thought.

"God will decide that."

"Your blessing might help her."

She finally nodded.

Here was my plan: I would let her give Zelda the blessing, and then I would kneel before her to receive my blessing too. But just as she prayed over my head, I would lunge forward, taking her off-balance. I would go straight for the spoon, snatch it from her, have it, take it back home up the sleeve of my royal-plum dress that was certainly no shroud.

Zelda went down on her knees, and the nun's hand went up. I thought Leopolda would be a good half hour at her blessing prayer, so much did she enjoy this chance. Her right hand made numerous signs of the cross or rested skeletal on the hair of my girl. Her left hand gripped the spoon forgetfully. But she did not put it down.

I was about to make some move to get this over, when Leopolda came to the end of her speech and wound it up. She made a few parting waves overhead, and Zelda staggered to her feet. I kneeled down then, at the side of the bed, and rested my folded hands on the coverlet in good reaching distance.

Kneeling there, I was surprised how it affected me.

My heart was beating in my throat. It was like I had gone back years and years to the old Marie who was spoken to by the dark. It was like I had come full circle to that rough girl, again, for one last fight with Leopolda before she swirled off and was nothing.

When I smiled into her face she smiled back. It was the huge bleached grin of a skull. She lifted her hand.

But it was not the right hand of her blessing she lifted. It was the other hand, the left hand, still gripping the iron spoon. The hand went up. Our eyesights locked. She lifted half out of bed, with her deathly strength, to give herself the leverage she needed to connect a heavy blow.

I went up with her, drawn by her gaze, knowing her intention as if she spoke it. The arm smacked down, but I somehow had grasped her wrist, and now we leaned into each other, balanced by hate.

"Down!" she said.

"No!"

And then, with my other hand, I tried to take the spoon from her weakened grip. But she clung to the iron handle with both hands and kept grinning into my face. I grinned back at her, just to even things, and that was when I felt she got the better of me, for suddenly my face stretched and the air around me flattened. On her breath, in which I kneeled, was the smell of turned earth. Her gaze, in which I struggled, was a deep square hole. Her strength was the strict progress of darkness.

"Hold on!" I yelled, frightened, for it seemed just as if I was falling fast into her eyes and would be covered up by flowers and clods of earth unless she pulled me back.

And she did pull. She stood me up, and then I sat down on the bed with her. Once I was there I let go of the spoon. It dropped heavily on her starved breast and lay as spent of power as she.

Her body was so shallow I could hardly tell if she breathed, the covering of her bones so frail I could see the heart pumping in her breast.

I sat with her a long while, in silence.

The earth was so mild and deep. By spring she would be placed there, alone, and there was no rescue. There was nothing I could do after hating her all these years.

We were quiet walking back down the hill, through the woods. The path in the trees was shadowy and almost cold after the blaze of road. The sun flickered in the brush. Each leaf balanced in the air. Watching Zelda walk in front of me, so sure of herself and thin, with a cutting edge, with a mind that wasn't made up, with pure white anklets and careful curls, I felt an amazement. I remembered the year I carried her. It was summer. I sat under the clothesline, breathing quiet so she would move, feeling the hand or foot knock just beneath my heart. We had been in one body then, yet she was a stranger. We were not as close now, yet perhaps I knew her better.

Her black hair swung calmly with each step. She looked so young.

"I might go up there someday," she said, "up the hill."

"And stay with them?"

"Yes."

That did not surprise me. Yet I felt a sinking surge, a regret, a feeling like I should clutch her by the shoulders, although it plagued me that she couldn't make up her mind. "Don't make any hasty decision about your life," I said.

"I should get a job like Gordie did!"

"No! You shouldn't!"

I was on the verge of saying how I needed her, at the house, but I didn't say it. After all, I thought, she should be free to go.

As we came through the woods to the field, I heard Nector's shotgun. The boys were hunting ducks at the slough. The house looked quiet. I could see Aurelia moping in the yard with Eugene and Patsy, the little ones I left in her care. No doubt she wanted to be hunting with the boys and June.

"Go on after them," I said, as we walked in the yard. Aurelia got up and ran. She did not have to be convinced. She liked a boy down the road, a friend of Gordie's. She never had trouble making up her mind.

Zelda went in the house before me, to change to her overhalls. I stood in the yard. Nector was not home. I picked up the baby I was keeping for a young girl across the road, because he cried when he saw me. I looked over at the door.

Zelda was standing there, shadowy, behind the screen.

"Hurry up and change," I said. The cow was bawling.

But she didn't move when I told her to move. She said nothing. It gripped me in the throat that there was something wrong.

As if he would protect us, I kept the baby in my arms. I walked up the steps and stood on the other side of the screen. She looked at me, steady, and then I pulled the handle toward me.

"Here, Mama," she said, handing me the letter.

I stood in the kitchen, with the letter in my hand, not moving.

"Go on," I said, "change."

So she went. I opened the paper and I read.

Dear Marie,

Can't see going on with this when every day I'm going down even worse. Sure I loved you once, but all this time I am seeing Lulu also. Now she pressured me and the day has come I must get up and go. I apologize. I found true love with her. I don't have a choice. But that doesn't mean Nector Kashpaw will ever forget his own.

I folded the paper back up and put it in my dress pocket. Zelda stepped back into the room.

"Where did you get this?" I asked her.

"Under the sugar jar."

She pointed at the table and then we both looked, as if the table would tell us what to do next. I concentrated very hard on what I saw. The box of spoons. The butter plate. The can of salt. Somehow these things looked more full of special meaning than the sugar jar. It was just smooth clear glass, decent and familiar in the sunlight, half full. I looked back at Zelda. We gazed at each other. Her eyes were wide, staring, but I wasn't sure if she had read the letter or just been scared by the oddness of a piece of paper with my name on it, sitting on that table. I couldn't tell.

"Listen to that cow," I said. I felt my heart bang hard. My throat shut. I wouldn't have been able to say another word.

Zelda listened. She turned slowly, put her hands in her pockets, and walked outside. I went into the other room with the baby and sat on the bed. The paper crackled in my pocket. I needed the quiet. I could hear Patsy humming outside the window. She was safe. The cow went still. The rest of them were occupied. I could think.

What should I think first? It seemed like it didn't matter. So I didn't know what to think, because of course I knew it mattered, and yet there was nothing to think about. I remembered how Mary Bonne, who lived in town, found her husband in their own bed with a La Chien woman. She went back in her kitchen, took a knife off the wall, and even thought to sharpen the blade on her stone before she went back and cut them. She only gave them a few cuts, but there was blood. I thought the sight of Lamartine's blood would do me good. I saw her face, painted up and bold, and I thought I would cut it right off her neck.

Yet really, I wasn't angry. I didn't even feel like I was inside my body. For I fed the child until it was full and slept, a dead weight in my arms, and I never noticed. I was wondering how I could raise the children without their father. I thought of Eli, how he had gone quieter and hardly came out of the woods anymore. He would not come around. He never thought of women. He was like a shy animal himself when he got trapped in a house.

Then I said right out loud in that bedroom, "He's a man!"

But that didn't make any sense. It meant nothing. That all men were like Nector wasn't true. I thought of Henry Lamartine. Before he was killed on the tracks, he surely knew that his wife went with anybody in the bushes. When she had the boys, all colors of humans, he could tell they were not his. He took care of them. I understood Henry, and I felt for him as I sat. I knew why he had parked his Dodge square on the tracks and let the train bear down.

He must have loved her. But I wouldn't park myself on the tracks for Nector.

"I'd see him in hell first," I said to the room. I realized the child was very heavy and put him on the bed. My arms ached. My throat was tight and dry. I saw that Patsy had come in the door and thrown herself on the bed, limp and exhausted as a doll made of rags. She was sleeping too. The afternoon was getting on, and I was still sitting there without having thought what I should do next.

"I should peel the potatoes," I told myself. No doubt they would bring in a duck at least.

So I went in the kitchen and sat down with a bowl of potatoes. I had peeled enough potatoes in my life so far to feed every man, woman, child of the Chippewas. Still I had more of them to go. It was calming to remove the rough skin, the eye sprouts, and get down to the smooth whiteness. I ate a raw slice. I would eat a raw potato like some people ate an apple. Zelda helped me cook at night. She would fry up the potatoes. After I peeled enough of them I went to the door and called her.

And then, when she never answered, I knew that she was gone. I knew that she read the letter. She had gone after Nector.

It wasn't hard to figure. What else would she do?

I went back in the house and sat down with the potatoes, and I cursed the girl for doing what she did. I should have done it. I should have gone to Lamartine's and dragged him out of her bed and beat him hard with a stick. And after I beat him and he was lying on the floor, I should have turned around and made the Lamartine miserable.

Yet in time, as I calmed down, I knew I'd thought better of going there for a reason. A good reason. The letter said that he loved her. I began peeling more potatoes, I don't know what for, but now I'd struck the comfortless heart I could not ignore. He loved the Lamartine, which was different from all the other things he did that caused me shame and disconvenienced my life. Him loving her, him finding *true love with her,* was what drove me to peel all the potatoes in that house.

I heard Aurelia, June, and the boys coming in the yard, fighting over whose turn it was to clean the birds. I guess they all cleaned their goose. I heard them behind the barn for a while. I put some potatoes on to boil. My hands hurt, full of acids, blistered by the knife. I was like a person in a dream, but my oldest boy never noticed.

Gordie came in with a tough goose.

"It should have flew higher than that," he said. "I got it on the wing."

He looked around at the dishpans and the washtubs of peeled potatoes. Three empty gunnysacks were laying on the floor, crumpled like drawers a man had stepped out of in haste.

"Why'd you do that?" he said.

I only looked at him. I shrugged. He shrugged. He was Nector's son. I thought to myself, he wouldn't go after Nector and bring him home. I was sure Gordie wouldn't do that, even though, like with Zelda, there was a time we had been in the same body. He wouldn't go, even though I had nursed him. We were closer when I carried him, when we never knew each other, I thought now. I did not trust him.

"It's too hot in here for more fire," I said. "Make one outside and roast your birds. I'm washing my floor."

"At night?" he said.

The sun was going down very fast.

"You heard me."

He went out and made a fire in the backyard where we had an old fieldstone range made to cook on in the summer. They all stayed out there. I fed Patsy a mashed potato. I fed her milk. I let the baby play and roll across the floor. I sat and watched them while I decided how I would wash the floor. I looked at my linoleum carefully, all the worn spots and cracks, all the places where the tin stripping had to be hammered flat. It was one of my prides to keep that floor shined up. Under the gray swirls and spots and leaves of the pattern, I knew there was tar paper and bare wood that could splinter a baby's feet. I knew, because I bought and paid for and put down that linoleum myself. It was a good solid covering, but under it the boards creaked.

There wasn't any use in thinking. I put the baby to sleep. I filled the tin bucket with hot water and spirits. I hauled the potatoes out of my way. Then I took up my brush. Outside they were talking. They had a fire. They could stay there. I never went down on my knees to God or anyone, so maybe washing my floor was an excuse to kneel that night. I felt better, that's all I know, as I scrubbed off the tarnished wax and dirt. I felt better as I recognized myself in the woman who kept her floor clean even when left by her husband.

I had been on a high horse. Now I was kneeling. I was washing the floor in my good purple dress. I never did laugh at myself in any situation, but I had to laugh now. I thought of cutting up a shroud. The nun was clever. She knew where my weakness had been.

But I was not going under, even if he left me. I could leave off my fear of ever being a Lazarre. I could leave off my fear, even of losing Nector, since he was gone and I was able to scrub down the floor.

I took my wax. I started polishing a little at a time.

Love had turned my head away from what was going on between my husband and Lamartine. There was something still left that Nector could hurt me with, and now I hurt for love and not because the old hens would squawk.

They would say Marie Kashpaw was down in the dirt. They would say how her husband had left her for dirt. They would say I got all that was coming, head so proud. But I would not care if Marie Kashpaw had to wear an old shroud. I would not care if Lulu Lamartine ended up the wife of the chairman of the Chippewa Tribe. I'd still be Marie. Marie. Star of the Sea! I'd shine when they stripped off the wax!

I had to laugh. I heard the dogs. I had waxed myself up to the table. I knew that I was hearing Nector and Zelda come home, walking in the yard. I wrung my rag out. I had waxed myself in. I thought of the letter in my pocket. Then I thought very suddenly of what this Marie who was interested in holding on to Nector should do. I took the letter. I did what I never would expect of myself. I lifted the sugar jar to put the letter back. Then I thought. I put the sugar down and picked up the can of salt. This was much more something I would predict of Marie.

I folded the letter up, exactly as it had been found, and I put it beneath the salt can. I did this for a reason. I would never talk about this letter but instead let him wonder. Sometimes he'd look at me, I'd smile, and he'd think to himself: salt or sugar? But he would never be sure.

I sat down in a chair. I put my legs in another chair, off the floor, and I waited for him to walk up the steps. When he did, I let him come. Step by step. I let him listen to hear if I was inside. I let him open the door. Only when we saw each other did I stop him.

"I just put the wax down," I said. "You have to wait."

He stood there looking at me over that long, shiny space. It rolled and gleamed like a fine lake between us. And it deepened. I saw that he was about to take the first step, and I let him, but halfway into the room his eyes went dark. He was afraid of how deep this was going to become. So I did for Nector Kashpaw what I learned from the nun. I put my hand through what scared him. I held it out there for him. And when he took it with all the strength of his arms, I pulled him in.

A BRIDGE

(1973)

It was the harsh spring that everybody thought would never end. All the way down to Fargo on the Jackrabbit bus Albertine gulped the rank, enclosed, passenger breath as though she could encompass the strangeness of so many other people by exchanging air with them, by replacing her own scent with theirs. She didn't close her eyes to nap even once during travel, because this was the first time she'd traveled anywhere alone. She was fifteen years old, and she was running away from home. When the sky deepened, casting bleak purple shadows along the snow ditches, she went even tenser than when she'd first walked up the ridged stairs of the vehicle.

She watched carefully as the dark covered all. The yard lights of farms, like warning beacons upon the sea or wide-flung constellations of stars, blinked on, deceptively close.

The bus came upon the city and the lights grew denser, reflecting up into the cloud cover, a transparent orange-pink that floated over the winking points of signs and low black buildings. The streets looked slick, deep green, from the windows of the bus.

The driver made a small rasping sound into the microphone and announced their arrival at the Fargo terminal.

Stepping into the bus station, the crowd of people in the hitched, plastic seats looked to Albertine like one big knot, a linked and doubled chain of coats, scarves, black-and-gray Herbst shopping bags, broad pale cheeks and noses. She wasn't sure what to do next. A chair was open. Beside it a standing ashtray bristled with butts, crushed soft-drink cups, flattened straws. Albertine sat down in the chair and stared at the clock. She frowned as though she were impatient for the next bus, but that was just a precaution. How long would they let her sit? This was as far as she had money to go. The compressed bundle of her jeans and underwear, tied in a thick sweater, felt reassuring as a baby against her stomach, and she clutched it close.

Lights of all colors, vaguely darkened and skewed in the thick glass doors, zipped up and down the sides of buildings. She glanced all around and back to the clock again. Minutes passed. Slow fright took her as she sat in the chair; she would have to go out soon. How many hours did she have left? The clock said eight. She sat stiffly, counting the moments, waiting for something to tell her what to do.

Now that she was in the city, all the daydreams she'd had were useless. She had not foreseen the blind crowd or the fierce activity of the lights outside the station. And then it seemed to her that she had been sitting in the chair too long. Panic tightened her throat. Without considering, in an almost desperate shuffle, she took her bundle and entered the ladies' room.

Fearing thieves, she took the bundle into the stall and held it awkwardly on her lap. Afterward, she washed her face, combed and redid the tin barrette that held her long hair off her forehead, then sat in the lobby. She let her eyes close. Behind her eyelids dim shapes billowed outward. Her body seemed to shrink and contract as in childish fever dreams when she lost all sense of the actual proportion of things and knew herself as bitterly small. She had come here for some reason, but couldn't remember what that was.

As it happened, then, because she didn't have anything particular in mind, the man seemed just what she needed when he appeared.

He needed her worse, but she didn't know that. He stood for an instant against the doors, long enough for Albertine to notice that his cropped hair was black, his skin was pale brown, thick and rough. He wore a dull green army jacket. She caught a good look at his profile, the blunt chin, big nose, harsh brow.

He was handsome, good-looking at least, and could have been an Indian. He even could have been a Chippewa. He walked out into the street.

She started after him. Partly because she didn't know what she was looking for, partly because he was a soldier like her father, and partly because he could have been an Indian, she followed. It seemed to her that he had cleared a path of safety through the door into the street. But when she stepped outside he had disappeared. She faltered, then told herself to keep walking toward the boldest lights.

Northern Pacific Avenue was the central thoroughfare of the dingy feel-good roll of Indian bars, western-wear stores, pawn shops, and Christian Revival Missions that Fargo was trying to eradicate. The strip had diminished under the town's urban-renewal project: asphalt plains and swooping concrete interchanges shouldered the remaining bars into an intricate huddle, lit for action at this hour. The giant cartoon outline of a cat, eyes fringed in pink neon, winked and switched its glittering tail. Farther down the street a cowgirl tall as a building tossed her lariat in slow heart-shaped loops. Beneath her glowing heels men slouched, passing bags crimped back for bottlenecks.

The night was cold. Albertine stepped into the recessed door stoop of a small shop. Its window displayed secondhand toasters. The other side of the street was livelier. She saw two Indian men, hair falling in cowlicks over their faces, dragging a limp, dazed woman between them. An alley swallowed them. Another woman in a tiger-skin skirt and long boots posed briefly in a doorway. A short round oriental man sprang out of nowhere, gesturing emphatically to someone who wasn't there. He went up the stairs of a doorway labeled ROOMS. That was the doorway Albertine decided she would try for a place to sleep, when things quieted down. For now she was content to watch, shifting from foot to foot, arms crossed over her bundle.

Then she saw the soldier again.

He was walking quickly, duffel hoisted up his shoulder, along the opposite side of the street. Again she followed. Stepping from her doorway she walked parallel with him, bundle slung from her hand and bouncing off her legs. He must have been a little over six feet. She was tall herself and always conscious of the height of men. She stopped when he paused before a windowful of pearl-button shirts, buff Stetsons, and thick-nosed pawned pistols. He stayed there a long time, moving from one display to the next. He was never still. He smoked quickly, jittering, dragging hard and snapping the cigarette against his middle finger. He turned back and forth, constantly aware of who was passing or what was making what noise where.

He knew the girl had been following and watching.

He knew she was watching now. He had noticed her first in the bus station. Her straight brown hair and Indian eyes drew him, even though she was too young. She was tall, strong, twice the size of most Vietnamese. It had been a long time since he'd seen any Indian women, even a breed. He had been a soldier, was now a veteran, had seen nine months of combat in the Annamese Cordillera before the NVA captured him somewhere near Pleiku. They kept him half a year. He was released after an honorable peace was not achieved, after the evacuation. Returning home he had been fouled up in red tape, routinely questioned by a military psychiatrist, dismissed. It had been three weeks, only that, since the big C-141 and Gia Lam airfield.

He examined the pawnshop window again.

Enough of this, he thought. He turned to face her.

Her legs were long, slightly bowed. Jeans lapped her toed-in boots. She'd be good with a horse. One hand was tensed in the pocket of a cheap black nylon parka. Passing headlights periodically lit her face—wide with strong, jutting bones. Not pretty yet, a kid trying to look old. Jailbait. She stared back at him through traffic. She was carrying a knotted bundle.

He had seen so many with their children, possessions, animals tied in cloths across their backs, under their breasts, bundles dragged in frail carts. He had seen them bolting under fire, arms wrapped around small packages. Some of the packages, loosely held the way hers was, exploded. Henry Lamartine Junior carried enough shrapnel deep inside of him, still working its way out, to set off the metal detector in the airport. He had been physically searched there in a small curtained booth. When he told the guard what the problem was, the man just looked at him and said nothing, dumb as stone. Henry had wanted to crush that stupid face the way you crumple a ball of wax paper.

The girl did not look stupid. She only looked young. She turned away. He thought that she might walk off carrying that bundle. She could go anywhere. Possibility of danger. Contents of bundle that could rip through flesh and strike bone. It was as much the sense of danger, the almost sweet familiarity he had with risk by now, as it was the attraction for her that made him put his hands out, stopping traffic, and cross to where she stood.

He turned out to be from a family she knew. A crazy Lamartine boy. Henry.

"I know your brother Lyman," she said. "I heard about you. How'd you get loose?"

"I'm like my brother Gerry. No jail built that can hold me either."

He grinned when she told him her name.

"Old Man Kashpaw know you're hanging out on NP Avenue?"

Albertine took his arm. "I'm thirsty," she said.

They walked beneath the cowgirl's lariat and found a table in the Round-Up Bar. After two drinks there they moved down the street, and kept moving on. Somewhere later that night, in the whiskey, her hand brushed his. He would not let go.

"You know any bar tricks?" she asked. "Show me one."

He dropped her hand and she made it into a fist and shoved it in her pocket. She still clutched her bundle tight between her feet, under the table. He got three steak knives and two water glasses from the bartender and brought them back to the table. He set the glasses down half a foot apart. Then he interlapped the knives so they made a bridge between the glass lips, a bridge of knives suspended in air.

Albertine looked at the precarious, linked edges.

She was nervous, but she didn't recognize this feeling, because it was part of a whirl in her stomach that was like excitement.

When Henry and Albertine left the bar it was very late, past last call, past closing. The streets were quiet. He put his arm around her and she stumbled once beneath its weight.

A small black-and-white television flickered on a high shelf behind the hotel desk. President Nixon's face drooped across the screen. The night clerk took Henry's ten-dollar bill, and threw it into the cash drawer and sleepily shoved a pen and lined slip across the counter toward him. The clerk was a mound of flesh tapering into a small thick skull. Waiting for the soldier to sign, he yawned so hugely that tears sprang from his eyes. It did not interest him that the man and girl, both Indian or Mexicans, whatever, signed in as Mr. and Mrs. Howdy Doody and were shacking up for the night. Whatever. He yawned again.

Motherfucker, Henry thought, lazy motherfucker, aren't you? Drunk, he had taken a violent dislike to the man. I could off this fat shit, he told himself. But Albertine was there. "Advise restraint," he said out loud. She didn't seem to hear. The place was well off the avenue, and the short upstairs hall was quiet. Henry steered her easily before him, touching her shoulder blades through the bunched padding in the nylon jacket. He shook the thought of the fat clerk away, far as possible.

"Angel, where's your wings," he whispered into her hair. "They should be here." He pressed the ends of his fingers hard against her jutting bones.

Her laugh was high and soft. He fumbled for the key. He was not used to having keys again and always forgot where he put them. Groping, patting, he fished the room key from his jacket and put it to the lock. She was poised, half turned from what she might see when the door opened. He waved her in. Once she entered and stood in the hard overhead light, he saw that she was bone tired, sagging from the broad sawhorse shoulders down, her hair wrenched in a clump by the barrette. He was drunker than she was. She had stopped after a few and let him go on drinking, talking, until he spilled too many and knew it was time to taper off.

There was no table lamp. He turned off the overhead light and left on the one over the bathroom mirror.

"Wanna use the head?"

At first she shook her head dumbly, no, and looked at the floor. *But then I can close the door and he'll be out there*, she thought.

She walked past him. He heard water rush into the sink. The other sounds she tried to hide made him smile. Women are so fucking cute sometimes it hurts. It really hurts.

Don't ever want to come out of here. She leaned her forehead on cool tile.

"When angel showers," he was singing to her closed door, "come your way. They bring the flowers that bloom in May."

He steadied himself on the iron bed rails, tried to pull his boots off, went to his knees.

"Keep looking for a bluebird and listen. . . . I know by God you were pissing in there. I heard you. It sounded like rain on a tin roof."

Then he was beating his chest lightly, like in the cold mission church he had served in when he was eight.

"Mea culpa, mea culpa, I am not worthy that you should come under my roof."

He tried to stand.

Hearing the sounds of a toothbrush he swayed backward, laughing. It sounded ridiculous. Sitting on the floor, stiff legged, he took off his boots and socks, then stood up warily to ease off his pants, unbutton his shirt. He set the bottle of Four Roses on a chair where he could reach it and turned down the covers on the bed. Then he crawled in and watched the crack of light around all four sides of the bathroom door.

"It was rehung a size too small," he said in a loud critical voice. "Or else it shrunk in the frame." He laughed again.

He is out of his mind.

She came through the door, put some clothes down neatly folded, and disappeared again. "If I close my eyes and imagine very hard what you're doing . . ." He addressed the bottle, then unscrewed the top. With his eyes shut he drank the rough whiskey. It left a sweet burn going down, and when he looked again his vision had narrowed.

He said those men took trophies. Skin pressed in the pages of a book.

There was often a stage in his drunkenness where his eyesight tunneled, like looking through the wrong end of binoculars. He had to be very careful now to remember where he was. He did not dare take his eyes from the shrinking door. "Please . . . ," he urged the dark room, "don't . . . ," fearing something might break the concentration. But he kept tight control. Advise restraint. Advise restraint, his brain tapped. He began connecting each loud invisible rustle with a very specific movement that the woman must make as she undressed. From top to bottom. He undressed her mentally with slow deliberation and no desire. Then suddenly, naked. She had even rolled her socks and stuck them in her boots.

She should have come out then, but she didn't. His heart pumped.

Concentration began to slacken. The image of her fled. He rolled from the bed and started to the door, feeling his way along the edge of the mattress until he lost it and had to cross long steps of endless space, where he thought water lapped his ankles. The rustling stopped. Silence warns. He was going to kick and jump aside like in the village back there, but from somewhere he gained a measure of control. He gripped the handle. The door swung in. The light seemed to move around her in sheets, and the tunnel widened.

On the tiny square of floor, still dressed, the bundle she had carried opened and spread all around her, she crouched low.

And he saw her as the woman back there.

How the hell could you figure them?

She looked at him. They had used a bayonet. She was out of her mind. You, me, same. Same. She pointed to her eyes and his eyes. The Asian, folded eyes of some Chippewas. She was hemorrhaging.

Question her

Sir, she is dying, sir.

"And anyway, what could I have asked? Huh? What the hell?"

Albertine was looking at him, staring at him. He realized he had spoken out loud.

The brown hair swung over her face as she bent, smoothing a red handkerchief into a small square. She was wrapping things back into her bundle. He tucked a gray towel around his waist and lowered himself onto the edge of the stool. Her clothing was spread between them. He bent over and picked up a thin long-waisted pair of cotton underpants, doubled them, put them back.

"I'll help you," he said.

"I don't need any help."

He put his hands in his lap. He wanted cigarettes now, badly, but he didn't want to go back and look for them in the dark where the bed was.

"Would you get me my smokes? I'm drunk."

His voice caught in his throat. She did not answer or look at him but went out of the room.

I shouldn't stay here, she thought. *But all my things are here. He was talking to himself.*

While she was gone he noticed that his face, hands, chest were cold with sweat. His hands trembled when he lighted the Marlboro.

Weak, he thought, holding the smoke in his lungs. But now he was used to the shaking, this kind of shaking, which meant that the tightness was lowering, lowering him. He lit one cigarette from another and dropped the ends in the bowl beneath his hip. As he watched her, his breathing gradually calmed. The blackness edging his vision dropped away. The movements of her hands were humble and certain. She had a long curved back and those jutting shoulder blades, like wings of horn.

How long can I sit here and let him watch me like this? She felt like she was still riding on the bus. Her blood rocked.

"Please," he said finally, when she had put everything in order several times, "can we go to bed? I won't touch you. Too drunk anyhow."

"All right."

He took her hand and led her from the bathroom, half shutting the door.

"I'm going to leave the light on if that's okay with you."

She nodded silently.

She took her jeans, boots, socks off, then slid into bed. She was wearing a long-sleeved shirt and underwear. Once beside him, although she had been half asleep as she folded her clothes, she became completely alert, conscious of his lightest movement.

Good night. *I'm going to shut my eyes and pretend to sleep.*

But the pretense just increased her sensitivity to his breathing, to the way the sheets scratched against his body.

The CREDIT sign across the street ticked on by slow stages until the letters completed, flared three times in silence. She turned to him. She propped herself on her elbow and unbuttoned her shirt. He took her hand away and worked the cloth off her shoulders. She wore a thick cotton brassiere. He put both arms around her and undid the hook. Once she was naked beneath him, he could hold off no longer. In panic, he tried to surge inside of her.

Her fear excited him so much, though, that he came helplessly, pressed against her, before he was even hard. She was quiet, waiting for him to say something. She touched his face, but he did not speak, so she rolled away from him.

Henry was not drunk anymore, not in the least. He knew that in a moment he would want her again, the right way, and in this expectation he listened as she pretended to sleep. Her back curved, a warm slope. The length and breadth of her seemed edgeless. He felt wonder and moved closer. She tensed. Her breathing changed.

She gave off a fetid traveler's warmth, cigarette smoke, bus-seat smell, a winy undertone from what they'd drunk, the crackery smell of snow melted into unwashed hair, a flowery heat from her armpits.

He thought of diving off a riverbank, a bridge.

He closed his eyes and saw the water, the whirling patterns, below. He pushed her over, face down, and pinned her from behind. He spread her legs with his knees and pulled her toward him.

Muffled, slogged in pillows, she gripped the head bars. He pushed into her. She made a harsh sound. Her back was board hard, resistant. Then she gave with a cry. He touched her with the cushioned part of his fingers until she softened to him. She opened. The bones of her pelvis creaked wide, like the petals of a wooden flower, and he thought she came. Then he did, too. Wobbling then surging smoothly forward, he came whispering that he loved her.

Afterward, he let her go, put his face in dark hair behind her ear, and was about to whisper love talk, but she rolled out from under his chest.

She got as far away from him as possible. It was, to Henry, as if she had crossed a deep river and disappeared. He lay next to her, divided from her, just outside and with no way to follow.

At last she slept. Her even breath was a desolate comfort. He wound his hand in a long hank of her hair and, eventually, slept, too.

Near dawn Albertine could not remember where she was. She could not remember about the dull ache between her legs. She turned to the man and made the mistake of touching him in his sleep. His name came back to her. She was about to say his name.

He shrieked. Exploded.

She was stunned on the floor, gasping for breath against the wall before the syllables of his name escaped. Outside their room a door opened and shut. Somewhere in the room she heard his breath, a slow animal wheeze that froze her to the wall. He moved. The scent of his harsh fear hit her first as he came toward her.

In reflex, she crossed her arms before her face. A dark numbing terror had stopped her mind completely. But when he touched her he was weeping.

THE RED CONVERTIBLE

(1974)

LYMAN LAMARTINE

I was the first one to drive a convertible on my reservation. And of course it was red, a red Olds. I owned that car along with my brother Henry Junior. We owned it together until his boots filled with water on a windy night and he bought out my share. Now Henry owns the whole car, and his younger brother Lyman (that's myself), Lyman walks everywhere he goes.

How did I earn enough money to buy my share in the first place? My one talent was I could always make money. I had a touch for it, unusual in a Chippewa. From the first I was different that way, and everyone recognized it. I was the only kid they let in the American Legion Hall to shine shoes, for example, and one Christmas I sold spiritual bouquets for the mission door to door. The nuns let me keep a percentage. Once I started, it seemed the more money I made the easier the money came.

Everyone encouraged it. When I was fifteen I got a job washing dishes at the Joliet Café, and that was where my first big break happened.

It wasn't long before I was promoted to bussing tables, and then the short-order cook quit and I was hired to take her place. No sooner than you know it I was managing the Joliet. The rest is history. I went on managing. I soon become part owner, and of course there was no stopping me then. It wasn't long before the whole thing was mine.

After I'd owned the Joliet for one year, it blew over in the worst tornado ever seen around here. The whole operation was smashed to bits. A total loss. The fryalator was up in a tree, the grill torn in half like it was paper. I was only sixteen. I had it all in my mother's name, and I lost it quick, but before I lost it I had every one of my relatives, and their relatives, to dinner, and I also bought that red Olds I mentioned, along with Henry.

The first time we saw it! I'll tell you when we first saw it. We had gotten a ride up to Winnipeg, and both of us had money. Don't ask me why, because we never mentioned a car or anything, we just had all our money. Mine was cash, a big bankroll from the Joliet's insurance. Henry had two checks—a week's extra pay for being laid off, and his regular check from the Jewel Bearing Plant.

We were walking down Portage anyway, seeing the sights, when we saw it. There it was, parked, large as life. Really as *if* it was alive. I thought of the word *repose*, because the car wasn't simply stopped, parked, or whatever. That car reposed, calm and gleaming, a FOR SALE sign in its left front window. Then, before we had thought it over at all, the car belonged to us and our pockets were empty. We had just enough money for gas back home.

We went places in that car, me and Henry. We took off driving all one whole summer. We started off toward the Little Knife River and Mandaree in Fort Berthold and then we found ourselves down in Wakpala somehow, and then suddenly we were over in Montana on the Rocky Boys, and yet the summer was not even half over. Some people hang on to details when they travel, but we didn't let them bother us and just lived our everyday lives here to there.

I do remember this one place with willows. I remember I laid under those trees and it was comfortable. So comfortable. The branches bent down all around me like a tent or a stable. And quiet, it was quiet, even though there was a powwow close enough so I could see it going on. The air was not too still, not too windy either. When the dust rises up and hangs in the air around the dancers like that, I feel good. Henry was asleep with his arms thrown wide. Later on, he woke up and we started driving again. We were somewhere in Montana, or maybe on the Blood Reserve—it could have been anywhere. Anyway it was where we met the girl.

All her hair was in buns around her ears, that's the first thing I noticed about her. She was posed alongside the road with her arm out, so we stopped. That girl was short, so short her lumber shirt looked comical on her, like a nightgown. She had jeans on and fancy moccasins and she carried a little suitcase.

"Hop on in," says Henry. So she climbs in between us.

"We'll take you home," I says. "Where do you live?"

"Chicken," she says.

"Where the hell's that?" I ask her.

"Alaska."

"Okay," says Henry, and we drive.

We got up there and never wanted to leave. The sun doesn't truly set there in summer, and the night is more a soft dusk. You might doze off, sometimes, but before you know it you're up again, like an animal in nature. You never feel like you have to sleep hard or put away the world. And things would grow up there. One day just dirt or moss, the next day flowers and long grass. The girl's name was Susy. Her family really took to us. They fed us and put us up. We had our own tent to live in by their house, and the kids would be in and out of there all day and night. They couldn't get over me and Henry being brothers, we looked so different. We told them we knew we had the same mother, anyway.

One night Susy came in to visit us. We sat around in the tent talking of this thing and that. The season was changing. It was getting darker by that time, and the cold was even getting just a little mean. I told her it was time for us to go. She stood up on a chair.

"You never seen my hair," Susy said.

That was true. She was standing on a chair, but still, when she unclipped her buns the hair reached all the way to the ground. Our eyes opened. You couldn't tell how much hair she had when it was rolled up so neatly. Then my brother Henry did something funny. He went up to the chair and said, "Jump on my shoulders." So she did that, and her hair reached down past his waist, and he started twirling, this way and that, so her hair was flung out from side to side.

"I always wondered what it was like to have long pretty hair," Henry says. Well we laughed. It was a funny sight, the way he did it. The next morning we got up and took leave of those people.

On to greener pastures, as they say. It was down through Spokane and across Idaho then Montana and very soon we were racing the weather right along under the Canadian border through Columbus, Des Lacs, and then we were in Bottineau County and soon home. We'd made most of the trip, that summer, without putting up the car hood at all. We got home just in time, it turned out, for the army to remember Henry had signed up to join it.

I don't wonder that the army was so glad to get my brother that they turned him into a Marine. He was built like a brick outhouse anyway. We liked to tease him that they really wanted him for his Indian nose. He had a nose big and sharp as a hatchet, like the nose on Red Tomahawk, the Indian who killed Sitting Bull, whose profile is on signs all along the North Dakota highways. Henry went off to training camp, came home once during Christmas, then the next thing you know we got an overseas letter from him. It was 1970, and he said he was stationed up in the northern hill country. Whereabouts I did not know. He wasn't such a hot letter writer, and only got off two before the enemy caught him. I could never keep it straight, which direction those good Vietnam soldiers were from.

I wrote him back several times, even though I didn't know if those letters would get through. I kept him informed all about the car. Most of the time I had it up on blocks in the yard or half taken apart, because that long trip did a hard job on it under the hood.

I always had good luck with numbers, and never worried about the draft myself. I never even had to think about what my number was. But Henry was never lucky in the same way as me. It was at least three years before Henry came home. By then I guess the whole war was solved in the government's mind, but for him it would keep on going. In those years I'd put his car into almost perfect shape. I always thought of it as his car while he was gone, even though when he left he said, "Now it's yours," and threw me his key.

"Thanks for the extra key," I'd said. "I'll put it up in your drawer just in case I need it." He laughed.

When he came home, though, Henry was very different, and I'll say this: the change was no good. You could hardly expect him to change for the better, I know. But he was quiet, so quiet, and never comfortable sitting still anywhere but always up and moving around. I thought back to times we'd sat still for whole afternoons, never moving a muscle, just shifting our weight along the ground, talking to whoever sat with us, watching things. He'd always had a joke, then, too, and now you couldn't get him to laugh, or when he did it was more the sound of a man choking, a sound that stopped up the throats of other people around him. They got to leaving him alone most of the time, and I didn't blame them. It was a fact: Henry was jumpy and mean.

I'd bought a color TV set for my mom and the rest of us while Henry was away. Money still came very easy. I was sorry I'd ever bought it though, because of Henry. I was also sorry I'd bought color, because with black-and-white the pictures seem older and farther away. But what are you going to do? He sat in front of it, watching it, and that was the only time he was completely still. But it was the kind of stillness that you see in a rabbit when it freezes and before it will bolt. He was not easy. He sat in his chair gripping the armrests with all his might, as if the chair itself was moving at a high speed and if he let go at all he would rocket forward and maybe crash right through the set.

Once I was in the room watching TV with Henry and I heard his teeth click at something. I looked over, and he'd bitten through his lip. Blood was going down his chin. I tell you right then I wanted to smash that tube to pieces. I went over to it but Henry must have known what I was up to. He rushed from his chair and shoved me out of the way, against the wall. I told myself he didn't know what he was doing.

My mom came in, turned the set off real quiet, and told us she had made something for supper. So we went and sat down. There was still blood going down Henry's chin, but he didn't notice it and no one said anything, even though every time he took a bite of his bread his blood fell onto it until he was eating his own blood mixed in with the food.

While Henry was not around we talked about what was going to happen to him. There were no Indian doctors on the reservation, and my mom was afraid of trusting Old Man Pillager because he courted her long ago and was jealous of her husbands. He might take revenge through her son. We were afraid that if we brought Henry to a regular hospital they would keep him.

"They don't fix them in those places," Mom said; "they just give them drugs."

"We wouldn't get him there in the first place," I agreed, "so let's just forget about it."

Then I thought about the car.

Henry had not even looked at the car since he'd gotten home, though like I said, it was in tip-top condition and ready to drive. I thought the car might bring the old Henry back somehow. So I bided my time and waited for my chance to interest him in the vehicle.

One night Henry was off somewhere. I took myself a hammer. I went out to that car and I did a number on its underside. Whacked it up. Bent the tail pipe double. Ripped the muffler loose. By the time I was done with the car it looked worse than any typical Indian car that has been driven all its life on reservation roads, which they always say are like government promises—full of holes. It just about hurt me, I'll tell you that! I threw dirt in the carburetor and I ripped all the electric tape off the seats. I made it look just as beat up as I could. Then I sat back and waited for Henry to find it.

Still, it took him over a month. That was all right, because it was just getting warm enough, not melting, but warm enough to work outside.

"Lyman," he says, walking in one day, "that red car looks like shit."

"Well it's old," I says. "You got to expect that."

"No way!" says Henry. "That car's a classic! But you went and ran the piss right out of it, Lyman, and you know it don't deserve that. I kept that car in A-one shape. You don't remember. You're too young. But when I left, that car was running like a watch.

Now I don't even know if I can get it to start again, let alone get it anywhere near its old condition."

"Well you try," I said, like I was getting mad, "but I say it's a piece of junk."

Then I walked out before he could realize I knew he'd strung together more than six words at once.

After that I thought he'd freeze himself to death working on that car. He was out there all day, and at night he rigged up a little lamp, ran a cord out the window, and had himself some light to see by while he worked. He was better than he had been before, but that's still not saying much. It was easier for him to do the things the rest of us did. He ate more slowly and didn't jump up and down during the meal to get this or that or look out the window. I put my hand in the back of the TV set, I admit, and fiddled around with it good, so that it was almost impossible now to get a clear picture. He didn't look at it very often anyway. He was always out with that car or going off to get parts for it. By the time it was really melting outside, he had it fixed.

I had been feeling down in the dumps about Henry around this time. We had always been together before. Henry and Lyman. But he was such a loner now that I didn't know how to take it. So I jumped at the chance one day when Henry seemed friendly. It's not that he smiled or anything. He just said, "Let's take that old shitbox for a spin." Just the way he said it made me think he could be coming around.

We went out to the car. It was spring. The sun was shining very bright. My only sister, Bonita, who was just eleven years old, came out and made us stand together for a picture. Henry leaned his elbow on the red car's windshield, and he took his other arm and put it over my shoulder, very carefully, as though it was heavy for him to lift and he didn't want to bring the weight down all at once.

"Smile," Bonita said, and he did.

That picture. I never look at it anymore. A few months ago, I don't know why, I got his picture out and tacked it on the wall. I felt good about Henry at the time, close to him. I felt good having his picture on the wall, until one night when I was looking at television. I was a little drunk and stoned. I looked up at the wall and Henry was staring at me. I don't know what it was, but his smile had changed, or maybe it was gone. All I know is I couldn't stay in the same room with that picture. I was shaking. I got up, closed the door, and went into the kitchen. A little later my friend Ray came over and we both went back into that room. We put the picture in a brown bag, folded the bag over and over tightly, then put it way back in a closet.

I still see that picture now, as if it tugs at me, whenever I pass that closet door. The picture is very clear in my mind. It was so sunny that day Henry had to squint against the glare. Or maybe the camera Bonita held flashed like a mirror, blinding him, before she snapped the picture. My face is right out in the sun, big and round. But he might have drawn back, because the shadows on his face are deep as holes. There are two shadows curved like little hooks around the ends of his smile, as if to frame it and try to keep it there—that one, first smile that looked like it might have hurt his face. He has his field jacket on and the worn-in clothes he'd come back in and kept wearing ever since. After Bonita took the picture, she went into the house and we got into the car. There was a full cooler in the trunk. We started off, east, toward Pembina and the Red River because Henry said he wanted to see the high water.

The trip over there was beautiful. When everything starts changing, drying up, clearing off, you feel like your whole life is starting. Henry felt it, too. The top was down and the car hummed like a top. He'd really put it back in shape, even the tape on the seats was very carefully put down and glued back in layers. It's not that he smiled again or even joked, but his face looked to me as if it was clear, more peaceful. It looked as though he wasn't thinking of anything in particular except the bare fields and windbreaks and houses we were passing.

The river was high and full of winter trash when we got there. The sun was still out, but it was colder by the river. There were still little clumps of dirty snow here and there on the banks. The water hadn't gone over the banks yet, but it would, you could tell. It was just at its limit, hard swollen, glossy like an old gray scar. We made ourselves a fire, and we sat down and watched the current go. As I watched it I felt something squeezing inside me and tightening and trying to let go all at the same time. I knew I was not just feeling it myself; I knew I was feeling what Henry was going through at that moment. Except that I couldn't stand it, the closing and opening. I jumped to my feet. I took Henry by the shoulders and I started shaking him. "Wake up," I says, "wake up, wake up, wake up!" I didn't know what had come over me. I sat down beside him again.

His face was totally white and hard. Then it broke, like stones break all of a sudden when water boils up inside them.

"I know it," he says. "I know it. I can't help it. It's no use."

We start talking. He said he knew what I'd done with the car. It was obvious it had been whacked out of shape and not just neglected. He said he wanted to give the car to me for good now, it was no use. He said he'd fixed it just to give it back and I should take it.

"No way," I says, "I don't want it."

"That's okay," he says, "you take it."

"I don't want it, though," I says back to him, and then to emphasize, just to emphasize, you understand, I touch his shoulder. He slaps my hand off.

"Take that car," he says.

"No," I say, "make me," I say, and then he grabs my jacket and rips the arm loose. That jacket is a class act, suede with tags and zippers. I push Henry backwards, off the log. He jumps up and bowls me over. We go down in a clinch and come up swinging hard, for all we're worth, with our fists. He socks my jaw so hard I feel like it swings loose. Then I'm at his ribcage and land a good one under his chin so his head snaps back. He's dazzled. He looks at me and I look at him and then his eyes are full of tears and blood and at first I think he's crying. But no, he's laughing. "Ha! Ha!" he says. "Ha! Ha! Take good care of it."

"Okay," I says, "okay, no problem. Ha! Ha!"

I can't help it, and I start laughing, too. My face feels fat and strange, and after a while I get a beer from the cooler in the trunk, and when I hand it to Henry he takes his shirt and wipes my germs off. "Hoof-and-mouth disease," he says. For some reason this cracks me up, and so we're really laughing for a while, and then we drink all the rest of the beers one by one and throw them in the river and see how far, how fast, the current takes them before they fill up and sink.

"You want to go on back?" I ask after a while. "Maybe we could snag a couple nice Kashpaw girls."

He says nothing. But I can tell his mood is turning again.

"They're all crazy, the girls up here, every damn one of them."

"You're crazy too," I say, to jolly him up. "Crazy Lamartine boys!"

He looks as though he will take this wrong at first. His face twists, then clears, and he jumps up on his feet. "That's right!" he says. "Crazier 'n hell. Crazy Indians!"

I think it's the old Henry again. He throws off his jacket and starts swinging his legs out from the knees like a fancy dancer. He's down doing something between a grouse dance and a bunny hop, no kind of dance I ever saw before, but neither has anyone else on all this green growing earth. He's wild. He wants to pitch whoopee! He's up and at me and all over. All this time I'm laughing so hard, so hard my belly is getting tied up in a knot.

"Got to cool me off!" he shouts all of a sudden. Then he runs over to the river and jumps in.

There's boards and other things in the current. It's so high. No sound comes from the river after the splash he makes, so I run right over. I look around. It's getting dark. I see he's halfway across the water already, and I know he didn't swim there but the current took him. It's far. I hear his voice, though, very clearly across it.

"My boots are filling," he says.

He says this in a normal voice, like he just noticed and he doesn't know what to think of it. Then he's gone. A branch comes by. Another branch. And I go in.

By the time I get out of the river, off the snag I pulled myself onto, the sun is down. I walk back to the car, turn on the high beams, and drive it up the bank. I put it in first gear and then I take my foot off the clutch. I get out, close the door, and watch it plow softly into the water. The headlights reach in as they go down, searching, still lighted even after the water swirls over the back end. I wait. The wires short out. It is all finally dark. And then there is only the water, the sound of it going and running and going and running and running.

SCALES

(1980)

ALBERTINE JOHNSON

I was sitting before my third or fourth Jellybean, which is anisette, grain alcohol, a lit match, and small wet explosion in the brain. On my left sat Gerry Nanapush of the Chippewa Tribe. On my right sat Dot Adare of the has-been, of the never-was, of the what's-in-front-of-me people. Still in her belly and tensed in its fluids coiled the child of their union, the child we were waiting for, the child whose name we were making a strenuous and lengthy search for in a cramped and littered bar at the very edge of that Dakota town.

Gerry had been on the wagon for thirteen years. He was drinking a tall glass of tonic water in which a crescent of soiled lemon bobbed, along with a Maraschino cherry or two. He was thirty-five years old and had been in prison, or out of prison and on the run, for almost half of those years. He was not in the clear yet nor would he ever be, that is why the yellow tennis player's visor was pulled down to the rim of his eyeglass frames. The bar was dimly lit and smoky; his glasses were very dark. Poor visibility must have been the reason Officer Lovchik saw him first.

Lovchik started toward us with his hand on his hip, but Gerry was over the backside of the booth and out the door before Lovchik got close enough to make a positive identification.

"Siddown with us," said Dot to Lovchik, when he neared our booth. "I'll buy you a drink. It's so dead here. No one's been through all night."

Lovchik sighed, sat, and ordered a blackberry brandy.

"Now tell me," she said, staring at him, "honestly. What do you think of the name Ketchup Face?"

It was through Gerry that I first met Dot, in a bar like that one only denser with striving drinkers, construction crews who had come into town because a new interstate highway was passing near it. I was stuck there, having run out of money and ideas of where to go next. I was twenty-two and knew I'd soon have to do something different with my life. But no matter what that would be, I had to make some money first.

I had heard Gerry Nanapush was around, and because he was famous for leading a hunger strike at the state pen, as well as having been Henry Lamartine's brother and some kind of boyfriend to Aunt June, I went to look for him. He was not hard to find, being large. I sat down next to him and we struck up a conversation, during the long course of which we became friendly enough for Gerry to put his arm around me.

Dot entered at exactly the wrong moment. She was quick-tempered anyway, and being pregnant (Gerry had gotten her that way on a prison visit six months previous) increased her irritability. It was only natural then, I guess, that she would pull the barstool out from under me and threaten my life. Only I didn't believe she was threatening my life at the time. I had a false view of pregnant women. I thought of them as wearing invisible halos, not committing mayhem.

"I'm gonna bend you out of shape," she said, flexing her hands over me. Her hands were small, broad, capable, with pointed nails. I used to do the wrong thing sometimes when I was drinking, and that time I did the wrong thing, even though I was stretched out on the floor beneath her. I started laughing at her because her hands were so small (though strong and determined looking—I should have been more conscious of that). She was about to dive on top of me, six-month belly and all, but Gerry caught her in midair and carried her, yelling, out the door. The next morning I reported for work. It was my first day on the job, and the only other woman on the construction site besides me was Dot Adare.

That day Dot just glared toward me from a distance. She worked in the weigh shack, and I was hired to press buttons on the conveyor belt. All I had to do was adjust the speeds on the belt for sand, rocks, or gravel and make sure it was aimed toward the right pile. There was a pyramid for each type of material, which was used to make hot-mix and cement. Across the wide yard, I saw Dot emerge from the little weigh shack from time to time. I couldn't tell whether she recognized me, but I thought, by the end of the day, that she probably didn't. I found out differently the next morning when I went to the company truck for coffee.

She got me alongside of the truck somehow, away from the men. She didn't say a word, just held the buck knife out where I could see it, blade toward me. She jiggled the handle, and the tip waved like the pointy head of a pit viper. Blind. Heat seeking. I was completely astonished. I had just put the plastic cover on my coffee and it steamed between my hands.

"Well, I'm sorry I laughed," I said. She stepped back. I peeled the lid off my coffee, took a sip, and then I said the wrong thing again.

"And I wasn't going after your boyfriend."

"Why not?" she said at once. "What's wrong with him?"

I saw that I was going to lose this argument no matter what I said, so for once I did the right thing. I threw my coffee in her face and ran. Later on that day Dot came out of the weigh shack and yelled, "Okay then!" I was close enough to see that she even grinned. I waved. From then on things were better between us, which was lucky, because I turned out to be such a good button presser that within two weeks I was promoted to the weigh shack, to help Dot.

It wasn't that Dot needed help weighing trucks, it was just a formality for the state highway department. I never quite understood, but it seems Dot had been both the truck weigher and the truck-weight inspector for a while, until someone caught wind of this. The company hired me to actually weigh the trucks, and Dot was hired by the state to make sure I recorded accurate weights. What she really did was sleep, knit, or eat all day. Between truckloads I did the same. I didn't even have to get off my stool to weigh the trucks, because the arm of the scale projected through a rectangular hole and the weights appeared right in front of me. The standard back dumps, bellydumps, and yellow company trucks eased onto a platform built over the arm next to the shack. I wrote their weight on a little pink slip, clipped the paper in a clothespin attached to a broom handle, and handed it up to the driver. I kept a copy of the pink slip on a yellow slip that I put in a metal filebox. No one ever picked up the filebox, so I never knew what the yellow slips were for. The company paid me very well.

It was early July when Dot and I started working together. At first I sat as far away from her as possible and never took my eyes off her knitting needles, although it made me a little dizzy to watch her work. It wasn't long before we came to an understanding, though, and after this I felt perfectly comfortable with Dot. She was nothing but direct, you see, and told me right off that only three things made her angry. Number one was someone flirting with Gerry. Number two was a cigarette leech, someone who was always quitting but smoking yours. Number three was a piss-ant. I asked her what that was. "A piss-ant," she said, "is a man with fat buns who tries to sell you things. A Jaycee, an Elk, a Kiwanis." I always knew where I stood with Dot, so I trusted her. I knew that if I fell out of her favor she would threaten me and give me time to run before she tried anything physical.

By mid-July our shack was unbearable, for it drew heat in from the bare yard and held it. We sat outside most of the time, moving around the shack to catch what shade fell, letting the raw hot wind off the beetfields suck the sweat from our armpits and legs. But the seasons change fast in North Dakota. We spent the last day of August jumping from foot to numb foot before Hadji, the foreman, dragged a little column of bottled gas into the shack. He lit the spoked wheel on its head, it bloomed, and from then on we huddled close to the heater, eating, dozing, or sitting mindless in its small radius of dry warmth.

By that time Dot weighed over two hundred pounds, most of it peanut-butter cups and egg-salad sandwiches. She was a short, broad-beamed woman with long yellow eyes and spaces between each of her strong teeth. When we began working together, her hair was cropped close. By the cold months it had grown out in thick quills—brown at the shank, orange at the tip. The orange dye job had not suited her coloring. By that time, too, Dot's belly was round and full, for she was due in October. The child rode high, and she often rested her forearms on it while she knitted. One of Dot's most peculiar feats was transforming that gentle task into something perverse. She knit viciously, jerking the yarn around her thumb until the tip whitened, pulling each stitch so tightly that the little garments she finished stood up by themselves like miniature suits of mail.

I thought that the child would need those tight stitches when it was born. Although Dot as expecting mother lived a fairly calm life, it was clear that she had also moved loosely among the dangerous elements. The child, for example, had been conceived in a visiting room at the state prison. Dot had straddled Gerry's lap in a corner the closed-circuit TV did not quite scan. Through a hole ripped in her pantyhose and a hole ripped in Gerry's jeans they somehow managed to join and, miraculously, to conceive. Not long after my conversation with Gerry in the bar, he was caught. That time he went back peacefully, and didn't put up a fight. He was mainly in the penitentiary for breaking out of it, anyway, since for his crime of assault and battery he had received three years and time off for good behavior. He just never managed to serve those three years or behave well. He broke out time after time, and was caught each time he did it, regular as clockwork.

Gerry was talented at getting out, that's a fact. He boasted that no steel or concrete shitbarn could hold a Chippewa, and he had eellike properties in spite of his enormous size. Greased with lard once, he squirmed into a six-foot-thick prison wall and vanished. Some thought he had stuck there, immured forever, and that he would bring luck, like the bones of slaves sealed in the wall of China. But Gerry rubbed his own belly for luck and brought luck to no one else, for he appeared, suddenly, at Dot's door, and she was hard-pressed to hide him.

She managed for nearly a month. Hiding a six-foot-plus, two-hundred-and-fifty-pound Indian in the middle of a town that doesn't like Indians in the first place isn't easy. A month was quite an accomplishment, when you know what she was up against. She spent most of her time walking to and from the grocery store, padding along on her swollen feet, astonishing the neighbors with the size of what they thought was her appetite. Stacks of pork chops, whole fryers, thick steaks disappeared overnight, and since Gerry couldn't take the garbage out by day, sometimes he threw the bones out the windows, where they collected, where dogs soon learned to wait for a handout and fought and squabbled over whatever there was.

The neighbors finally complained, and one day, while Dot was at work, Lovchik knocked on the door of the trailer house. Gerry answered, sighed, and walked over to their car. He was so good at getting out of the joint and so terrible at getting caught. It was as if he couldn't stay out of their hands. Dot knew his problem and told him that he was crazy to think he could walk out of prison and then live like a normal person. Dot told him that didn't work. She told him to get lost for a while on the reservation or to let his mother, Lulu, who had a long successful history of hiding men, keep him under cover. She told him to change his name, to let the straggly hairs above his lip grow, disguising his face. But Gerry wouldn't do any of that. He simply knew he did not belong in prison, although he admitted it had done him some good when he was younger, hadn't known how to be a criminal, and so had taken lessons from professionals. Now that he knew all there was to know, however, he couldn't see the point of staying in a prison and taking the same lessons over and over. "A hate factory," he called it once, and said it manufactured black poisons in his stomach that he couldn't get rid of although he poked a finger down his throat and retched and tried to be a clean and normal person in spite of everything.

Gerry's problem, you see, was he believed in justice, not laws. He felt he had paid for his crime, which was done in a drunk heat and to settle the question with a cowboy of whether a Chippewa was also a nigger. Gerry said that the two had never settled it between them, but that the cowboy at least knew that if a Chippewa was a nigger he was sure also a hell of a mean and low-down fighter. For Gerry did not believe in fighting by any rules but reservation rules, which is to say the first thing Gerry did to the cowboy, after they squared off, was kick his balls.

It hadn't been much of a fight after that, and since there were both white and Indian witnesses, Gerry thought it would blow over if it ever reached court. But there is nothing more vengeful and determined in this world than a cowboy with sore balls, and Gerry soon found this out. He also found that white people are good witnesses to have on your side, because they have names, addresses, social security numbers, and work phones. But they are terrible witnesses to have against you, almost as bad as having Indians witness for you.

Not only did Gerry's friends lack all forms of identification except their band cards, not only did they disappear (out of no malice but simply because Gerry was tried during powwow time), but the few he did manage to get were not interested in looking judge or jury in the eyes. They mumbled into their laps. Gerry's friends, you see, had no confidence in the United States judicial system. They did not seem comfortable in the courtroom, and this increased their unreliability in the eyes of judge and jury. If you trust the authorities, they trust you better back, it seems. It looked that way to Gerry, anyhow.

A local doctor testified on behalf of the cowboy's testicles, and said his fertility might be impaired. Gerry got a little angry at that, and said right out in court that he could hardly believe he had done that much damage since the cowboy's balls were very small targets, it had been dark, and his aim was off anyway because of two, or maybe it was three, beers. That made matters worse, of course, and Gerry was socked with a sentence that was heavy for a first offense, but not bad for an Indian. Some said he got off lucky.

Only one good thing came from the whole experience, said

Gerry, and that was that maybe the cowboy would not have any little cowboys, although, Gerry also said, he had nightmares sometimes that the cowboy did manage to have little cowboys, all born with full sets of grinning teeth, Stetson hats, and little balls hard as plum pits.

So you see, it was difficult for Gerry, as an Indian, to retain the natural good humor of his ancestors in these modern circumstances. He tried though, and since he believed in justice, not laws, Gerry knew where he belonged—out of prison, in the bosom of his new family. And in spite of the fact that he was untrained in the honest life, he wanted it. He was even interested in getting a job. It didn't matter what kind of job. "Anything for a change," Gerry said. He wanted to go right out and apply for one, in fact, the moment he was free. But of course Dot wouldn't let him. And so, because he wanted to be with Dot, he stayed hidden in her trailer house even though they both realized, or must have, that it wouldn't be long before the police came asking around or the neighbors wised up and Gerry Nanapush would be back at square one again. So it happened. Lovchik came for him. And Dot now believed she would have to go through the end of her pregnancy and the delivery all by herself.

Dot was angry about having to go through it alone, and besides that, she loved Gerry with a deep and true love—that was clear. She knit his absences into thick little suits for the child, suits that would have stopped a truck on a dark road with their colors—Bazooka pink, bruise blue, the screaming orange flaggers wore.

The child was as restless a prisoner as its father, and grew more anxious and unruly as the time of release neared. As a place to spend a nine-month sentence in, Dot wasn't much. Her body was inhospitable. Her skin was loose, sallow, and draped like upholstery fabric over her short, boardlike bones. Like the shack we spent our days in, she seemed jerry-built, thrown into the world with loosely nailed limbs and lightly puttied joints. Some pregnant women's bellies look like they always have been there. But Dot's stomach was an odd shape, almost square, and had the tacked-on air of a new and unpainted bay window. The child was clearly ready for a break and not interested in earning its parole, for it kept her awake all night by pounding reasonlessly at her inner walls or beating against her bladder until she swore. "Kid wants out, bad," poor Dot would groan. "You think it might be premature?" From the outside, anyway, the child looked big enough to stand and walk and maybe even run straight out of the maternity ward the moment it was born.

The sun, at the time, rose around seven, and we got to the weigh shack while the frost was still thick on the gravel. Each morning I started the gas heater, turning the nozzle and standing back, flipping the match at it the way you would feed a fanged animal. Then one morning I saw the red bud through the window, lit already. But when I opened the door the shack was empty. There was, however, evidence of an overnight visitor—cigarette stubs, a few beer cans crushed to flat disks. I swept these things out and didn't say a word about them to Dot when she arrived.

She seemed to know something was in the air, however; her face lifted from time to time all that morning. She sniffed, and even I could smell the lingering odor of sweat like sour wheat, the faint reek of slept-in clothes and gasoline. Once, that morning, Dot looked at me and narrowed her long, hooded eyes. "I got pains," she said, "every so often. Like it's going to come sometime soon. Well, all I can say is he better drag ass to get here, that Gerry." She closed her eyes then, and went to sleep.

Ed Rafferty, one of the drivers, pulled in with a load. It was overweight, and when I handed him the pink slip he grinned. There were two scales, you see, on the way to the cement plant, and if a driver got past the state-run scale early, before the state officials were there, the company would pay for whatever he got away with. But it was not illicit gravel that tipped the wedge past the red mark on the balance. When I walked back inside I saw the weight had gone down to just under the red. Ed drove off, still laughing, and I assumed that he had leaned on the arm of the scale, increasing the weight.

"That Ed," I said, "got me again."

But Dot stared past me, needles poised in her fist like a picador's lances. It gave me a start, to see her frozen in such a menacing pose. It was not the sort of pose to turn your back on, but I did turn, following her gaze to the door, which a man's body filled suddenly.

Gerry, of course it was Gerry. He'd tipped the weight up past the red and leapt down, cat-quick for all his mass, and silent. I hadn't heard his step. Gravel crushed, evidently, but did not roll beneath his tight, thin boots.

He was bigger than I remembered from the bar, or perhaps it was just that we'd been living in that dollhouse of a weigh shack so long that everything else looked huge. He was so big that he had to hunker one shoulder beneath the lintel and back his belly in, pushing the doorframe wider with his long, soft hands. It was the hands I watched as Gerry filled the shack. His plump fingers looked so graceful and artistic against his smooth mass. He used them prettily. Revolving agile wrists he reached across the few inches left between himself and Dot. Then his littlest fingers curled like a woman's at tea, and he disarmed his wife. He drew the needles out of Dot's fists, and examined the little garment that hung like a queer fruit beneath.

"S'very, very nice," he said, scrutinizing the tiny, even stitches. "S'for the kid?"

Dot nodded solemnly and dropped her eyes to her lap. It was an almost tender moment. The silence lasted so long that I got embarrassed and would have left had I not been wedged firmly behind his hip in one corner.

Gerry stood there, smoothing black hair behind his ears. Again, there was a queer delicacy about the way he did this. So many things Gerry did might remind you of the way that a beautiful courtesan, standing naked before a mirror, would touch herself—lovingly, conscious of her attractions. He nodded encouragingly. "Let's go then," said Dot.

Suave, grand, gigantic, they moved across the construction site and then, by mysterious means, slipped their bodies into Dot's compact car. I expected the car to belly down, thought the muffler would scrape the ground behind them. But instead they flew, raising a great spume of dust that hung in the air a long time after they were out of sight.

I went back into the weigh shack when the air behind them had settled. I was bored, dead bored. And since one thing meant about as much to me as another, I picked up her needles and began knitting, as well as I could anyway, jerking the yarn back after each stitch, becoming more and more absorbed in my work until, as it happened, I came suddenly to the end of the garment, snipped the yarn, and worked the loose ends back into the collar of the thick little suit.

I missed Dot in the days that followed, days so alike they welded seamlessly to one another and took your mind away. I seemed to exist in a suspension and spent my time sitting at the window watching nothing until the sun went down, bruising the whole sky as it dropped, clotting my heart. I couldn't name anything I felt anymore, although I knew it was a kind of boredom. I had been living the same life too long. I did jumping jacks and pushups and stood on my head in the little shack to break the tedium, but too much solitude rots the brain. I wondered how Gerry had stood it. Sometimes I grabbed drivers out of their trucks and talked loudly and quickly and inconsequentially as a madwoman. There were other times I couldn't talk at all because my tongue had rusted to the roof of my mouth.

Sometimes I daydreamed about Dot and Gerry. I had many choice daydreams, but theirs was my favorite. I pictured them in Dot's long tan trailer house, both hungry. Heads swaying, clasped hands swinging between them like hooked trunks, they moved through the kitchen feeding casually from boxes and bags on the counters, like ponderous animals alone in a forest. When they had fed, they moved on to the bedroom and settled themselves upon Dot's king-size and sateen-quilted spread. They rubbed together, locked and unlocked their parts. They set the trailer rocking on its cement-block-and-plywood foundation and the tremors spread, causing cups to fall, plates to shatter in the china hutches of their more established neighbors.

But what of the child there, suspended between them. Did it know how to weather such tropical storms? It was a week past the week it was due, and I expected the good news to come any moment. I was anxious to hear the outcome, but still, I was surprised when Gerry rumbled to the weigh-shack door on a huge and ancient, rust-pocked, untrustworthy-looking machine that was like no motorcycle I'd ever seen before.

"She asst for you," he hissed. "Quick, get on!"

I hoisted myself up behind him, although there wasn't room on the seat. I clawed his smooth back for a handhold and finally perched, or so it seemed, on the rim of his heavy belt. Flylike, glued to him by suction, we rode as one person, whipping a great wind around us. Cars scattered, the lights blinked and flickered on the main street. Pedestrians swiveled to catch a glimpse of us—a mountain tearing by balanced on a toy, and clinging to the sheer northwest face, a scrawny half-breed howling something that Dopplered across the bridge and faded out, finally, in the parking lot of Saint Adalbert's Hospital.

In the waiting room we settled on chairs molded of orange plastic. The spike legs splayed beneath Gerry's mass but managed to support him the four hours we waited. Nurses passed, settling like field gulls among reports and prescriptions, eyeing us with reserved hostility. Gerry hardly spoke. He didn't have to. I watched his ribs and the small of his back darken with sweat. For that well-lighted tunnel, the waiting room, the tin rack of magazines, all were the props and inevitable features of institutions. From time to time Gerry paced in the time-honored manner of the prisoner or expectant father. He made lengthy trips to the bathroom. All the quickness and delicacy of his movements had disappeared, and he was only a poor tired fat man in those hours, a husband worried about his wife, menaced, tired of getting caught.

At last the gulls emerged and drew Gerry in among them. He visited Dot for perhaps half an hour, and then came out of her room. Again he settled, the plastic chair twitched beneath him. He looked bewildered and silly and a little addled with what he had seen. The shaded lenses of his glasses kept slipping down his nose. Beside him, I felt the aftermath of the shock wave traveling from the epicenter deep in his flesh outward from part of him that had shifted along a crevice. The tremors moved in widening rings. When they reached the very surface of him, and when he began trembling, Gerry stood suddenly. "I'm going after cigars," he said, and walked quickly away.

His steps quickened to a near run as he moved down the corridor. Waiting for the elevator, he flexed his nimble fingers. Dot told me she had once sent him to the store for a roll of toilet paper. It was eight months before she saw him again, for he'd met the local constabulary on the way. So I knew, when he flexed his fingers, that he was thinking of pulling the biker's gloves over his knuckles, of running. It was perhaps the very first time in his life he had something to run for.

It seemed to me, at that moment, that I should at least let Gerry know it was all right for him to leave, to run as far and fast as he had to now. Although I felt heavy—my body had gone slack, and my lungs ached with smoke—I jumped up. I signaled him from the end of the corridor. Gerry turned, unwillingly turned. He looked my way just as two of our local police—Officers Lovchik and Harriss—pushed open the fire door that sealed off the staircase behind me. I didn't see them and was shocked at first that my wave caused such an extreme reaction in Gerry.

His hair stiffened. His body lifted like a hot-air balloon filling suddenly. Behind him there was a wide, tall window. Gerry opened it and sent the screen into thin air with an elegant chorus-girl kick. Then he followed the screen, squeezing himself unbelievably through the frame like a fat rabbit disappearing down a hole. It was three stories down to the cement and asphalt parking lot.

Officers Lovchik and Harriss gained the window. The nurses followed. I slipped through the fire exit and took the back stairs down into the parking lot, believing I would find him stunned and broken there.

But Gerry had chosen his window with exceptional luck, for the officers had parked their car directly underneath. Gerry landed just over the driver's seat, caving the roof into the steering wheel. He bounced off the hood of the car and then, limping, a bit dazed perhaps, straddled his bike. Out of duty, Lovchik released several rounds into the still trees below him. The reports were still echoing when I reached the front of the building.

I was just in time to see Gerry Nanapush, emboldened by his godlike leap and recovery, pop a wheelie and disappear between the neat shrubs that marked the entrance to the hospital.

Two weeks later Dot and her girl, who was finally named Shawn, like most girls born that year, came back to work at the scales. Things went on as they had before, except that Shawn kept us occupied during the long hours. She was large, of course, and had a sturdy pair of lungs she used often. When she cried, she screwed her face into fierce baby wrinkles and would not be placated with sugar tits or pacifiers. Dot unzipped her parka halfway, pulled her blouse up, and let her nurse for what seemed like hours. We could scarcely believe her appetite. Dot was a diligent producer of milk, however. Her breasts, like overfilled inner tubes, strained at her nylon blouses. Sometimes when she thought no one was looking, Dot rose and carried them in the crooks of her arms, for her shoulders were growing bowed beneath their weight.

The trucks came in on the hour, or half hour. I heard the rush of air brakes, gears grinding only inches from my head. It occurred to me that although I measured many tons every day, I would never know how heavy a ton was unless it fell on me. I wasn't lonely now that Dot had returned. The season would end soon, and we wondered what had happened to Gerry.

There were only a few weeks left of work when we heard that Gerry was caught again. He'd picked the wrong reservation to hide on—Pine Ridge. As always, it was overrun with federal agents and armored vehicles. Weapons were stashed everywhere and easy to acquire. Gerry got himself a weapon. Two men tried to arrest him. Gerry would not go along, and when he started to run and the shooting started, Gerry shot and killed a clean-shaven man with dark hair and light eyes, a state trooper, a man whose picture was printed in all the papers.

They sent Gerry to prison in Marion, Illinois. He was placed in the control unit. He receives visitors in a room where no touching is allowed, where the voice is carried by phone, glances meet through sheets of Plexiglas, and no children will ever be engendered.

Dot and I continued to work the last weeks together. Once we weighed baby Shawn. We unlatched her little knit suit, heavy as armor, and bundled her in a light, crocheted blanket. Dot went into the shack to adjust the weights. I stood there with Shawn. She was such a solid child, she seemed heavy as lead in my arms.

I placed her on the ramp between the wheel sights and held her steady for a moment, then took my hands slowly away. She stared calmly into the rough distant sky. She did not flinch when the wind came from every direction, wrapping us tight enough to squeeze the very breath from a stone. She was so dense with life, such a powerful distillation of Dot and Gerry, it seemed she might weigh about as much as any load. But that was only a thought, of course. For as it turned out, she was too light and did not register at all.

CROWN OF THORNS

(1981)

A month after June died Gordie took the first drink, and then the need was on him like a hook in his jaw, tipping his wrist, sending him out with needles piercing his hairline, his aching hands. From the beginning it was his hands that made him drink. They remembered things his mind could not—curve of hip and taut breast. They remembered farther back, to the times he spent with June when the two were young. They had always been together, like brother and sister, stealing duck eggs, blowing crabgrass between their thumbs, chasing cows. They got in trouble together. They fought but always made up easy and quick, until they were married.

His hands remembered things he forced his mind away from—how they flew out from his sides in rage so sudden that he could not control the force and the speed of their striking. He'd been a boxer in the Golden Gloves. But what his hands remembered now were the times they struck June.

They remembered this while they curled around the gold-colored can of beer he had begged down the road at Eli's.

"You gone too far now," Eli said. Gordie knew he was sitting at his Uncle Eli's table again because the orange spots in the oil-cloth were there beneath his eyes. Eli's voice came from the soft pure blackness that stretched out in all directions from the lighted area around the beer can. Gordie's hands felt unclean. The can felt cold and pure. It was as though his hands were soiling something never touched before. The way the light fell it was as though the can were lit on a special altar.

"I'm contaminated," Gordie said.

"You sure are." Eli spoke somewhere beyond sight. "You're going to land up in the hospital."

That wasn't what he'd meant, Gordie struggled to say, but he was distracted suddenly by the size of his hands. So big. Strong.

"Look at that," said Gordie wonderingly, opening and closing his fist. "If only they'd let me fight the big one, huh? If only they'd gave me a chance."

"You did fight the big one," said Eli. "You got beat."

"That's right," said Gordie. "It wasn't even no contest. I wasn't even any good."

"You forget those things," said Eli. He was moving back and forth behind the chair.

"Eat this egg. I fixed it over easy."

"I couldn't," said Gordie, "or this bun either. I'm too sick."

His hands would not stay still. He had noticed this. They managed to do an alarming variety of things while he was not looking. Now they had somehow crushed the beer can into a shape. He took his hands away and studied the can in its glowing spotlight. The can was bent at the waist and twisted at the hips like the torso of a woman. It rocked slightly side to side in the breeze from the window.

"She's empty!" he realized suddenly, repossessing the can. "I don't think it was full to begin with. I couldn't've."

"What?" asked Eli. Patiently, his face calm, he spooned the egg and fork-toasted bread into his mouth. His head was brown and showed through the thin gray stubble of his crew cut. A pale light lifted and fell in the room. It was six A.M.

"Want some?" Eli offered steaming coffee in a green plastic mug, warped and stained. It was the same color as his work clothes.

Gordie shook his head and turned away. Eli drank from the cup himself.

"You wouldn't have another someplace that you forgot?" said Gordie sadly.

"No," said Eli.

"I've got to make a raise then," said Gordie.

The two men sat quietly, then Gordie shook the can, put it down, and walked out of the door. Once outside, he was hit by such a burst of determination that he almost walked normally, balanced in one wheel rut, down Eli's little road. Some of his thick hair stuck straight up in a peak, and some was crushed flat. His face sagged. He'd hardly eaten that week, and his pants flapped beneath his jacket, cinched tight, the zipper shamefully unzipped.

Eli watched from his chair, sipping the coffee to warm his blood. He liked the window halfway open although the mornings were still cold. When June lived with him she'd slept on the cot beside the stove, a lump beneath the quilts and army blankets when he came in to get her up for the government school bus. Sometimes they'd sat together looking out the same window into cold blue dark. He'd hated to send her off at that lonely hour. Her coat was red. All her clothes were from the nuns. Once he'd bought June a plastic dish of bright bath-oil beads. Before he could stop her she had put one in her mouth, not understanding what it was. She'd swallowed it down, too. Then, when she'd started crying out of disappointment and shame, bubbles had popped from her lips and nose.

Eli laughed out loud, then stopped. He saw her face and the shocked look. He sat there thinking of her without smiling and watched Gordie disappear.

Two cars passed Gordie on the road but neither stopped. It was too early to get anything in town, but he would have appreciated a ride to his house. It was a mile to his turnoff, and his need grew worse with each step he took. He shook with the cold, with the lack. The world had narrowed to this strip of frozen mud. The trees were slung to either side in a dense mist, and the crackle his feet made breaking ice crystals was bad to hear. From time to time he stopped to let the crackle die down. He put his hands to his mouth to breathe on them. He touched his cold cheeks. The skin felt rubbery and dead. Finally the turnoff came and he went down to the lake where his house was. Somehow he gained the stairs and door then crawled across the carpet to the phone. He even looked the number up in the book.

"Royce there?" he asked the woman's voice. She put her husband on without a word.

"You still drinking?" said Royce.

"Could you bring me some quarts? Three, four, last me out. I'll pay you when I get my check."

"I don't make house calls or give no credit."

"Cousin . . . you know I work."

There was a pause.

"All right then. Credit's one dollar on the bottle, and house call's two."

Gordie babbled his thanks. The phone clicked. Knowing it would come, Gordie felt much stronger, clearer in the brain. He knew he would sleep once he got the wine. He noticed he'd landed underneath the table, that he'd brought the phone down. He lay back restfully. It was a good place to stay.

A lot of time went by, hours or days, and the quarts were gone. More wine appeared. One quart helped and the next didn't. Nothing happened. He'd gone too far. He found himself sitting at the kitchen table in a litter of dried bread, dishes he must have eaten something from, bottles and stubbed cigarettes. Either the sun was rising or the sun was going down, and although he did not feel that he could wait to find out which it was, he knew he had no choice. He was trapped there with himself. He didn't know how long since he had slept.

Gordie's house was simple and very small. It was a rectangle divided in half. The kitchen and the living room were in one half and the bedroom and the bathroom were in the other. A family of eight had lived here once, but that was long ago in the old days before government housing. Gordie bought the place after June left. He'd fixed it up with shag carpeting, linoleum tile, paint and Sheetrock and new combination windows looking out on the lake. He had always wanted to live by a lake, and now he did. All the time he had been living there he both missed June and was relieved to be without her. Now he couldn't believe that she would not return. He had been together with her all his life. There was nothing she did not know about him. When they ran away from everybody and got married across the border in South Dakota, it was just a formality for the records. They already knew each other better than most people who were married a lifetime. They knew the good things, but they knew how to hurt each other, too.

"I was a bastard, but so were you," he insisted to the room. "We were even."

The sun was setting, he decided. The air was darker. The waves rustled and the twigs scraped together outside.

"I love you, little cousin!" he said loudly. "June!" Her name burst from him. He wanted to take it back as soon as he said it. Never, never, ever call the dead by their names, Grandma said. They might answer. Gordie knew this. Now he felt very uneasy. Worse than before.

The sounds from the lake and trees bothered him, so he switched on the television. He turned the volume up as loud as possible. There was a program on with sirens and shooting. He kept that channel. Still he could not forget that he'd called June. He felt as though a bad thing was pushing against the walls from outside. The windows quivered. He stood in the middle of the room, unsteady, listening to everything too closely. He turned on the lights. He locked each window and door. Still he heard things. The waves rustled against each other like a woman's stockinged legs. Acorns dropping on the roof clicked like heels. There was a low murmur in the breeze.

An old vacuum cleaner was plugged in the corner. He switched that on and the vibrations scrambled the sounds in the air. That was better. Along with the television and the buzz of the lights, the vacuum cleaner was a definite help. He thought of other noises he might produce indoors. He remembered about the radio in the bedroom and lurched through the doorway to turn that on too. Full blast, a satisfying loud music poured from it, adding to the din. He went into the bathroom and turned on his electric shaver. There were no curtains in the bathroom, and something made him look at the window.

Her face. June's face was there. Wild and pale with a bloody mouth. She raised her hand, thin bones, and scratched sadly on the glass. When he ran from the bathroom she got angry and began to pound. The glass shattered. He heard it falling like music to the bathroom floor. Everything was on, even the oven. He stood in the humming light of the refrigerator, believing the cold radiance would protect him. Nothing could stop her though.

There was nothing he could do, and then he did the wrong thing. He plugged the toaster into the wall.

There was a loud crack. Darkness. A ball of red light fell in his hands. Everything went utterly silent, and she squeezed through the window in that instant.

Now she was in the bedroom pulling the sheets off the bed and arranging her perfume bottles. She was coming for him. He lurched for the door. His car key. Where was it? Pants pocket. He slipped through the door and fell down the stairs somehow pitching onto the hood of the Malibu parked below. He scrambled in, locked up tight, then roared the ignition. He switched the headlamps on and swung blindly from the yard, moving fast, hitting the potholes and bottoming out until he met the gravel road.

At first he was so relieved to escape that he forgot how sick he was. He drove competently for a while, and then the surge of fear that had gotten him from the house wore off and he slumped forward, half sightless, on the wheel. A car approached, white light that blinded. He pulled over to catch his senses. His mind lit in warped hope on another bottle. He'd get to town. Another bottle would straighten him out. The road was five miles of bending curves and the night was moonless, but he would make it. He dropped his head a few moments and slept to gain his strength.

He came to when the light roared by, dazzling him with noise and its closeness. He'd turned his own lights off, and the car had swerved to avoid him. Blackness closed over the other car's red taillights, and Gordie started driving. He drove with slowness and utter drunken care, craning close to the windshield, one eye shut so that the road would not branch into two before him. Gaining confidence, he rolled down his window and gathered speed. He knew the road to town by heart. The gravel clattered the wheel wells and the wind blew cold, sweet in his mouth, eager and watery. He felt better. So much better. The turn came so quickly he almost missed it. But he spun the wheel and swerved, catching himself halfway across the concrete road.

Just there, as he concentrated on controlling the speed of the turn, he hit the deer. It floated into the shadow of his headbeams. The lamps blazed stark upon it. A sudden ghost, it vanished. Gordie felt the jolt somewhat after he actually must have hit it, because, when he finally stopped the car, he had to walk back perhaps twenty yards before he found it sprawled oddly on its belly, legs splayed.

He stood over the carcass, nudged it here and there with his foot. Someone would trade it for a bottle, even if it was a tough old doe. It was surprising, Gordie thought, to find one like this, barren from the looks of her, unless her fawn was hidden in the ditch. He looked around, saw nothing, but then the brush was tall, the air black as ink.

Bending slowly, he gripped the delicate fetlocks and pulled her down the road.

When he reached the car, he dropped the deer and fumbled with his pocket. He found the only key he had was the square-headed one for the ignition. He tried to open the trunk, but the key did not fit. The trunk unlocked only with the rounded key he'd left at home.

"Damn their hides," he shouted. Everything worked against him. He could not remember when this had started to happen. Probably from the first, always and ever afterward, things had worked against him. He leaned over the slope of the trunk then turned onto his back. He was shaking hard all over, and his jaw had locked shut. The sky was an impenetrable liquid, starless and grim. He had never really understood before but now, because two keys were made to open his one car, he saw clearly that the setup of life was rigged and he was trapped.

He was shaking dead sick, locked out of his car trunk, with a doe bleeding slowly at his feet.

"I'll throw her in the back then," he said, before confusion smashed down. The seat was vinyl. It was important that he get a bottle, several bottles, to stop the rattling. Once the shaking got a good start on him nothing would help. It would whip him back and forth in its jaws like a dog breaks the spine of a gopher.

He opened the rear door and then, holding the deer under the front legs and cradled with its back against him, ducked into the backseat and pulled her through. She fit nicely, legs curled as if to run, still slightly warm. Gordie opened the opposite door and climbed out. Then he walked around the front and sat down in the driver's seat. He started the car and moved onto the highway. It was harder now to see the road. The night had grown darker or the shaking had obscured his vision. Or maybe the deer had knocked out a headlight. Clearly, he was sure of it, there was less light. He tried to accommodate the shaking. To keep it under control he took deep shuddering breaths that seemed to temporarily loosen its hold, but then it would be back, fiercely jolting him from side to side in his seat, so that the wheel twisted in his hands. He drove with impossible slowness now, hardly able to keep his course. A mile passed slowly. Perhaps another. Then he came to the big settlement of the Fortiers. Their yard blazed with light. He drove a few yards past their gate, and then something made him even more uncomfortable than the shaking. He sensed someone behind him and glanced in the rearview mirror.

What he saw made him stamp the brake in panic and shock. The deer was up. She'd only been stunned.

Ears pricked, gravely alert, she gazed into the rearview and met Gordie's eyes.

Her look was black and endless and melting pure. She looked through him. She saw into the troubled thrashing woods of him, a rattling thicket of bones. She saw how he'd woven his own crown of thorns. She saw how although he was not worthy he'd jammed this relief on his brow. Her eyes stared into some hidden place but blocked him out. Flat black. He did not understand what he was going to do. He bent, out of her gaze, and groped beneath the front seat for the tire iron, a flat-edged crowbar thick as a child's wrist.

Then he raised it. As he turned he brought it smashing down between her eyes. She sagged back into the seat again. Gordie began to drive.

This time, when the shaking started, there was no limit to the depth. It was in the bones, then the marrow of the bones. It ran all through him. His head snapped back. He stopped the car. The crowbar was in his lap in case she came to life again. He held it, fusing his hands to the iron to keep them still.

He sat there in the front seat, holding tight to the bar, shaking violently all around it. He heard loud voices. The windshield cracked into a spider's nest. The dash fell open and the radio shrieked. The crowbar fell, silencing that too.

The shaking stopped, a sudden lull that surprised him.

In that clear moment it came to his attention that he'd just killed June.

She was in the backseat, sprawled, her short skirt hiked up over her hips. The sheer white panties glowed. Her hair was tossed in a dead black swirl. What had he done this time? Had he used the bar? It was in his hands.

"Get rid of the evidence," he said, but his fingers locked shut around the iron, as if frozen to it. He would never be able to open his hands again. He was cracking, giving way. Control was caving like weathered ground. The blood roared in his ears. He could not see where he was falling, but he knew, at length, that he'd landed in an area of terrible vastness where nothing was familiar.

Sister Mary Martin de Porres played the clarinet and sometimes, when she was troubled or sleep was elusive, wrote her own music. Tonight she woke, staring, from an odd dream. For a long moment she vaguely believed she was at home in Lincoln. She had been drawing a cool bath for herself, filling the clawed tub, stirring the water with her hands. The water smelled sharp, of indestructible metals. The cicadas buzzed outside, and the pods were blackening on the catalpas. She thought that once she stripped herself and crawled into the tub, she would change, she would be able to breathe under water. But she woke first. She turned on her side, found she was in her room at Sacred Heart, and reached for her eyeglasses. Her clock said one. She watched the glowing minute hand glide forward and knew, without even attempting to close her eyes again, that it was another of "her nights," as the others put it on those days when she was unusually out of sorts. "Sister Mary Martin's had one of her nights again."

Her nights were enjoyable while she was having them, which was part of the problem. Once she woke in a certain mood and thought of the clarinet, sleep seemed dull, unnecessary even, although she knew for a fact that she was not a person who could go sleepless without becoming irritable. She rolled out of bed. She was a short, limber, hardworking woman, who looked much younger than she was, that is, she looked thirtyish instead of forty-two. Most of the others, people noticed, looked younger than their true ages, also.

"It's no darn use anyway," she mumbled, slipping on her old green robe. Already she felt excited about rising alone, seeing no one. Her own youthfulness surprised her on nights like this. Her legs felt springy and lean, her body taut like a girl's. She raised her arms over her head, stretched hard, and brought them down. Then she eased through her door. It was the one at the end of the halls, the quietest room of all. She walked soundlessly along the tiles, down the stairs, through another corridor, and back around the chapel into a small sitting room impossibly cluttered with afghans and pillows.

She turned on the floor lamp and pulled her instrument case from beneath the sofa. Kneeling with it, she lifted the pieces from the crushed and molded velvet and fit them together. She took a small, lined music notebook from a shelf of books. A sharpened pencil was already attached to the spine with a string. Last of all, before she sat down, she draped an enormous bee-yellow afghan around her shoulders. Then she settled herself, hooked her cold feet in the bottom of the knit blanket, wet the reed, and began to play.

Sometimes it put her to sleep in half an hour. Other times she hit on a tune and scribbled, wherever it took her, until dawn. The sitting room was newly attached to the main convent and insulated heavily, so her music disturbed no one. On warm nights she even opened windows and let the noises drift in, clear in the dry air, from the town below. They were wild noises—hoarse wails, reeling fiddle music, rumble of unmufflered motors, and squeals of panicked acceleration. Then after three or four in the morning a kind of dazed blue silence fell, and there was nothing but her own music and the black crickets in the wall.

Tonight, perhaps because of her dream, which was both familiar and something she did not understand, the music was both faintly menacing and full of wonder. It took her in circles of memories. A shape rose in her mind, a tree that was fully branched like the main candelabrum on the altar of the Blessed Virgin. It had been her favorite tree to climb on as a child, but at night she had feared the rasp of its branches.

She stopped, particularly struck by a chance phrase, and played it over with slight variations until it seemed too lovely to discard. Then she wrote it down. She worked in silence for a while after, seeing something that might become a pattern, approaching and retreating from the strength of her own design.

An hour or perhaps two hours passed. The air was still. Sister Mary Martin heard nothing but the music, even when she stopped playing to write down the notes. A slim gravel path led around the back of the convent, but perhaps, she thought later, the man had walked through the wet grass, for she did not hear him approaching and only realized his presence at the window when the sill rattled. He'd tried to knock, but had fallen instead against the frame. Mary Martin froze in her chair and laid the clarinet across her lap.

"Who's there?" she said firmly. There was no answer. She was annoyed, first to have her night invaded and then with herself for not having drawn the blinds, because the sky was black and she could not see even the shadow of the prowler's shape while she herself was perfectly exposed, as on a stage.

"What do you want?" There was still no answer, and her heart sped, although the windows were screened and secure. She could always rouse the others if she had to. But she was consistently the one called upon to lift heavy boxes and jumpstart the community's car. Probably it would be up to her to scare off this intruder herself, even if the others came downstairs.

She reached up and switched the lamp off. The room went utterly dark. Now she heard his breath rasp, his shudder lightly ring the screen. Her eyes adjusted, and she saw the blunt outline of him, hang-dog, slumped hard against the window.

"What do you want?" she repeated, rising from the chair. She began to lower the clarinet to the carpet, then held it. If he came through the screen she could poke him with the playing end. She walked over to the dense shadow of the bookshelf, near the window and against the wall, where she thought it would be impossible for him to see her.

A breeze blew through the screen and she smelled the sour reek of him. Drunk. Probably half conscious.

But now he roused himself with a sudden jerk and spoke.

"I come to take confession. I need to confess it."

She stood against the wall, next to the window, arms folded against her chest.

"I'm not a priest."

"Bless me Father for I have sinned. . . ."

The voice was blurred, stupidly childish.

"I'll go get a priest for you," she said.

"It's been, shit, ten years since my last confession." He laughed, then he coughed.

The wind blew up, suddenly, a cold gust from the garden, and a different, specifically evil, smell came from his clothes, along with the smell of something undefinably worse.

"What do you want?" she said for the third time.

He banged the screen with his elbow. He turned, hugging himself, pounding his arms with his fists, and threw his forehead against the window frame. He was weeping, she recognized at last. This was the soundless violent way that this particular man wept.

"All right," she said, knowing and not wanting to know. It would be a very bad thing that he had to say. "Tell me."

And then he tried to tell her, stumbling and stuttering, about the car and the crowbar and how he'd killed June.

A low humming tension collected in the dark around Mary Martin as she sorted through his jumbled story. He could not stop talking. He went on and on. Finally it became real for her also. He had just now killed his wife. Her throat went dry. She held the clarinet across her chest with both hands, fingers pressed on the warm valves and ebony. She listened. Clarity. She could not think. The word fell into her mind, but her mind was not clear. The metal valve caps were silky smooth. She thought she smelled the blood on him. A knot of sickness formed in her stomach and uncurled, rising in her throat, burning. She wanted urgently to get away from him and sleep. She needed to lie down.

"*Stop,*" she begged. Her throat closed. He fell silent on her word. But it was too late. She saw the woman clubbed, distinctly heard the bar smash down, saw the vivid blood.

Her fists were tight knobs. Tears had filled the slight cup where her glasses frames touched her cheeks, and they leaked straight down from there along the corners of her mouth. The tears dropped on her hands. She had to say something.

"Are you sure that she's dead?"

His silence told her that he was. He seemed to have relaxed, breathing easier, as if telling her had removed some of the burden from him already. She heard him fumble through his clothes. A match snicked. There was a brief glare of light, and then tobacco curled faintly through the window and disappeared in the black room. Something lit furiously in Mary Martin when she heard him take the smoke in with a grateful sigh. Light pinwheeled behind her eyes, red and jagged, giving off a tide of heat that swept her to the window. For what she did not know.

Now she stood, trembling, inches from him and spoke into the shadow of his face.

"Where is she?"

"Outside in my car."

"Take me to see her then," said Mary Martin.

To get to the portico of the back entryway, she had to pass through the dark chapel. A candle burned, soft orange in its jar, before the small wooden sacristy where the host was kept. She walked by without genuflecting or making the sign of the cross, then made herself stop and go back. The calm of the orange glow reproached her. But after she had bent her knee and crossed herself she felt no different. She left her clarinet on one of the chairs and walked out to unlatch the back door. She stepped into the cool night air. He had gone before her and was already partway down the path walking bowlegged for balance. She stamped out the glowing cigarette stub he flipped in the grass. He stopped twice, giving in to a spasm of rolling shivers against a drainpipe then again where the gate opened out to the front yard. His car was parked in the lot, askew. She saw it right off—a long, low-slung green car directly lit by the yard light. He stopped at the edge of the gravel lot, swaying slightly, and put his hand to his mouth.

She had not seen his face yet, and now, as she stood beside him, forced herself to look, to find something, before she went to the car, that would make it impossible to hate him.

But his face was the puckered, dull mask of a drunk, and she turned quickly away. She walked over to the car, leaving him where he stood. The backseat was lit from one side, she saw, and so she walked up to it, taking deep breaths before she bent and gazed through the window.

Mary Martin had prepared herself so strictly for the sight of a woman's body that the animal jolted her perhaps more than if the woman had been there. At the first sight of it, so strange and awful, a loud cackle came from her mouth. Her legs sagged, suddenly old, and a fainting surge of weakness spread through her. She managed to open the door. There was no mistake—dun flanks, flag tail, curled legs, and lolling head. The yard light showed it clearly. But she had to believe. She bent into the car, put her hands straight out, and lowered them carefully onto the deer. The flesh was stiff, but the short hair seemed warm and alive. The smell hit her—the same frightening smell that had been on the man—some death musk that deer give off, acrid and burning and final. Suddenly and without warning, like her chest were cracking, the weeping broke her. It came out of her with hard violence, loud in her ears, a wild burst of sounds that emptied her.

When it was over, she found herself in the backseat wedged against the animal's body.

Night was lifting. The sky was blue gray. She thought she could smell the dew in the dust and silence. Then, almost dreamily, she shook her head toward the light, blank for a moment as a waking child. She heard the wailing voice, an echo of hers, and remembered the man at the edge of the gravel lot.

She crawled from the car, shook the cramps from her legs, and started toward him. Her hands made gestures in the air, but no sound came from her mouth. When he saw that she was coming at him he stopped in the middle of a bawl. He stiffened, windmilled his arms, and stumbled backward in a cardboard fright. Lights were on behind him in the convent. Mary Martin began to run. He whirled to all sides, darting glances, then fled with incredible quickness back along the sides of the building to the long yard where there were orchards, planted pines, then the reservation grass and woods.

She followed him, calling now, into the apple trees but lost him there, and all that morning, while they waited for the orderlies and the tribal police to come with cuffs and litters and a court order, they heard him crying like a drowned person, howling in the open fields.

LOVE MEDICINE

(1982)

LIPSHA MORRISSEY

I never really done much with my life, I suppose. I never had a television. Grandma Kashpaw had one inside her apartment at the Senior Citizens, so I used to go there and watch my favorite shows. For a while she used to call me the biggest waste on the reservation and hark back to how she saved me from my own mother, who wanted to tie me in a potato sack and throw me in a slough. Sure, I was grateful to Grandma Kashpaw for saving me like that, for raising me, but gratitude gets old. After a while, stale. I had to stop thanking her. One day I told her I had paid her back in full by staying at her beck and call. I'd do anything for Grandma. She knew that. Besides, I took care of Grandpa like nobody else could, on account of what a handful he'd gotten to be.

But that was nothing. I know the tricks of mind and body inside out without ever having trained for it, because I got the touch. It's a thing you got to be born with. I got secrets in my hands that nobody ever knew to ask. Take Grandma Kashpaw with her tired veins all knotted up in her legs like clumps of blue snails. I take my fingers and I snap them on the knots. The medicine flows out of me. The touch. I run my fingers up the maps of those rivers of veins or I knock very gentle above their hearts or I make a circling motion on their stomachs, and it helps them. They feel much better. Some women pay me five dollars.

I couldn't do the touch for Grandpa, though. He was a hard nut. You know, some people fall right through the hole in their lives. It's invisible, but they come to it after time, never knowing where. There is this woman here, Lulu Lamartine, who always had a thing for Grandpa. She loved him since she was a girl and always said he was a genius. Now she says that his mind got so full it exploded.

How can I doubt that? I know the feeling when your mental power builds up too far. I always used to say that's why the Indians got drunk. Even statistically we're the smartest people on the earth. Anyhow with Grandpa I couldn't hardly believe it, because all my youth he stood out as a hero to me. When he started getting toward second childhood he went through different moods. He would stand in the woods and cry at the top of his shirt. It scared me, scared everyone, Grandma worst of all.

Yet he was so smart—do you believe it?—that he *knew* he was getting foolish.

He said so. He told me that December I failed school and come back on the train to Hoopdance. I didn't have nowhere else to go. He picked me up there and he said it straight out: "I'm getting into my second childhood." And then he said something else I still remember: "I been chosen for it. I couldn't say no." So I figure that a man so smart all his life—tribal chairman and the star of movies and even pictured in the statehouse and on cans of snuff—would know what he's doing by saying yes. I think he was called to second childhood like anybody else gets a call for the priesthood or the army or whatever. So I really did not listen too hard when the doctor said this was some kind of disease old people got eating too much sugar. You just can't tell me that a man who went to Washington and gave them bureaucrats what for could lose his mind from eating too much Milky Way. No, he put second childhood on himself.

Behind those songs he sings out in the middle of Mass, and back of those stories that everybody knows by heart, Grandpa is thinking hard about life. I know the feeling. Sometimes I'll throw up a smokescreen to think behind. I'll hitch up to Winnipeg and play the Space Invaders for six hours, but all the time there and back I will be thinking some fairly deep thoughts that surprise even me, and I'm used to it. As for him, if it was just the thoughts there wouldn't be no problem. Smokescreen is what irritates the social structure, see, and Grandpa has done things that just distract people to the point they want to throw him in the cookie jar where they keep the mentally insane. He's far from that, I know for sure, but even Grandma had trouble keeping her patience once he started sneaking off to Lamartine's place. He's not supposed to have his candy, and Lulu feeds it to him. That's *one* of the reasons why he goes.

Grandma tried to get me to put the touch on Grandpa soon after he began stepping out. I didn't want to, but before Grandma started telling me again what a bad state my bare behind was in when she first took me home, I thought I should at least pretend.

I put my hands on either side of Grandpa's head. You wouldn't look at him and say he was crazy. He's a fine figure of a man, as Lamartine would say, with all his hair and half his teeth, a beak like a hawk, and cheeks like the blades of a hatchet. They put his picture on all the tourist guides to North Dakota and even copied his face for artistic paintings. I guess you could call him a monument all of himself. He started grinning when I put my hands on his templates, and I knew right then he knew how come I touched him. I knew the smokescreen was going to fall.

And I was right: just for a moment it fell.

"Let's pitch whoopee," he said across my shoulder to Grandma.

They don't use that expression much around here anymore, but for damn sure it must have meant something. It got her goat right quick.

She threw my hands off his head herself and stood in front of him, overmatching him pound for pound, and taller too, for she had a growth spurt in middle age while he had shrunk, so now the length and breadth of her surpassed him. She glared up and spoke her piece into his face about how he was off at all hours tomcatting and chasing Lamartine again and making a damn old fool of himself.

"And you got no more whoopee to pitch anymore anyhow!" she yelled at last, surprising me so my jaw just dropped, for us kids all had pretended for so long that those rustling sounds we heard from their side of the room at night never happened. She sure had pretended it, up till now, anyway. I saw that tears were in her eyes. And that's when I saw how much grief and love she felt for him. And it gave me a real shock to the system. You see I thought love got easier over the years so it didn't hurt so bad when it hurt, or feel so good when it felt good. I thought it smoothed out and old people hardly noticed it. I thought it curled up and died, I guess. Now I saw it rear up like a whip and lash.

She loved him. She was jealous. She mourned him like the dead.

And he just smiled into the air, trapped in the seams of his mind.

So I didn't know what to do. I was in a laundry then. They was like parents to me, the way they had took me home and reared me. I could see her point for wanting to get him back the way he was so at least she could argue with him, sleep with him, not be shamed out by Lamartine. She'd always love him. That hit me like a ton of bricks. For one whole day I felt this odd feeling that cramped my hands. When you have the touch, that's where longing gets you. I never loved like that. It made me feel all inspired to see them fight, and I wanted to go out and find a woman who I would love until one of us died or went crazy. But I'm not like that really. From time to time I heal a person all up good inside, however when it comes to the long shot I doubt that I got staying power.

And you need that, staying power, going out to love somebody. I knew this quality was not going to jump on me with no effort. So I turned my thoughts back to Grandma and Grandpa. I felt her side of it with my hands and my tangled guts, and I felt his side of it within the stretch of my mentality. He had gone out to lunch one day and never came back. He was fishing in the middle of Lake Turcot. And there was big thoughts on his line, and he kept throwing them back for even bigger ones that would explain to him, say, the meaning of how we got here and why we have to leave so soon. All in all, I could not see myself treating Grandpa with the touch, bringing him back, when the real part of him had chose to be off thinking somewhere. It was only the rest of him that stayed around causing trouble, after all, and we could handle most of it without any problem.

Besides, it was hard to argue with his reasons for doing some things. Take Holy Mass. I used to go there just every so often, when I got frustrated mostly, because even though I know the Higher Power dwells everyplace, there's something very calming about the cool greenish inside of our mission. Or so I thought, anyway. Grandpa was the one who stripped off my delusions in this matter, for it was he who busted right through what Father Upsala calls the sacred serenity of the place.

We filed in that time. Me and Grandpa. We sat down in our

pews. Then the rosary got started up pre-Mass and that's when Grandpa filled up his chest and opened his mouth and belted out them words.

HAIL MARIE FULL OF GRACE.

He had a powerful set of lungs.

And he kept on like that. He did not let up. He hollered and he yelled them prayers, and I guess people was used to him by now, because they only muttered theirs and did not quit and gawk like I did. I was getting red-faced, I admit. I give him the elbow once or twice, but that wasn't nothing to him. He kept on. He shrieked to heaven and he pleaded like a movie actor and he pounded his chest like Tarzan in the Lord I Am Not Worthies. I thought he might hurt himself. Then after a while I guess I got used to it, and that's when I wondered: how come?

So afterwards I out and asked him. "How come? How come you yelled?"

"God don't hear me otherwise," said Grandpa Kashpaw.

I sweat. I broke right into a little cold sweat at my hairline because I knew this was perfectly right and for years not one damn other person had noticed it. God's been going deaf. Since the Old Testament, God's been deafening up on us. I read, see. Besides the dictionary, which I'm constantly in use of, I had this Bible once. I read it. I found there was discrepancies between then and now. It struck me. Here God used to raineth bread from clouds, smite the Phillipines, sling fire down on red-light districts where people got stabbed. He even appeared in person every once in a while. God used to pay attention, is what I'm saying.

Now there's your God in the Old Testament and there is Chippewa Gods as well. Indian Gods, good and bad, like tricky Nanabozho or the water monster, Missepeshu, who lives over in Lake Turcot. That water monster was the last God I ever heard to appear. It had a weakness for young girls and grabbed one of the Blues off her rowboat. She got to shore all right, but only after this monster had its way with her. She's an old lady now. Old Lady Blue. She still won't let her family fish that lake.

Our Gods aren't perfect, is what I'm saying, but at least they come around. They'll do a favor if you ask them right. You don't have to yell. But you do have to know, like I said, how to ask in the right way. That makes problems, because to ask proper was an art that was lost to the Chippewas once the Catholics gained ground. Even now, I have to wonder if Higher Power turned it back, if we got to yell, or if we just don't speak its language.

I looked around me. How else could I explain what all I had seen in my short life—King smashing his fist in things, Gordie drinking himself down to the Bismarck hospitals, or Aunt June left by a white man to wander off in the snow. How else to explain the times my touch don't work, and farther back, to the old-time Indians who was swept away in the outright germ warfare and dirty-dog killing of the whites. In those times, us Indians was so much kindlier than now.

We took them in.

Oh yes, I'm bitter as an old cutworm just thinking of how they done to us and doing still.

So Grandpa Kashpaw just opened my eyes a little there. Was there any sense relying on a God whose ears was stopped? Just like the government? I says then, right off, maybe we got nothing but ourselves. And that's not much, just personally speaking. I know I don't got the cold hard potatoes it takes to understand everything. Still, there's things I'd like to do. For instance, I'd like to help some people like my Grandpa and Grandma Kashpaw get back some happiness within the tail ends of their lives.

I told you once before I couldn't see my way clear to putting the direct touch on Grandpa's mind, and I kept my moral there, but something soon happened to make me think a little bit of mental adjustment wouldn't do him and the rest of us no harm.

It was after we saw him one afternoon in the sunshine courtyard of the Senior Citizens with Lulu Lamartine. Grandpa used to like to dig there. He had his little dandelion fork out, and he was prying up them dandelions right and left while Lamartine watched him.

"He's scratching up the dirt, all right," said Grandma, watching Lamartine watch Grandpa out the window.

Now Lamartine was about half the considerable size of Grandma, but you would never think of sizes anyway. They were different in an even more noticeable way. It was the difference between a house fixed up with paint and picky fence, and a house left to weather away into the soft earth, is what I'm saying. Lamartine was jacked up, latticed, shuttered, and vinyl sided, while Grandma sagged and bulged on her slipped foundations and let her hair go the silver gray of rain-dried lumber. Right now, she eyed the Lamartine's pert flowery dress with such a look it despaired me. I knew what this could lead to with Grandma. Alterating tongue storms and rock-hard silences was hard on a man, even one who didn't notice, like Grandpa. So I went fetching him.

But he was gone when I popped through the little screen door that led out on the courtyard. There was nobody out there either, to point which way they went. Just the dandelion fork quibbling upright in the ground. That gave me an idea. I snookered over to the Lamartine's door and I listened in first, then knocked. But nobody. So I went walking through the lounges and around the card tables. Still nobody. Finally it was my touch that led me to the laundry room. I cracked the door. I went in. There they were. And he was really loving her up good, boy, and she was going hell for leather. Sheets was flapping on the lines above, and washcloths, pillowcases, shirts was also flying through the air, for they was trying to clear out a place for themselves in a high-heaped but shallow laundry cart. The washers and the dryers was all on, chock full of quarters, shaking and moaning. I couldn't hear what Grandpa and the Lamartine was billing and cooing, and they couldn't hear me.

I didn't know what to do, so I went inside and shut the door.

The Lamartine wore a big curly light-brown wig. Looked like one of them squeaky little white-people dogs. Poodles they call them. Anyway, that wig is what saved us from the worse. For I could hardly shout and tell them I was in there, no more could I try and grab him. I was trapped where I was. There was nothing I could really do but hold the door shut. I was scared of somebody else upsetting in and really getting an eyeful. Turned out though, in the heat of the clinch, as I was trying to avert my eyes you see, the Lamartine's curly wig jumped off her head. And if you ever been in the midst of something and had a big change like that occur in the someone, you can't help know how it devastates your basic urges. Not only that, but her wig was almost with a life of its own. Grandpa's eyes were bugging at the change already, and swear to God if the thing didn't rear up and pop him in the face like it was going to start something. He scrambled up, Grandpa did, and the Lamartine jumped up after him all addled looking. They just stared at each other, huffing and puffing, with quizzical expression. The surprise seemed to drive all sense completely out of Grandpa's mind.

"The letter was what started the fire," he said. "I never would have done it."

"What letter?" said the Lamartine. She was stiff-necked now, and elegant, even bald, like some alien queen. I gave her back the wig. The Lamartine replaced it on her head, and whenever I saw her after that, I couldn't help thinking of her bald, with special powers, as if from another planet.

"That was a close call," I said to Grandpa after she had left.

But I think he had already forgot the incident. He just stood there all quiet and thoughtful. You really wouldn't think he was crazy. He looked like he was just about to say something important, explaining himself. He said something, all right, but it didn't have nothing to do with anything that made sense.

He wondered where the heck he put his dandelion fork. That's when I decided about the mental adjustment.

Now what was mostly our problem was not so much that he was not all there, but that what was there of him often hankered after Lamartine. If we could put a stop to that, I thought, we might be getting someplace. But here, see, my touch was of no use. For what could I snap my fingers at to make him faithful to Grandma? Like the quality of staying power, this faithfulness was invisible. I know it's something that you got to acquire, but I never known where from. Maybe there's no rhyme or reason to it, like my getting the touch, and then again maybe it's a kind of magic.

It was Grandma Kashpaw who thought of it in the end. She knows things. Although she will not admit she has a scrap of Indian blood in her, there's no doubt in my mind she's got some Chippewa. How else would you explain the way she'll be sitting there, in front of her TV story, rocking in her armchair and suddenly she turns on me, her brown eyes hard as lake-bed flint.

"Lipsha Morrissey," she'll say, "you went out last night and got drunk."

How did she know that? I'll hardly remember it myself. Then she'll say she just had a feeling or ache in the scar of her hand or a creak in her shoulder. She is constantly being told things by little aggravations in her joints or by her household appliances. One time she told Gordie never to ride with a crazy Lamartine boy. She had seen something in the polished-up tin of her bread toaster. So he didn't. Sure enough, the time came we heard how Lyman and Henry went out of control in their car, ending up in the river. Lyman swam to the top, but Henry never made it.

Thanks to Grandma's toaster, Gordie was probably spared.

Someplace in the blood Grandma Kashpaw knows things. She also remembers things, I found. She keeps things filed away. She's got a memory like them video games that don't forget your score. One reason she remembers so many details about the trouble I gave her in early life is so she can flash back her total when she needs to.

Like now. Take the love medicine. I don't know where she remembered that from. It came tumbling from her mind like an asteroid off the corner of the screen.

Of course she starts out by mentioning the time I had this accident in church and did she leave me there with wet overhalls? No she didn't. And ain't I glad? Yes I am. Now what you want now, Grandma?

But when she mentions them love medicines, I feel my back prickle at the danger. These love medicines is something of an old Chippewa specialty. No other tribe has got them down so well. But love medicines is not for the layman to handle. You don't just go out and get one without paying for it. Before you get one, even, you should go through one hell of a lot of mental condensation. You got to think it over. Choose the right one. You could really mess up your life grinding up the wrong little thing.

So anyhow, I said to Grandma I'd give this love medicine some thought. I knew the best thing was to go ask a specialist like Old Man Pillager, who lives up in a tangle of bush and never shows himself. But the truth is I was afraid of him, like everyone else. He was known for putting the twisted mouth on people, seizing up their hearts. Old Man Pillager was serious business, and I have always thought it best to steer clear of that whenever I could. That's why I took the powers in my own hands. That's why I did what I could.

I put my whole mentality to it, nothing held back. After a while I started to remember things I'd heard gossiped over.

I heard of this person once who carried a charm of seeds that looked like baby pearls. They was attracted to a metal knife, which made them powerful. But I didn't know where them seeds grew. Another love charm I heard about I couldn't go along with, because how was I suppose to catch frogs in the act, which it required. Them little creatures is slippery and fast. And then the powerfullest of all, the most extreme, involved nail clips and such. I wasn't anywhere near asking Grandma to provide me all the little body bits that this last love recipe called for. I went walking around for days just trying to think up something that would work.

Well I got it. If it hadn't been the early fall of the year, I never would have got it. But I was sitting underneath a tree one day down near the school just watching people's feet go by when something tells me, look up! Look up! So I look up, and I see two honkers, Canada geese, the kind with little masks on their faces, a bird what mates for life. I see them flying right over my head naturally preparing to land in some slough on the reservation, which they certainly won't get off of alive.

It hits me, anyway. Them geese, they mate for life. And I think to myself, just what if I went out and got a pair? And just what if I fed some part—say the goose heart—of the female to Grandma and Grandpa ate the other heart? Wouldn't that work? Maybe it's all invisible, and then maybe again it's magic. Love is a stony road. We know that for sure. If it's true that the higher feelings of devotion get lodged in the heart like people say, then we'd be home free. If not, eating goose heart couldn't harm nobody anyway. I thought it was worth my effort, and Grandma Kashpaw thought so, too. She had always known a good idea when she heard one. She borrowed me Grandpa's gun.

So I went out to this particular slough, maybe the exact same slough I never got thrown in by my mother, thanks to Grandma Kashpaw, and I hunched down in a good comfortable pile of rushes. I got my gun loaded up. I ate a few of these soft baloney sandwiches Grandma made me for lunch. And then I waited. The cattails blown back and forth above my head. Them stringy blue herons was spearing up their prey. The thing I know how to do best in this world, the thing I been training for all my life, is to wait. Sitting there and sitting there was no hardship on me. I got to thinking about some funny things that happened. There was this one time that Lulu Lamartine's little blue tweety bird, a paraclete, I guess you'd call it, flown up inside her dress and got lost within there. I recalled her running out into the hallway trying to yell something shaking. She was doing a right good jig there, cutting the rug for sure, and the thing is it *never* flown out. To this day people speculate where it went. They fear she might perhaps of crushed it in her corsets. It sure hasn't ever yet been seen alive. I thought of funny things for a while, but then I used them up, and strange things that happened started weaseling their way into my mind.

I got to thinking quite naturally of the Lamartine's cousin named Wristwatch. I never knew what his real name was. They called him Wristwatch because he got his father's broken wristwatch as a young boy when his father passed on. Never in his whole life did Wristwatch take his father's watch off. He didn't care if it worked, although after a while he got sensitive when people asked what time it was, teasing him. He often put it to his ear like he was listening to the tick. But it was broken for good and forever, people said so, at least that's what they thought.

Well I saw Wristwatch smoking in his pickup one afternoon and by nine that evening he was dead.

He died sitting at the Lamartine's table, too. As she told it, Wristwatch had just eaten himself a good-size dinner and she said would he take seconds on the hot dish when he fell over to the floor. They turnt him over. He was gone. But here's the strange thing: when the Senior Citizen's orderly took the pulse he noticed that the wristwatch Wristwatch wore was now working. The moment he died the wristwatch started keeping perfect time. They buried him with the watch still ticking on his arm.

I got to thinking. What if some gravediggers dug up Wristwatch's casket in two hundred years and that watch was still going? I thought what question they would ask and it was this: Whose hand wound it?

I started shaking like a piece of grass at just the thought.

Not to get off the subject or nothing. I was still hunkered in the slough. It was passing late into the afternoon and still no honkers had touched down. Now I don't need to tell you that the waiting did not get to me, it was the chill. The rushes was very soft, but damp. I was getting cold and debating to leave, when they landed. Two geese swimming here and there as big as life, looking deep into each other's little pinhole eyes. Just the ones I was looking for. So I lifted Grandpa's gun to my shoulder and I aimed perfectly, and *blam*! *Blam*! I delivered two accurate shots. But the thing is, them shots missed. I couldn't hardly believe it. Whether it was that the stock had warped or the barrel got bent someways, I don't quite know, but anyway them geese flown off into the dim sky, and Lipsha Morrissey was left there in the rushes with evening fallen and his two cold hands empty. He had before him just the prospect of another day of bone-cracking chill in them rushes, and the thought of it got him depressed.

Now it isn't my style, in no way, to get depressed.

So I said to myself, Lipsha Morrissey, you're a happy S.O.B. who could be covered up with weeds by now down at the bottom of this slough, but instead you're alive to tell the tale. You might have problems in life, but you still got the touch. You got the power, Lipsha Morrissey. Can't argue that. So put your mind to it and figure out how not to be depressed.

I took my advice. I put my mind to it. But I never saw at the time how my thoughts led me astray toward a tragic outcome none could have known. I ignored all the danger, all the limits, for I was tired of sitting in the slough and my feet were numb. My face was aching. I was chilled, so I played with fire. I told myself love medicine was simple. I told myself the old superstitions was just that—strange beliefs. I told myself to take the ten dollars Mary MacDonald had paid me for putting the touch on her arthritis joint, and the other five I hadn't spent yet from winning bingo last Thursday. I told myself to go down to the Red Owl store.

And here is what I did that made the medicine backfire. I took an evil shortcut. I looked at birds that was dead and froze.

All right. So now I guess you will say, "Slap a malpractice suit on Lipsha Morrissey."

I heard of those suits. I used to think it was a color clothing quack doctors had to wear so you could tell them from the good ones. Now I know better that it's law.

As I walked back from the Red Owl with the rock-hard, heavy turkeys, I argued to myself about malpractice. I thought of faith. I thought to myself that faith could be called belief against the odds and whether or not there's any proof. How does that sound? I thought how we might have to yell to be heard by Higher Power, but that's not saying it's not *there*. And that is faith for you. It's belief even when the goods don't deliver. Higher Power makes promises we all know they can't back up, but anybody ever go and slap an old malpractice suit on God? Or the U.S. government? No they don't. Faith might be stupid, but it gets us through. So what I'm heading at is this. I finally convinced myself that the real actual power to the love medicine was not the goose heart itself but the faith in the cure.

I didn't believe it, I knew it was wrong, but by then I had waded so far into my lie I was stuck there. And then I went one step further.

The next day, I cleaned the hearts away from the paper packages of gizzards inside the turkeys. Then I wrapped them hearts with a clean hankie and brung them both to get blessed up at the mission. I wanted to get official blessings from the priest, but when Father answered the door to the rectory, wiping his hands on a little towel, I could tell he was a busy man.

"Booshoo, Father," I said. "I got a slight request to make of you this afternoon."

"What is it?" he said.

"Would you bless this package?" I held out the hankie with the hearts tied inside it.

He looked at the package, questioning it.

"It's turkey hearts," I honestly had to reply.

A look of annoyance crossed his face.

"Why don't you bring this matter over to Sister Martin," he said. "I have duties."

And so, although the blessing wouldn't be as powerful, I went over to the Sisters with the package.

I rung the bell, and they brought Sister Martin to the door. I had her as a music teacher, but I was always so shy then. I never talked out loud. Now, I had grown taller than Sister Martin. Looking down, I saw that she was not feeling up to snuff. Brown circles hung under her eyes.

"What's the matter?" she said, not noticing who I was.

"Remember me, Sister?"

She squinted up at me.

"Oh yes," she said after a moment. "I'm sorry, you're the youngest of the Kashpaws. Gordie's brother."

Her face warmed up.

"Lipsha," I said, "that's my name."

"Well, Lipsha," she said, smiling broad at me now, "what can I do for you?"

They always said she was the kindest-hearted of the Sisters up the hill, and she was. She brought me back into their own kitchen and made me take a big yellow wedge of cake and a glass of milk.

"Now tell me," she said, nodding at my package. "What have you got wrapped up so carefully in those handkerchiefs?"

Like before, I answered honestly.

"Ah," said Sister Martin. "Turkey hearts." She waited.

"I hoped you could bless them."

She waited some more, smiling with her eyes. Kindhearted though she was, I began to sweat. A person could not pull the wool down over Sister Martin. I stumbled through my mind for an explanation, quick, that wouldn't scare her off.

"They're a present," I said, "for Saint Kateri's statue."

"She's not a saint yet."

"I know," I stuttered on, "in the hopes they will crown her."

"Lipsha," she said, "I never heard of such a thing."

So I told her. "Well the truth is," I said, "it's a kind of medicine."

"For what?"

"Love."

"Oh Lipsha," she said after a moment, "you don't need any medicine. I'm sure any girl would like you exactly the way you are."

I just sat there. I felt miserable, caught in my pack of lies.

"Tell you what," she said, seeing how bad I felt, "my blessing won't make any difference anyway. But there is something you can do."

I looked up at her, hopeless.

"Just be yourself."

I looked down at my plate. I knew I wasn't much to brag about right then, and I shortly became even less. For as I walked out the door I stuck my fingers in the cup of holy water that was sacred from their touches. I put my fingers in and blessed the hearts, quick, with my own hand.

I went back to Grandma and sat down in her little kitchen at the Senior Citizens. I unwrapped them hearts on the table, and her hard agate eyes went soft. She said she wasn't even going to cook those hearts up but eat them raw so their power would go down strong as possible.

I couldn't hardly watch when she munched hers. Now that's true love. I was worried about how she would get Grandpa to eat his, but she told me she'd think of something and don't worry. So I did not. I was supposed to hide off in her bedroom while she put dinner on a plate for Grandpa and fixed up the heart so he'd eat it. I caught a glint of the plate she was making for him. She put that heart smack on a piece of lettuce like in a restaurant and then attached to it a little heap of boiled peas.

He sat down. I was listening in the next room.

She said, "Why don't you have some mash potato?" So he had some mash potato. Then she gave him a little piece of boiled meat. He ate that. Then she said, "Why you didn't never touch your salad yet. See that heart? I'm feeding you it because the doctor said your blood needs building up."

I couldn't help it, at that point I peeked through a crack in the door.

I saw Grandpa picking at that heart on his plate with a certain look. He didn't look appetized at all, is what I'm saying. I doubted our plan was going to work. Grandma was getting worried, too. She told him one more time, loudly, that he had to eat that heart.

"Swallow it down," she said. "You'll hardly notice it."

He just looked at her straight on. The way he looked at her made me think I was going to see the smokescreen drop a second time, and sure enough it happened.

"What you want me to eat this for so bad?" he asked her uncannily.

Now Grandma knew the jig was up. She knew that he knew

she was working medicine. He put his fork down. He rolled the heart around his saucer plate.

"I don't want to eat this," he said to Grandma. "It don't look good."

"Why it's fresh grade-A," she told him. "One hundred percent."

He didn't ask percent what, but his eyes took on an even more warier look.

"Just go on and try it," she said, taking the salt shaker up in her hand. She was getting annoyed. "Not tasty enough? You want me to salt it for you?" She waved the shaker over his plate.

"All right, skinny white girl!" She had got Grandpa mad. Oopsy-daisy, he popped the heart into his mouth. I was about to yawn loudly and come out of the bedroom. I was about ready for this crash of wills to be over, when I saw he was still up to his old tricks. First he rolled it into one side of his cheek. "Mmmmm," he said. Then he rolled it into the other side of his cheek. "Mmmmmmm," again. Then he stuck his tongue out with the heart on it and put it back, and there was no time to react. He had pulled Grandma's leg once too far. Her goat was got. She was so mad she hopped up quick as a wink and slugged him between the shoulderblades to make him swallow.

Only thing is, he choked.

He choked real bad. A person can choke to death. You ever sit down at a restaurant table and up above you there is a list of instructions what to do if something slides down the wrong pipe? It sure makes you chew slow, that's for damn sure. When Grandpa fell off his chair better believe me that little graphic illustrated poster fled into my mind. I jumped out the bedroom. I done everything within my power that I could do to unlodge what was choking him. I squeezed underneath his ribcage. I socked him in the back. I was desperate. But here's the factor of decision: he wasn't choking on the heart alone. There was more to it than that. It was other things that choked him as well. It didn't seem like he wanted to struggle or fight. Death came and tapped his chest, so he went just like that. I'm sorry all through my body at what I done to him with that heart, and there's those who will say Lipsha Morrissey is just excusing himself off the hook by giving song and dance about how Grandpa gave up.

Maybe I can't admit what I did. My touch had gone worthless, that is true. But here is what I seen while he lay in my arms.

You hear a person's life will flash before their eyes when they're in danger. It was him in danger, not me, but it was *his* life come over me. I saw him dying, and it was like someone pulled the shade down in a room. His eyes clouded over and squeezed shut, but just before that I looked in. He was still fishing in the middle of Lake Turcot. Big thoughts was on his line and he had half a case of beer in the boat. He waved at me, grinned, and then the bobber went under.

Grandma had gone out of the room crying for help. I bunched my force up in my hands and I held him. I was so wound up I couldn't even breathe. All the moments he had spent with me, all the times he had hoisted me on his shoulders or pointed into the leaves was concentrated in that moment. Time was flashing back and forth like a pinball machine. Lights blinked and balls hopped and rubber bands chirped, until suddenly I realized the last ball had gone down the drain and there was nothing. I felt his force leaving him, flowing out of Grandpa never to return. I felt his mind weakening. The bobber going under in the lake. And I felt the touch retreat back into the darkness inside my body, from where it came.

One time, long ago, both of us were fishing together. We caught a big old snapper what started towing us around like it was a motor. "This here fishline is pretty damn good," Grandpa said. "Let's keep this turtle on and see where he takes us." So we rode along behind that turtle, watching as from time to time it surfaced. The thing was just about the size of a washtub. It took us all around the lake twice, and as it was traveling, Grandpa said something as a joke. "Lipsha," he said, "we are glad your mother didn't want you because we was always looking for a boy like you who would tow us around the lake."

"I ain't no snapper. Snappers is so stupid they stay alive when their head's chopped off," I said.

"That ain't stupidity," said Grandpa. "Their brain's just in their heart, like yours is."

When I looked up, I knew the fuse had blown between my heart and my mind and that a terrible understanding was to be given.

Grandma got back into the room and I saw her stumble. And then she went down too. It was like a house you can't hardly believe has stood so long, through years of record weather, suddenly goes down in the worst yet. It makes sense, is what I'm saying, but you still can't hardly believe it. You think a person you know has got through death and illness and being broke and living on commodity rice will get through anything. Then they fold and you see how fragile were the stones that underpinned them. You see how instantly the ground can shift you thought was solid. You see the stop signs and the yellow dividing markers of roads you traveled and all the instructions you had played according to vanish. You see how all the everyday things you counted on was just a dream you had been having by which you run your whole life. She had been over me, like a sheer overhang of rock dividing Lipsha Morrissey from outer space. And now she went underneath. It was as though the banks gave way on the shores of Lake Turcot, and where Grandpa's passing was just the bobber swallowed under by his biggest thought, her fall was the house and the rock under it sliding after, sending half the lake splashing up to the clouds.

Where there was nothing.

You play them games never knowing what you see. When I fell into the dream alongside of both of them I saw that the dominions I had defended myself from anciently was but delusions of the screen. Blips of light. And I was scot-free now, whistling through space.

I don't know how I come back. I don't know from where. They was slapping my face when I arrived back at Senior Citizens and they was oxygenating her. I saw her chest move, almost unwilling. She sighed the way she would when somebody bothered her in the middle of a row of beads she was counting. I think it irritated her to no end that they brought her back. I knew from the way she looked after they took the mask off, she was not going to forgive them disturbing her restful peace. Nor was she forgiving Lipsha Morrissey. She had been stepping out onto the road of death, she told the children later at the funeral. I asked was there any stop signs or dividing markers on that road, but she clamped her lips in a vise the way she always done when she was mad.

Which didn't bother me. I knew when things had cleared out she wouldn't have no choice. I was not going to speculate where the blame was put for Grandpa's death. We was in it together. She had slugged him between the shoulders. My touch had failed him, never to return.

All the blood children and the took-ins, like me, came home from Minneapolis and Chicago, where they had relocated years ago. They stayed with friends on the reservation or with Aurelia or slept on Grandma's floor. They were struck down with grief and bereavement to be sure, every one of them. At the funeral I sat down in the back of the church with Albertine. She had gotten all skinny and ragged haired from cramming all her years of study into two or three. She had decided that to be a nurse was not enough for her so she was going to be a doctor. But the way she was straining her mind didn't look too hopeful. Her eyes were bloodshot from driving and crying. She took my hand. From the back we watched all the children and the mourners as they hunched over their prayers, their hands stuffed full of Kleenex. It was someplace in that long sad service that my vision shifted. I began to see things different, more clear. The family kneeling down turned to rocks in a field. It struck me how strong and reliable grief was, and death. Until the end of time, death would be our rock.

So I had perspective on it all, for death gives you that. All the Kashpaw children had done various things to me in their lives—shared their folks with me, loaned me cash, beat me up in secret—and I decided, because of death, then and there I'd call it quits. If I ever saw King again, I'd shake his hand. Forgiving somebody else made the whole thing easier to bear.

Everybody saw Grandpa off into the next world. And then the Kashpaws had to get back to their jobs, which was numerous and impressive. I had a few beers with them and I went back to Grandma, who had sort of got lost in the shuffle of everybody being sad about Grandpa and glad to see one another.

Zelda had sat beside her the whole time and was sitting with her now. I wanted to talk to Grandma, say how sorry I was, that it wasn't her fault, but only mine. I would have, but Zelda gave me one of her looks of strict warning as if to say, "I'll take care of Grandma. Don't horn in on the women."

If only Zelda knew, I thought, the sad realities would change her. But of course I couldn't tell the dark truth.

It was evening, late. Grandma's light was on underneath a crack in the door. About a week had passed since we buried Grandpa. I knocked first but there wasn't no answer, so I went right in. The door was unlocked. She was there but she didn't notice me at first. Her hands were tied up in her rosary, and her gaze was fully absorbed in the easy chair opposite her, the one that had always been Grandpa's favorite. I stood there, staring with her, at the little green nubs in the cloth and plastic armrest covers and the sad little hair-tonic stain he had made on the white doily where he laid his head. For the life of me I couldn't figure what she was staring at. Thin space. Then she turned.

"He ain't gone yet," she said.

Remember that chill I luckily didn't get from waiting in the slough? I got it now. I felt it start from the very center of me, where fear hides, waiting to attack. It spiraled outward so that in minutes my fingers and teeth were shaking and clattering. I knew she told the truth. She seen Grandpa. Whether or not he had been there is not the point. She had *seen* him, and that meant anybody else could see him, too. Not only that but, as is usually the case with these here ghosts, he had a certain uneasy reason to come back. And of course Grandma Kashpaw had scanned it out.

I sat down. We sat together on the couch watching his chair out of the corner of our eyes. She had found him sitting in his chair when she walked in the door.

"It's the love medicine, my Lipsha," she said. "It was stronger than we thought. He came back even after death to claim me to his side."

I was afraid. "We shouldn't have tampered with it," I said. She agreed. For a while we sat still. I don't know what she thought, but my head felt screwed on backward. I couldn't accurately consider the situation, so I told Grandma to go to bed. I would sleep on the couch keeping my eye on Grandpa's chair. Maybe he would come back and maybe he wouldn't. I guess I feared the one as much as the other, but I got to thinking, see, as I lay there in darkness, that perhaps even through my terrible mistakes some good might come. If Grandpa did come back, I thought he'd return in his right mind. I could talk with him. I could tell him it was all my fault for playing with power I did not understand.

Maybe he'd forgive me and rest in peace. I hoped this. I calmed myself and waited for him all night.

He fooled me though. He knew what I was waiting for, and it wasn't what he was looking to hear. Come dawn I heard a blood-splitting cry from the bedroom and I rushed in there. Grandma turnt the lights on. She was sitting on the edge of the bed and her face looked harsh, pinched-up, gray.

"He was here," she said. "He came and laid down next to me in bed. And he touched me."

Her heart broke down. She cried. His touch was so cold. She laid back in bed after a while, as it was morning, and I went to the couch. As I lay there, falling asleep, I suddenly felt Grandpa's presence and the barrier between us like a swollen river. I felt how I had wronged him. How awful was the place where I had sent him. Behind the wall of death, he'd watched the living eat and cry and get drunk. He was lonesome, but I understood he meant no harm.

"Go back," I said to the dark, afraid and yet full of pity. "You got to be with your own kind now," I said. I felt him retreating, like a sigh, growing less. I felt his spirit as it shrunk back through the walls, the blinds, the brick courtyard of Senior Citizens. "Look up Aunt June," I whispered as he left.

I slept late the next morning, a good hard sleep allowing the sun to rise and warm the earth. It was past noon when I awoke. There is nothing, to my mind, like a long sleep to make those hard decisions that you neglect under stress of wakefulness. Soon as I woke up that morning, I saw exactly what I'd say to Grandma. I had gotten humble in the past week, not just losing the touch but getting jolted into the understanding that would prey on me from here on out. Your life feels different on you, once you greet death and understand your heart's position. You wear your life like a garment from the mission bundle sale ever after—lightly because you realize you never paid nothing for it, cherishing because you know you won't ever come by such a bargain again. Also you have the feeling someone wore it before you and someone will after. I can't explain that, not yet, but I'm putting my mind to it.

"Grandma," I said, "I got to be honest about the love medicine."

She listened. I knew from then on she would be listening to me the way I had listened to her before. I told her about the turkey hearts and how I had them blessed. I told her what I used as love medicine was purely a fake, and then I said to her what my understanding brought me.

"Love medicine ain't what brings him back to you, Grandma. No, it's something else. He loved you over time and distance, but he went off so quick he never got the chance to tell you how he loves you, how he doesn't blame you, how he understands. It's true feeling, not no magic. No supermarket heart could have brung him back."

She looked at me. She was seeing the years and days I had no way of knowing, and she didn't believe me. I could tell this. Yet a look came on her face. It was like the look of mothers drinking sweetness from their children's eyes. It was tenderness.

"Lipsha," she said, "you was always my favorite."

She took the beads off the bedpost, where she kept them to say at night, and she told me to put out my hand. When I did this, she shut the beads inside of my fist and held them there a long minute, tight, so my hand hurt. I almost cried when she did this. I don't really know why. Tears shot up behind my eyelids, and yet it was nothing. I didn't understand, except her hand was so strong, squeezing mine.

The earth was full of life and there were dandelions growing out the window, thick as thieves, already seeded, fat as big yellow plungers. She let my hand go. I got up. "I'll go out and dig a few dandelions," I told her.

Outside, the sun was hot and heavy as a hand on my back. I felt it flow down my arms, out my fingers, arrowing through the ends of the fork into the earth. With every root I prized up there was return, as if I was kin to its secret lesson. The touch got stronger as I worked through the grassy afternoon. Uncurling from me like a seed out of the blackness where I was lost, the touch spread. The spiked leaves full of bitter mother's milk. A buried root. A nuisance people dig up and throw in the sun to wither. A globe of frail seeds that's indestructible.

THE GOOD TEARS

(1983)

LULU LAMARTINE

1.

No one ever understood my wild and secret ways. They used to say Lulu Lamartine was like a cat, loving no one, only purring to get what she wanted. But that's not true. I was in love with the whole world and all that lived in its rainy arms. Sometimes I'd look out on my yard and the green leaves would be glowing. I'd see the oil slick on the wing of a grackle. I'd hear the wind rushing, rolling, like the far-off sound of waterfalls. Then I'd open my mouth wide, my ears wide, my heart, and I'd let everything inside.

After some time I'd swing my door shut and walk back into the house with my eyes closed. I'd sit there like that in my house. I'd sit there with my eyes closed on beauty until it was time to make the pickle brine or smash the boiled berries or the boys came home. But for a while after letting the world in I would be full. I wouldn't want anything more but what I had.

And so when they tell you that I was heartless, a shameless man-chaser, don't ever forget this: I loved what I saw. And yes, it is true that I've done all the things they say. That's not what gets them. What aggravates them is I've never shed one solitary tear. I'm not sorry. That's unnatural. As we all know, a woman is supposed to cry.

There were times.

I'm going to tell you about the men. There were times I let them in just for being part of the world. I believe that angels in the body make us foreign to ourselves when touching. In this way I'd slip my body to earth, like a heavy sack, and for a few moments I would blend in with all that forced my heart. There was this one man I kept trying to forget. The handsome, distinguished man who burnt my house down. He did it after I got married the third and last time. The fire balded me completely. I doubt I'll ever marry again.

There's no time for it anyway. By getting married to Nector Kashpaw I could have perhaps forgot him, but he dawdled. This way, that. He was my first love. We were young. Some nights we'd talk behind the mission dance hall, and by midnight we'd have set the date. Then I wouldn't see him as the day grew closer. At length I knew he loved, or at least was taken up with, someone else.

After I had figured that out, I married a riffraff Morrissey for hurt and spite. Then I married again out of fondness. That made twice. All through this time I made a great pretense to ignore Nector Kashpaw.

"Hello." I'd see him in town. "How the world have you been?" And I'd have dreamed about sitting in his lap naked while the green dark rolled down. Or I'd have dreamed about his hands undoing everything.

The one I married for fondness, Henry, died one winter on a dangerous train crossing. I always knew they should have put some automatic bars up out there. He stalled in the middle of a soybean field, or maybe the train did not blow its warning whistle. There's really no way to ever tell. After the funeral, though, my secret wildness took me over.

The more I think about it, I just never got Nector where I wanted him. At my mercy, I suppose, so that I could have my will. That's how I got most of them, strange to say, for I was never any looker. It was just that I kept my youth. They couldn't take that away. Even bald and half blinded as I am at present, I have my youth and my pleasure. I still let in the beauty of the world.

It's a sad world, though, when you can't get love right even after trying it as many times as I have.

After Henry's funeral I came home and soaked in the pity of my eight sons, big boys, not a one of them the child of Henry in the factual sense. They were his spawn by force of habit, though. They kept me company through loneliness. And they would look aside and never notice what my wildness made me do.

It doesn't seem like twenty-six years ago, but indeed it was that long since I had my house on a beautiful hill that the tribe owned. Henry had raised it there. It was in that house, during the dead of night, that Kashpaw would visit me after Henry died. I kept a window open on the yard, and he always had himself a pocketful of meat scraps to feed our half-wild dogs. After he climbed in, when he touched me, I would smell that at first. A ripe animal-death smell. I kept a bowl of soap and water by the bed, for I was frightened to have that smell upon my body.

It brought such pictures to mind.

Nobody knows this. When I was seven I found the body of a dead man in the woods. I used to go out there and sweep my secret playhouse, clean my broken pots with leaves, tend to my garden of rocks and feathers. I would go out there and stay for hour upon hour. Nobody knew where to find me, or really looked very hard, anyway. They were used to my going off alone.

My square of swept dirt in the woods is where I found the man. He laid across my front door as though to guard it from strangers, like a dog. He was so relaxed on his back, hat tipped on his face, that at first I did not think he was dead. I hid in a Juneberry bush and waited for him to wake, to stretch, get up and leave. He was an old ragged bum, dark and lean. His clothes were earthen, a dim cloth of dirt and holes. When he did not move for a long time I stepped out. I was never a patient thing. Bold and nervous, I took his hat off his face to wake him up.

He had been staring into it. I mean the dark bowl of his little brown cap. And now he stared into an endless ceiling of sky and leaves. I knew how wrong it was. My body slacked before my mind made up the right words to describe him. Death was something I had never come upon until then, but let me tell you, I knew it when I saw it. Death was him. Staring into the ragged confinement of leaves. I put the cap back on his face. Then I left him, stepping over him. I went and sat in my playhouse to think.

I kept my eyes on him. After I put his cap back on his face he seemed asleep again. I sat there for a whole afternoon. He never moved. He never woke. He never seemed to know the passage of time. So after a while, I knew that he was mine.

I never told anybody else he was there. He was the best thing I'd ever discovered. I went back to visit him the next morning while the dew was still wet on his clothes. I took the cap off his face and I saw how his eyes had changed, clouded like marbles. I touched the middle of his eye with the tip of a blade of grass, and he never blinked. It still surprised me, but I was less and less afraid. It seemed to me that he had come to my secret place for some reason. As young girls are, I was no different. I was curious. Well maybe I was more curious than most.

He was so desperate poor that his clothing was nearly ripped off his body. The day went by. I cleaned up my house and then I cooked. Acorns, beetles, patty dirt. I made some kind of food that was even deader than him and put a spoonful between his lips. He had a strange jagged mouth. It was slightly open, as though it froze in the middle of an unspellable word.

It was just that time of summer before school starts, before the leaves turn yellow and fall off overnight, before I would have to get on the government bus and go off to boarding school. Some children never did come home, I'd heard. It was just that time of summer when your life smarts and itches. When even your clothing hurts.

That's why I did it. That's why I did the worst.

Holes, dirt, with nothing but an old red scarf for a pants belt. That was all he had on anyway. At first the cold hard stone of him surprised me. I only grazed him by accident. I did not really want to touch. I untied the knotted scarf, and his pants fell open from the waist. It was so easy I jumped backward. His pants were worn and rotted. I can't remember what I saw, or even how long I stayed. But soon after that the leaves came off the trees in yellow drifts, and every time I got close to my secret house a wall of smell rose up. I veered away. Then I went down to school on the government bus.

It was on that bus that Lulu Lamartine cried all the tears she would ever cry in her life. I don't know why, but after that they just dried up.

Everyone who knows me will say I am a happy person. I go through life like a breeze. I try to greet the world without a grudge. I can beat the devil himself at cards because I play for the sheer amusement. I never worry half as much as other people. Things pass by. I suppose that Kashpaw was the one exception in my life.

I clung to him like no other. I wanted to get the best of him.

And I did. But for a time it seemed he had me over the barrel of his love. He came sneaking in my house with bad smells on his hands, and I made him wash before he touched me. But when he smelled like my lilac bath soap it would be blackness, deep blackness, and feathered insects with ruby eyes that watched us calmly in the dark. Nobody else ever knew of us. Nobody, if they don't read this, ever will. We were that cautious. He had a wife who lost a boy and girl in fever, then took on too many children for anyone to count.

It went on for five years like that, until well after my youngest boy was born. Half Kashpaw. No wonder Lyman had money sense. Perhaps it would have gone like that for countless years more. I didn't want more than I could get, I was pretty well content. But then the politician showed his true stripe, a lily-white, and the love knot we had welded between us unbent.

All through my life I never did believe in human measurement. Numbers, time, inches, feet. All are just ploys for cutting nature down to size. I know the grand scheme of the world is beyond our brains to fathom, so I don't try, just let it in. I don't believe in numbering God's creatures. I never let the United States census in my door, even though they say it's good for Indians. Well, quote me. I say that every time they counted us they knew the precise number to get rid of.

I believed this way even before those yellow-bearded Chinooks in their tie boots came to measure the land around Henry's house. Henry Lamartine had never filed on or bought the land outright, but he lived there. He never took much stock in measurement, either. He knew like I did. If we're going to measure land, let's measure right. Every foot and inch you're standing on, even if it's on the top of the highest skyscraper, belongs to the Indians. That's the real truth of the matter.

Of course, since when were higher-ups interested in the truth?

One morning bright and early we got a regulation on our doorstep. It was signed with Kashpaw's hand as representing the tribal government. In turn, that was the red-apple court representing Uncle Sam.

Kashpaw knocked that night.

"Lulu," he said, "it don't mean nothing. Just let me in."

I stopped my ears and sicced the dogs on him. I was done with his lying hands.

I was the blood that pounded in his temples. I was the knock of his heart. I was the needle of desire. I worked my way through his body and sewed him up. Yet he was willing to turn me from my house.

Oh, they said they'd move it. Sure they did. How many times did we move? The Chippewas had started off way on the other side of the five great lakes. How we were shoved out on this lonesome knob of prairie my grandmother used to tell. It is too long a story to get into now. Let's just say that I refused to move one foot farther west. I was very much intent to stay where I was.

Around that time Henry's brother, Beverly, appeared out of nowhere. He wanted to get married. "I been waiting for you all these years," he said. I believed no such thing, but he seemed so lost and dazed it was as if he had been sleepwalking through his life up until the time he fell back into my arms. I had a fond spot in my heart for Beverly. He was a smooth, mild man, and I thought he wouldn't give me any trouble once I had him. I told Kashpaw about the marriage the next time I saw him in town, as though it were nothing to him.

"I'm tying the knot again. You know Bev Lamartine, from the Cities?"

Well Nector's long face went longer. His eyes went blacker. And what I saw in their hate pits made me cross my breast before I turned away. A love so strong brews the same strength of hate. "I'll kill him," the eyes said. "Or else I'll kill you."

I thought his passion would die down. We never do one-half the things we threaten. But that was my mistaken judgment, for I hadn't reckoned on the tribal mob.

Indian against Indian, that's how the government's money offer made us act. Here was the government Indians ordering their own people off the land of their forefathers to build a modern factory. To make it worse, it was a factory that made equipment of false value. Keepsake things like bangle beads and plastic war clubs. A load of foolishness, that was.

Dreamstuff. I used that word in the speech when I stood up to the tribal council. I came before them. Kashpaw recognized me. "Mrs. Lamartine has the floor," he said.

"She's had the floor and half the council on it," I heard a whispered voice say. But I paid no heed and kept my head up proud.

I spoke. I looked deep through Nector Kashpaw and let my voice rove through the postcard Indian handsomeness of his personal dreamstuff. Sweat had darkened patches on his workshirt beneath the arms. Perhaps he feared that I would tell how each night I made him wash his hands before he touched me, or what the insects saw us do with their blood-red eyes.

It was the stuff of dreams, I said. The cheap false longing that makes your money-grubbing tongues hang out. The United States government throws crumbs on the floor, and you go down so far to lick up those dollars that you turn your own people off the land. I got mad. "What's that but *merde?*" I yelled at them. "False value!" I said to them that this tomahawk factory mocked us all.

"She dyes her hair," I heard a voice behind me whisper. "Gray at the roots."

"The Lamartines lived all their life on that land," I said. "The Lamartine family deserves to stay."

A voice clapped itself over the mouth. But not before I heard it cry, "Bitch!" By then there were near a hundred people in the room. "All those Lamartine sons by different fathers." That voice was loud enough to be heard. And then it said: "Ain't the youngest Nector's?" So I had no choice in what I did. I turned around. I looked straight out at the people sitting in their unfolded chairs. There was many a man who found something to study on the floor.

"I'll name all of them," I offered in a very soft voice. "The fathers . . . I'll point them out for you right here."

There was silence, in which a motion was made from the floor. "Restitution for Lamartine," they said. "Monetary settlement."

Relief blew through the room, but I would have none of it.

"We don't want money," I said. "We're staying on our land."

Every one of them could see it in my face. They saw me clear. Before I'd move the Lamartine household I'd hit the tribe with a fistful of paternity suits that would make their heads spin. Some of them had forgotten until then that I'd even had their son. Still others must have wondered I could see the back neck hair on the wives all over that room prickle. So it was. Eventually the meeting broke up. But to where? For it was soon after that Henry's house burnt down.

I wish that Bev had gotten back from Minneapolis and stopped Kashpaw. Here was the strange thing. Bev and me were married by a judge in the presence of the boys. Then a week later he told me he already had a wife. I put my foot down, of course. I can be a hard woman when I'm pressed. I told him to go back there and get a divorce. I sent Gerry, my grown-up baby tough as nails, in the car with him to the Cities in order to make certain that he dumped her. Whoever she was, I needed Bev worse.

Neither Bev nor Gerry came back for a long time. Bev had liked the idea of Gerry going along with him, but got more than he bargained for. They threw my boy in detention, and to this day I think that Bev turned him in. I wasn't too worried over that, however, since no white man has made a jail that could hold the son of Old Man Pillager.

That's one father's name I gave away now, free. But of course Pillager was not sitting in the council room that night. And if he'd known about the fire, he would have scorched Kashpaw's hands with it.

How do I know? How can I say it was Kashpaw who lit my house?

I can say so because of what I saw in his eyes when I looked deeply through him, after I told him about my marriage on the street like he was just any passing acquaintance. My house was burning in his eyes, and I was trapped there, alone, on fire with my own fire. The red-eyed moths had come out of the trees where they hid themselves, looking exactly like dead leaves. Drawn by the bright flames, they'd come helplessly to burn.

That fated night the boys, all except for the youngest, Lyman, were off in town hanging at the outskirts of a large jackpot bingo. I left Lyman home just for a moment and went down across the road to Florentine's house to trade some commodity rice she had extra and would give me in exchange for cigarettes and powdered eggs. We had a cup of coffee while I was there. We talked of this and that. It was the chance they were watching my house to take. When she poured the second cup I saw the flames shooting out of the black liquid as it streamed from the pot. I got up and left without saying good-bye. To this day she tells how Lamartine saw her house was burning in the pour of her coffee.

She doesn't know I saw it first in Kashpaw's eyes.

She doesn't know what I saw when I got in eyeshot of my yard.

Smoke had unrolled from the windows and wrapped itself into a giant tube that fled straight toward heaven in that cloudless, windless dusk. I threw rice in the air like a hundred weddings and took to my heels. Already voices had stopped behind me, shouting on the road. I ran in a beeline wasting no breath, no time. I'd left Lyman sleeping in that house with the radio going in his ear. I ran straight in the door.

Of course I choked. I got down on my hands and knees, crawling like a toddler baby in and out the rooms under burdensome heat. Smoke. The roof was just about to cave and Lyman wasn't nowhere to be found. Yet a mother's heart was certain that her son was in the house. I stopped underneath my table to get my bearings, and then I knew. Sometimes he would go inside my private closet and lay against my clothes and shoes. He liked the dark of it, I guess. The woman smells of cloth and perfumes. Sometimes after I'd come home he would be sleeping on my closet floor.

I crawled in there. He was nuzzled in my nightgowns, overcome. I guess I heaved him out the bedroom window and fell after him into the hollyhocks. The tribal fire trucks were all broken down at the time. That was their plan.

And so, after all of us were safe, there was nothing to do but stand and watch it burn.

How come we've got these bodies? They are frail supports for what we feel. There are times I get so hemmed in by my arms and legs I look forward to getting past them. As though death will set me free like a traveling cloud. I'll get past the ragged leaves that dead bum of my youth looked into. I'll be out there as a piece of the endless body of the world feeling pleasures so much larger than skin and bones and blood.

After the house burnt to blackened sticks they came around. My people. "Lamartine," they said. "Poor Lulu. Come stay with us, will you?"

"No," I said. "I'm going to live right here."

And I did live on the very spot where the house had stood. For two months we camped there in a shack made out of bent sheets of tin siding, busted boards, burnt wood. We hauled water in cans. The summer was dry and hot. In the hulks of our busted-down cars my boys slept comfortably and well. People brought us food and beer. The Sisters gave us clothes. But we lived there like a pack of wild animals, and after a while it became a disgrace even to those who did not know the meaning of disgrace. The tribe finally built a crackerbox government house for us. They put it on a strip of land rightfully repurchased from a white farmer. That land was better than Henry's, even, with a view overlooking town. From there I could see everything. I accepted their restitution.

Time went fleetingly by until every one of my boys was a grown-up man. Some did me grief, though I was proud of them. Gerry was one. In and out of prison, yet inspiring the Indian people, that was his life. Like myself he could not hold his wildness in. The other one who went wild on me was unexpected. That was Henry Junior. All his life he did things right, and then the war showed him right was wrong. Something broke in him. His mind gave way. He was past all touch when he returned. I would catch his gaze sometimes and think I recognized it from somewhere. One day I knew. He had the same dead wide stare as the man in my playhouse. It did not surprise me so much, then, to hear the words on Lyman's mouth the day he hitchhiked from the river.

"It was an accident," Lyman said, coming in the door. He looked half gone himself. I threw an afghan on his shoulders.

"Don't say nothing." I led him over to a chair. He sat in shock.

"The car went in," he said. "Out of control." There was a false note in his voice, and I knew he had planned to say this. I also knew that no accident would have taken Henry Junior's life, not after he had the fortune to get through a war and a prison camp alive. But like the time they came to tell me the news of Henry Senior, I said nothing. I knew what people needed to believe.

For a while after Henry Junior died, Lyman was affected. He had always been carefree, a lover of nice things and ironed clothes like myself, with the golden touch for money from his father. He got morose. He could not snap out of it but slowly improved his outlook by working. He became a contractor, hired on his brothers, and in that way supported us all.

And so we stuck together on that strip of land that was once sun beat and bare of trees. Wives and children, in-laws, cousins, all collected there in trailers and more old car hulks. Box elder trees and oak scrub were planted and grew up. We even had a gooseberry patch. It became a regular nest of Lamartines. I'd had my first daughter, my last child, when I was almost fifty years old. Bonita's father was a Mexican who followed the sugar beet harvests. That's why her name was a little different. Our life went on. We saw the factory go up and then fall as it was meant to. Nobody cared whose land it stood on anymore. Even the biggest problems got long lost in time, careful time, that undid us all, like Kashpaw's hands with their flowered lies.

When I was over sixty-five and losing my sight, I had strings pulled to get a little two-room at the Senior Citizens. For years I'd just had the junk other people pawned off on me. Bouquets of plastic flowers that looked like they'd faded over graves, dishes of stained green plastic, clothes that went two for a quarter in the Bundles. I threw it all out and started over fresh. My apartment had painted block walls. I bought pictures of trees, dancers, wolves, and John Kennedy. I bought the classic called *Plunge of the Brave*, which everyone had whether they liked Kashpaw and wanted to venerate his youth, or did not like him and therefore made fun of his naked leap.

My boys went in together and bought me furniture. A matching set. And then, after my new plush rocker was set in the middle of the room, after they brought in my radio and straightened the place around, after my boys toasted me with beers and left for the Lamartine homesite once more, I sat there. I felt the liquid golden last days of my oats.

And that is where the second half of this story starts.

2.

I had nothing to do with the fact that Nector Kashpaw went foolish.

He had brains and heart to spare but never had to use them for himself. He never fought. So when his senses started slipping he just let them dribble out. At least that's the way I look at it, knowing him as I did.

I kept my grudge, although hard feelings were not as a rule my policy. But he'd done the worst that anyone had ever done to me. I could do without my hair, without my house. My pride was what he pricked. Perhaps my grudge against Nector reached the size it did because I never spread the bad feeling around. Nobody would have guessed.

I knew he was at the Senior Citizens, but I hadn't yet seen him or his wife, Marie, on the morning I went walking those halls. As it turned out I just about ran into him. My vision was so bad I only saw dim shapes or holes of space, and when I walked past the candy machine I thought that he was attached to it. But the less I saw the more I had developed my other senses, so I felt what I knew were a man's eyes upon me before I could tell where he was.

I turned toward the gaze and saw the shape I knew was Kashpaw, even though the outline of him was vague, cracked and shifting.

"Hello Nector," I said.

And now I heard his breath. He said no word.

"It's me. Lulu," I told him. "Have I changed so much?"

He repeated my name flatly as he would have said *doorknob*. Then he turned to the candy machine and gave it a hard shove. I heard the little paper packages in the slots whisk back and rustle. A strange complicated hesitation swept over me. Part of me wanted to walk away. People had told me that he was changed, but I guess I had not believed it. Now it was one way or the other. He was here. As much as I wanted to leave I also wanted to stay and put my arms around him, simply, in the broad daylight of our old age.

He shoved the tin box again then struck it with the flat of his hand. The way he gulped he could have been crying.

"Sometimes they just take your money," I said.

"Peanut butter cups." He turned from the machine's lit face. "I wanted a pack of them peanut butter cups," he said. And I realized that bit of candy was all he had in his mind. I was less than a chair or an old shoe to Nector.

Wasn't that just like him? People said Nector Kashpaw had changed, but the truth was he'd just become more like himself than ever. I left him mourning at the window of the glowing machine, staring at the array in a child's billow of frustration. It was too soon to tell what I felt for him. I suppose I felt sorry for what a greedy thing he'd been all along, and how it showed now. But I didn't go back and give him a quarter. I still cared enough about him not to do that.

Now as I said, his wife, Marie, also lived in the home. It might seem odd I never spoke of her yet, but really it's not. I never wanted to admit the existence of wives, you see, and they were just as anxious not to realize about Lulu Lamartine. If we could have snapped our fingers to get rid of each other we would have done that. But since we couldn't, we did the next best and ignored. That's not to say I didn't notice her. She was big and slightly hunched with bad legs. On hot days I guess it hurt her very much to move.

Marie was always good at taking care of things, and once she got to Senior Citizens she started right in with organizing pinochle nights. Sometimes I played cards with a magnifying glass and sometimes I just played by feel and what I could hear. My ears had seemed to grow like radar. That was how I heard my name come up in conversation under bids on the far side of the room.

"Standing by the candy machine with Lulu the other day . . ." I heard a voice tell another. Who? I had a feeling it was Marie. And sure enough I heard another voice I recognized as hers answer. "He's like a child now. He's just got to have his candy come what might."

I understood it was the nature of his disease Marie was talking about, and not the times Kashpaw came in my window. But it might as well have been that. The way it hit me she was correct. He always did have to have his candy come what might and whether Lulu or Marie was damaged by his taking it. All that mattered was his greed. And the odd thing was, I loved him for it. We were two of a kind. There is no getting around that. We took our pleasure without asking or thinking further than a touch. We were so deeply sunk in the land of our greed it took the court action of the tribe and a house on fire to pull us out.

Hearing her voice I tried imagining what Marie must have thought. He came each week in the middle of the night. She must have known he wasn't out taking walks to see the beauty of the dark heaven. I wondered. Of course, there was no way I could ask her. It was probably too late, after the fact and all, to get to know her. I thought of joining one of the entertainment or health committees she was on, but my nerve failed. And, besides, I was suffering worse from the eyesight every day, almost as if the longer I sat quiet in the Senior Citizens, reflecting on the human heart, the more inward turned my vision, until I was almost blind to the outside world.

Was it the blindness itself, so black it matched his lifelong greed? Was it the true remaining desire of my wants? Or was what happened just plain stupidity?

One day I was cutting back rhubarb in the courtyard when he came up behind me with a stick in his hand. I knew, as if by instinct, it was one of those dandelion diggers, forked like his tongue.

"Don't bother me," I said, walking back in the building. He followed. I had a load in the laundry room to check. He stepped into the room behind me, and then he shut the door. I turned to him, silent.

"Lulu, call the dogs off," he said.

After all the grudge, the pity, I could not help but take him in my arms. "Down boys," I whispered. "Leave Nector be."

He held me tightly, and we began to kiss. But things being what they were, what with him knocking off my wig and Lipsha Morrissey popping in unexpectedly to ask what was going on, nothing really went too far after that first surprising embrace. As soon as I got free I walked out of there leaving my laundry sitting in the tumblers. Dreamstuff. It was all I needed at this time. Once I gave the tribal council hell about their mortal illusions. And yet here I was making my one big mistake in life over again for the sake of illusion. What I felt for Nector was just elusive dreams but no less powerful for being false. He had no true memory or mind. I should have known that.

I was down in Grand Forks, surviving my operation, when Nector Kashpaw died. I saw no ghostly green light, heard no voice. Nothing unusual happened to inform me of his passing. Lyman told me about it the day after, when he came down to take me back to Senior Citizens. In a strange way I took the news calmly, but I was grateful the pads of cotton were taped over my eyes. I was glad not to show all I felt, and yet Lyman must have noticed something.

"He was your boyfriend once, wasn't he?" Lyman asked after my long silence. His voice was hesitating, almost sad. I pictured Lyman about ten years old. He was chubbier then and kept his dimes in an old Nesbits pop bottle.

"Where did you hear about me and Kashpaw?"

"Around."

"I was always a hot topic," I said.

I could feel that he didn't smile. He was never quite the same after Henry.

"You know what?" he sighed after a while. "I don't really want to know."

Of course, he did know that Kashpaw was his father. What he really meant was there was nothing to be done about it anymore. I felt the loss. I wanted to hold my son in my lap and let him cry. Even blind, a mother knows when her boy is holding in a painful silence. But we got packed and never said another word all the way home. The new expensive car, the first one he'd bought since the convertible, was cool and tight inside as a cave. It hadn't struck me, going down to the hospital, but on the way back I was sad at the thought that we would soon arrive at a place, break our silence, and leave the soft deep bucket seats.

"Let's go driving around someday," I said when he let me into my apartment.

But he didn't answer. He just said he had to go.

Nothing ever hurt me like the day Lyman walked into my trailer with mud in his hair. The worst thing was, every time I think back, that Henry Junior died by drowning. I could not get it from my head. Old Man Pillager told me, when we were on the closest terms, how drowning was the worst death for a Chippewa to experience. By all accounts, the drowned weren't allowed into the next life but forced to wander forever, broken shoed, cold, sore, and ragged. There was no place for the drowned in heaven or anywhere on earth. That is what I never found it easy to forget, and that is also the reason I broke custom very often and spoke Henry Junior's name, out loud, on my tongue.

I wanted him to know, if he heard, that he still had a home.

Nector Kashpaw did not die by drowning, but he wandered for a while.

Blind in my room I mourned Nector, although I knew we had really parted long ago, on the night my dogs tore the meat scraps out of his hands and then started in on him. I heard their brute cries following him over the next hill, out of my life. I screamed so hard inside, laughing at the cartoon picture of him running, that I had to stuff the corner of the pillow between my teeth. But after that night I thought he couldn't truly hurt me, even with his death.

It surprised me, after all, how much I felt.

There were so many things I never cried for. I knew if I started now I would have to waste all the rest of my last years. Besides that there weren't tears in me. I was incapable. The operation had my eyes so dried out. I was going to get someone to put the drops in, for Lyman said he couldn't. I wasn't ever supposed to stoop down, scream, or jig again because the stitching in my eye might slip.

That is why, after the funeral, when Nector came back from the other side to visit me, I kept still.

It was an odd time to remember doctor's orders, but I'd never been in quite the situation. Naturally I couldn't see him, but I woke up the minute he whispered my name. It was how he'd sometimes come to me in the old days, making his way through the window so soundlessly he'd be underneath my covers just as I woke up, and then I'd turn . . .

And he was there like so long ago. I remembered the doctor's advice to keep still. I felt the long weight of Nector, cold with the chill of early morning, and I smelled the lilac bath soap on his hands. All through my room the moths had lit their eyes. I felt their soft presences and the breeze of their fanning wings, tufted feelers, and the night passed in his arms, and the darkness did not lift.

New worlds, I thought, beyond this. Things of which I'd never heard.

Yet, when morning had apparently come, life went on even more usual than usual. I had put in my request for an aide at the desk but they didn't have enough aides for all who needed them. That's why Marie volunteered to take care of me. She knocked that morning. I let her in.

Things are new even at the age when we are supposed to have seen everything. We sat down for coffee and listened to the early-morning music hour on the radio. I thought her voice was like music in itself, ripe and quiet. I had gotten so good at listening I appreciated just the sound of it. I gave her a pillow I'd made out of those foam rubber petals they sell in kits.

"This is real nice," she said. "I never learned how to do this kind of thing."

"You were always too busy taking children in," I told her.

Then there was something I had to get off my chest.

"I appreciate you coming here to help me get my vision," I said. "But the truth is I have no regrets."

"That's all right." She was almost impersonal in her kindness. Her voice had lightened. "There's a pattern of three lines in the wood."

I didn't understand, so she put it another way.

"Somebody had to put the tears into your eyes."

We fell to hearing the music again.

She did not mention Nector's funeral. We did not talk about Nector. He was already there. Too much might start the floodgates flowing and our moment would be lost. It was enough just to sit there without words. We mourned him the same way together. That was the point. It was enough. For the first time I saw exactly how another woman felt, and it gave me deep comfort, surprising. It gave me the knowledge that whatever had happened the night before, and in the past, would finally be over once my bandages came off.

She got my eyedrops from the table. I tipped my head back and felt her gently peel the tape from my cheeks. She wiped my eyes with a warm washcloth. I blinked. The light was cloudy but I could already see. She swayed down like a dim mountain, huge and blurred, the way a mother must look to her just born child.

CROSSING THE WATER

(1984)

1.
HOWARD KASHPAW

He watched the women in their blue nightgowns with the jars on their heads. They went around and around the bathroom in rows. Sometimes they disappeared behind the cabinets, the toilet tank, or tub, but always they came out in single file again. They never stumbled. They never had to steady their jars. Their calm tread calmed him. Below the cracked tiles they walked in seamless gowns.

Now and then, outside, his father kicked the table.

"He's busted out again. I'm sunk."

A note that sounded childish even to the child was in the voice. Spoons, bowls, ashtrays, and bottles clinked together. That was not so bad. The bad part was his big voice ripping out, then getting childish. His mother screamed.

"What about us? What about us?"

She said his father could only think about himself. She screamed until the women on the wall trembled. King Junior's nightmare was to see their jars crack or their arms fall off while she screamed. But this did not happen. The miracle was that they stayed put together, flowing forward, moving around him in a circle.

In school, they called him *Howard*. It happened like this:

The first grade teacher had said to his mother, "Your boy is very bright, Mrs. Kashpaw. Did you teach him how to read?"

"I don't know how he learned it," his mother had said. "Unless from that TV program."

King Junior watched everything, but Sesame Street was what taught him. He read the backs of cereal boxes, labels on cans, the titles in her love magazines. He was ahead of the other children in kindergarten, and so they put him in the first grade.

"King Howard Kashpaw, Junior," said his new teacher. "Which of those names would you like to be called?"

He had never thought about it.

"Howard," he was surprised to hear himself answer. It was that simple. After that he was Howard at school.

They were cutting out red paper hearts one afternoon. Hearts to tack up on the bulletin boards. The teacher had a black Magic Marker. One by one the children went up to his desk and used his Magic Marker to write their names in the center of their hearts. The sharp-smelling ink soaked into the paper. PERMANENT, it said on the marker's label. "That means forever," said the teacher when Howard asked. "It won't erase."

"Good," said Howard.

He sat down and watched the teacher tape his heart on the wall. The wall was green. Placed against the wall, oddly, the heart seemed to pulse. In and out. He stared at the heart with his name firmly inside of it, and suddenly something moved inside of him. He felt a jolt of strangeness. For a moment he was heavy, full of meaning. *Howard* was sitting there. *Howard* was both familiar and different. *Howard* was living in this body like a house. *Howard* Kashpaw.

At home, the blue women continued to circle. A neighbor had come by and hit the door with a broom handle. Their voices went down after that. "What should we do? What should we do?" they said. He thought the police might come to get his father again. It had happened once before in the middle of a normal day. They had come to the door and snapped the circles on big King's wrists. Now he heard his father and mother go into the next room, then they were quiet. He leaned back against the porcelain tank. He could sleep now; whatever she screamed about was over.

2.
LIPSHA MORRISSEY

King Kashpaw was advising me:

"There's no way you're gonna lose the M.P. Shit. Turn yourself in! I know them bastards don't let up on you, man. I was in the Marines."

"You been a lot of places," Lynette told her husband roughly. "Stillwater Pen?"

"Fuck that for now. I was in Nam."

"He never got off the West Coast." Lynette leaned back to me with a bleery confiding look. Not that she'd been drinking. She seemed punch-addled or half asleep. "We listen to him anyway," she winked. "How he does blab on."

King glared at the little green-and-yellow-checkered mat in the middle of the table, but he didn't take up the challenge. In the past couple of years his face had pouched up and swelled. He was a wreck of a good-time boy now, with a soft belly in his T-shirt and eyes usually squeezed shut against the harsh light.

"Them bastards just won't let up on you," he repeated.

He was drinking cans of 7-Up. There was about a case of empties scattered all around the apartment. I had never seen him drinking pop before.

"Go bite," Lynette told him. "I wouldn't let those M.P.s get ahold of me." She shook her head in my direction. She'd frizzed her hair out in a solid-red halo. "What made you sign with the dumb-shit army anyway?" she asked.

"I had a feeling my mother would have wanted me to," I said.

They got uncomfortable quiet and gave each other a quick glance. That's when I knew they both knew the secret of who my mother was. They had both known all along. There was too many who had known. Too many for me to hate them one by one. So I just smiled, although my stomach was a churning washer full of dimes.

I was King's half brother, see, a bastard son of June's.

The old lady who told me this fact was the one who put the spell on Grandpa Kashpaw in his youth. Some said she caused him, later, to lose his senses. It was Lulu Lamartine—the jabwa witch whose foundation garments was a nightmare cage for little birds. I'd had a low-down opinion of Lulu, like most, but I'll respect her from now on because her motives was correct in telling me. She made an effort. She told me about June in a simple way that let me know that grown-up business was meant.

After she told me I tried, I really did try, to take it all in my grain of thought. But here, as you'll see in the eventual telling, I met with a failure of the heart. In the end that was the overbearing reason I joined up.

So to go on with the story, I was walking in the hall of the

Senior Citizens one day when Lulu opened her door and leaned out beckoning. She had red lacquer on her hooks, bangle jewelry all up her arms, and her head was like a closet of crows. A raging wig.

"Come on in here," she said. "Young man we got something to talk about."

"I don't think so, Mrs. Lamartine."

I was quite careful. To tell the truth I was afraid of her. She scared people after the bandages came off her eyes, because she seemed to know everybody else's business. No one understood that like I did. For you see, having what they call the near-divine healing touch, I know that such things are purely possible. If she had some kind of power, I wasn't one to doubt.

That time the Defender girl was less than two months pregnant Lulu knew about it just from touching her hand.

When Old Man Bunachi got a mistaken thousand-dollar credit from the government in his social security check, she asked him for a tiding-over loan. He had been keeping it a secret.

What about Germaine? She told Germaine to quit hoarding commodity flour and give it away because there was worms in it. How do you figure?

Insight. It was as though Lulu knew by looking at you what was the true bare-bone elements of your life. It wasn't like that before she had the operation on her eyes, but once the bandages come off she saw. She saw too clear for comfort.

Only Grandma Kashpaw wasn't one trifle out of current at the insight Lulu showed. She and Lulu was thick as thieves now. That too was odd. If you'll just picture them together knowing everybody's life, as if they had hotlines to everybody's private thoughts, you'll know why people started rushing past their doors. They feared one of them would reach out, grab them into their room, and tell them all the secrets they tried to hide from themselves.

Which is of course just what happened to Lipsha Morrissey.

Lulu grabbed me.

She might be soft and sweet as marshmallows, but in her biceps there was tension steel. She had run her nails beneath my collar, and I was whisked in before I could draw breath to yell. Clapped right down in her plastic armchair and scared to move for starting a fateful apartment-wide avalanche of sharp-edged ashtrays and painted poodles, I breathed a sigh. Caught but good, I thought. I wasn't really scared so much as irritated to be treated so abrupt. I was sure I knew all my secrets, see, and hadn't anything to hide.

But I was wrong. As soon as she'd said, *"I talked this over with your mother long ago,"* I knew she was going to tell me something on which I'd shut the door.

And when she said, "Not your stepmother, not Marie, but your mother in the flesh . . ." my worst thought was confirmed.

"I don't want to hear," I told Lulu flat out. "My real mother's Grandma Kashpaw. That's how I consider her, and why not? Seeing as my blood mother wanted to tie a rock around my neck and throw me in the slough."

"That's what you always been told," said Lulu calmly.

"Been told?"

Sure enough, I was hooked then. I took her bait.

"What do you mean?"

So she up and spilled the beans.

"You're nineteen years old now? That makes it twenty years ago this happened. My son Gerry—you know him, in Illinois doing time now—was just out of high school. One day he came home and told he how he'd got his eye set on this beautiful woman. 'She's got a beautiful shape,' he said. 'She has class.' He didn't say that she was also very bold, or that she was already married, or even that she had a child. He didn't tell me those facts! He just said, 'Mom I think I'll marry her.' He presented me with it. The only drawback was she was what you'd call an older woman.

More experienced. But who cares past a certain point anyhows? People talked, but those two went together and fell in love. Well, the inevitable happened pretty soon. That pretty woman started wearing a big wide tent dress. My boy left. Then I don't know what happened between them, because, not long after, a little baby was placed in your Grandma Kashpaw's arms. The woman went back to her husband, Gordie Kashpaw. As you know, they did not live very happily ever after. Neither did my Gerry. In fact, it looks like you had the best life of them all."

I couldn't take it in.

"You went and made this up for laughs," I said. "I ain't June Kashpaw's son."

"Her father was a Morrissey," said Lulu, "figure that."

So I figured. My head felt put on strange. A buzzing sound was starting in the room.

I looked at her, and all of a sudden here was the next odd thing: I saw that Lulu Lamartine and Lipsha Morrissey had the same nose. Hers was little, semi–squashed in, straight and flat. Mine was a bigger, flatter version of hers down to the squashed-in tip. It was like seeing something in a mirror that's not your face.

"I'm scared to death of you," I said. "Old witch, you tell me lies!"

"You spoilt child," she said. "Who else would you want to hear it from? They all know. Grandma Kashpaw, she's afraid to tell you because she loves you like a son. It frightens her to think you might run off. June's dead. My son Gerry's in the clink. Gordie's drying out, but he wouldn't tell you anyhow. They all know it though, all of them Kashpaws. What the heck is it anyway? Do you like being the only one that's ignorant?"

"No," I said.

She softened. Her hard little black eyes toned down and misted. That black crow feather duster on her head seemed to fold its wings and settle.

"I got a letter," she said, then she smiled. "Your dad Gerry's been so good they're going to transfer him back to the state pen. There ain't a prison that can hold the son of Old Man Pillager, a Nanapush man. You should be proud that you're one.

"I'm the only one that had nothing to lose by telling you all this," she went on after a short pause. "It's simple. I either gain a grandson or lose a young man who didn't like me in the first place."

I sat there in total quiet. She had caught me but good.

"Well," she said after a while, "which is it?"

Consideration got me no place the next day and a half. I thought at first I would pretend like nothing happened, and just go about my business. But as I walked here and there on the reservation, swept the bingo hall, cleaned up pop-tops in the playground, I could not help but dwell on the subject of myself. Lipsha Morrissey, who'd learned so much in his short life. Who had lost and regained the touch. Lipsha Morrissey who was now on the verge of knowing who he was.

I was confused.

Had my mother tried to sling me in the marsh? I went back to Lulu and asked.

"No," she said. "June was just real upset about the whole thing. Your Grandma Kashpaw took you on because the truth is she had a fond spot for June, just like she's got one for you. Besides that, Gordie couldn't handle another man's son. They're all jealous of Gerry Nanapush on this reservation."

I was still confused.

Had June mentioned me at all in the time I was growing up?

"Yes," said Lulu. "She watched you from a distance, and hoped you would forgive her some day. She wondered why you turned out odd."

"I turned out odd?"

"Well *I* never thought you was odd," she said. "Just troubled.

You never knew who you were. That's one reason why I told you. I thought it was a knowledge that could make or break you."

Again I sat there in total silence.

"Well," she said, "make or break?"

I didn't know. I was still trying to compass it all out. It was the taxingest problem my brain had ever had to work with. I know that Grandma Kashpaw tried to give me help. She used up her cans of commodity beef to keep my strength up. She fought Old Lady Blue at the mission bundle sales to acquire a Stetson practically new except for a burnt hole through the crown. One night she said that she didn't trust the banks no more and showed me where she'd stuck her money. She had it all tied up in a little pink hankie and stuck amid her underskirts.

"I'm an old woman," she said. "What do I need with this?"

Maybe I was misconstructing, but the more I thought about the way she looked at me when she said that, the more I felt like Grandma was offering me something. Bus fare, maybe, the chance to get away from here in my confusion. Whatever it was she really meant, I finally did the wicked act you might have already been expecting.

I stole into Grandma Kashpaw's apartment and sneaked the hankie full of money from her drawer.

As my hand was feeling for that hankie, I heard her breathing in the dark bed, pretending to be asleep. I was doing what she was afraid of and running away. More than anything I wanted to say I'd get back as soon as I could, reassure her somehow, but I couldn't. My throat choked up.

What could a sneak thief have to say anyhow? I thought.

I was drove to this crime by mass confusion. My soul was going to get whaled on for sure, if it was not already damned. As I walked out of that room, I justified. I justified my criminal act by being so unhappy I could die of it. Confusion. It was a bleak sadness sweeping through my brain. Sirens blowing. Random anger, which had never been my style before.

More than anything, I resented how they all had known.

So that's all there was to it, pretty much. I rode the bus across the missile bases and the sunflower fields until I came to our most popular border town, and then shame hit but good. Shame rolled over me in waves and a tidal wash. I was buried in it like a sink-hold. I took a room in a hotel for old veterans and, like them, I spent my daylight sitting in the window drinking 3.2 beer and my nights in the lobby watching cop shows. Shame had me by the neck. But at last, when it had played out to squirts and dribbles, I was able to look around me. I was able to walk the streets like the younger derelicts.

I walked back and forth then, all day, only vaguely curious about what I would do next. As I walked, I kept returning to one particular window. In it was the pictures of some clean-cut boys with monkey wrenches standing among a bank of red flowers. There was a caption. It said:

JOIN TODAY'S ACTION ARMY

Eventually, I walked into the office behind those grinning boys. Two shakes later, before I had thought twice, I was signing my name on a wad of paper.

After I had signed up for my monkey wrench and red flower, I went back to the hotel and watched Efrem Zimbalist Junior persecute some drug addicts. I happened to take a close look around me at one point, and then I realized something. I realized that if I went in the army, and then if I got lucky enough to come out, I would be a veteran like these guys—gumming the stubble on their chins, dreaming of long-hocked medals, curling up around their secret war wounds to comfort a lonesome night. Not much in that, less than nothing. It gave me a sick chill to think of ending up here, like foam throwed off the waves of the lake, spin drift, all warped and cracked like junk and left to rot.

This here was *yesterday's* action army, I thought.

Fear clenched down. If I wanted to evade the consequences, I was going to have to hightail it and run.

But where to? That was my problem. I couldn't bear going back home to the rez, where every damn Kashpaw cousin knew the secret of my background all those years. I was too galled. And yet I really didn't have nowhere else. There was no clear direction to follow, nothing to send me anywhere, until, as in this sort of case, I decided to ask myself point-blank what exactly I wanted.

The answer came quick and surprising.

"I want to meet my dad," I said aloud.

An old Sioux vet who said he was at Iwo Jima with Ira Hayes passed me a bagged flask of whiskey underneath the sign PLEASE DON'T DRINK HERE. THIS IS YOUR LOBBY. I took a long pull, slugged it down. Then I started crying. That is, tears came out. I made no sound.

"It often has that effect on me too, boy," the old man said. "It cleans you out."

So I let the tears fall. my hands shredding the bag, until the face of Old Grand Dad was revealed and the clerk told us to take it outside. By then I was half smashed. Everything seemed to hang in a sharp-edged silence. It was there, before the peeled, kicked-up doorway of the Rudolph Hotel that I got the word on what I should do.

"Ira's favorite brand," said my friend, gazing tenderly at the empty bottle. "What the hell."

As he walked away he threw it over his shoulder, and it hit me smack between the eyes.

Now as you know, as I have told you, I am sometimes blessed

with the talent to touch the sick and heal their individual problems without even knowing what they are. I have some powers which, now that I think of it, was likely come down from Old Man Pillager. And then there is the newfound fact of insight I inherited from Lulu, as well as the familiar teachings of Grandma Kashpaw on visioning what comes to pass within a lump of tinfoil.

It was all these connecting threads of power, you see, that gave me the flash of vision when I was knocked in the skull by Ira's favorite brand.

No concrete shitbarn prison's built that can hold a Chippewa, I thought. And I realized instantly that was a direct, locally known quote of my father, Gerry Nanapush, famous politicking hero, dangerous armed criminal, judo expert, escape artist, charismatic member of the American Indian Movement, and smoker of many pipes of kinnikinnick in the most radical groups.

That was . . . Dad.

According to my vision, he would make a break for freedom soon.

So that is how I got to the Twin Cities. After I got off the Greyhound I just started following the Indians whenever I saw one, and eventually ended up where I belonged. Now I was sitting across from King.

Let's get one thing straight: I never had much use for King. He did me dirt. Yet we know there were reasons to visit him. For one thing, I just had to see him knowing what I knew. Maybe things would change now that we were formally brothers. The other thing was that King had done time with Gerry Nanapush. I didn't think King knew Gerry was my father, but I knew there was some connection, a strong connection, maybe strong enough to lead me onward in my quest. I had to get down to the bottom of my heritage.

King once threatened to slice me up with a bread knife. I didn't hold that against him, since it was done during one of his frequent leaves of sense, but what I did hold against him was the manner he always took toward me.

"You little orphant," he'd say when we were young. "Who said *you* get a pork chop for dinner? That's for the *real* children." Or he'd steal my chunk of Spam. It didn't matter what we were having, he'd steal mine for the sheer spite.

"I'll thank you, hand over your Koolaid too," he'd say. "Only the *real* children get that."

And so forth, on and on. He did his best to make me feel like a beggar at the table of life. I was supposed to eat the *real* children's crumbs. He lorded over me until I got about his size and really let fly once. I'm not a regular strong guy, but push me too far and I might just go haywire. Punching and rolling, biting and kicking, I tore into him. He still beat me that time, but at least King learned I was no fun to tangle with. I wonder now why I never made sense of what happened after that. June ran out of the house and broke us up. And then, even though I was the one on the bottom, she beat my britches with uncommon vigor. I hadn't done King lasting harm. But I guess I had done her some.

King must have been ten years old when I punched his face. Since that time we'd come on the verge of blows, but he never harassed me the way he used to do at the table, and I in turn stayed out of his path as much as possible.

Now you know, when it comes to life, I stayed innocent for many years. I stayed simple. But I could not afford to be this anymore. I was on the run. I looked over at him sitting across the table. He was still King who had hounded me with dim conceptions. But he had changed. His bones had sunk back in his flesh. The booze was telling on him. Wear and tear of being mean had worn his temper so it balanced on a sliver. His eyes had a strange mocking glint.

"Have some pop, Sad Sack," he said, shoving me a can. "Just kidding. Haw. Today I'm on the wagon, ain't that right?"

"I guess you better be," said Lynette. Her lip was puffed up. She had a surly look about her. Maybe they were fighting or maybe it was the deranging effects of this apartment. I had never seen a place remotely so depressing; even the inside of the Rudolph at least had windows. This place was like a long dark closet. The narrow rooms was laid in a row. The air was smoky and thick. The walls was a most disturbing shade of mustard green. One side you could hear people trampling up and down the hall, while the other led out into a dim-lighted area. This was not outdoors, but a well with spooky gray light from the dirty skylight on the roof. I should mention, however, there was a couple attempts at doing something to reclaim this twilight zone. A corn plant in a flour bucket sagged like a drunk propped up a wall. One chubby little cactus, a fist in a glass, threatened you to touch it. There was the skin of a real live alligator nailed on the closet door. In the next room, over the television set, they had one of them velvet rugs that depict bulldogs playing cards.

I had gone to check the next room out.

"This here's nice," I said to Little King. The boy was glaring at TV. He didn't so much as look at me.

"Little King," I said. "Hey there, it's me."

"He don't call himself Little King anymore," Lynette said from the kitchen. "He thinks his name's Howard."

"Howard?"

The boy looked at me and nodded.

"He won't claim his dad no more," said King, standing in the doorway. "He's too good."

Which was true enough. You could see how smart that Howard was. The boy's black eyes had fairly swallowed me up in their short glance. He was a skinny little kid, with peakish hair the light brown color that Lynette's was when it had been natural.

The contrast between his light coloring and those deep black eyes was what made him so startling to look at. He turned back to the set. His face lit up for a moment, captured in the drama of old cartoon Coyote getting blown to bits for the fifty-millionth time by the Road Runner.

"Man that was decent," he said in a false little squeaky voice.

They showed the coyote all blasted and frayed.

I always thought, personally, the coyote deserved to roast that chipper bird on a spit.

"I feel sorry for old Wiley Coyote," I said.

The kid looked at me like I was a sad case.

"That don't matter," he said. "They still blow him up."

Or run him over with garbage trucks. That's what they did next. When he was flat as a pancake someone rolled him in a tube and mailed him C.O.D. to Tijuana.

It was just early evening, a typical Sunday night for the King Kashpaw family. I decided to put them out for dinner at the very least. I'd get paid back for the pork chops and Koolaid King had screwed me out of as a child. I could see my presence was not exactly welcome to them, however. They seemed to have something weighty on their minds. They kept sighing and looking out their windows, which led down the air shaft. No one appreciated me asking Lynette whether I could help with dinner. She hadn't actually looked like she was going to fix any. She sat back at the kitchen table, flicked her little red lighter, and blasted a ball of smoke in the air.

"I'm on strike," she said. "Tonight I'm improving my mind."

Across the table, King closed his eyes and popped a 7-Up.

"She thinks that's funny," he said, "which it is."

She had a long blue sweater on and a blouse that looked as if it was ripped whole from a shower curtain. There were magazines behind her in a cardboard box. She grabbed up a fistful of pages and went in to sit by the television. Me and King tipped back the 7-Ups.

Pretty soon the boy came in and opened the refrigerator. He took out a carton of milk and put it on the cupboard. Then he got himself a bowl and spoon. He poured the bowl full of milk. Then he reached under the sink and took out a box of cereal.

"He does it all backwards," observed King. "First he should put the cereal in his bowl, then the milk."

Howard didn't say nothing. He carried the bowl and the box of cereal very carefully in to the television. It was like he was going to make a religious offering. He and his mother would be huddled to the box, sitting there like cold spooks. I almost laughed. I was so tired from the bus that my mind was running wild. I asked, "Do you ever think about that summer you came to stay with Grandma Kashpaw? When you were little?"

"Not too much."

I wondered what the hell he did think about. And then I thought there was no harm in asking.

"Well what do you think about?" I asked.

You could have knocked me over with a straw at the way he started to answer that question. It was a big fat surprise, I'll tell you, to know that King Kashpaw could do much more than growl, whine, throw his weight around. I guess being on the wagon brought him out or something.

"Minnows," he said. "It's like I'm always stuck with the goddamn minnows. Every time I work my way up—say I'm next in line for the promotion—they shaft me. It's always something they got against me. I move on. Entry level. Stuck down at the bottom with the minnows."

He grit his teeth, picked the warm can up in his hand, then crushed it softly so it gurgled.

"I'm gonna rise," he said. "One day I'm gonna rise. They can't keep down the Indians. Right on brother, huh?"

"Yeah," I said.

I couldn't help it; the laugh behind my face was like a sneeze. He'd called me brother.

"What's so funny?"

"Don't know."

"My God," he said. "You'd think the Indians that got *up* there would look out for their own! Once they start earning twenty-five, thirty grand they move off in a suburb and forget about their cousins. They look down on you. Hey. You ever heard of the food chain?"

"I'm hungry," I said.

"You been smoking dope? Dopehead. Listen. The big fish eats the little fish and the little fish eats the littler fish. The one with the biggest mouth eats any damn old fish he wants."

I got up. They had another box of cereal under the counter. Lucky Charms. I poured some milk in my bowl and then dumped the cereal in, like Howard.

"Yeah," said King, "go ahead and eat anything you want. Like I was telling you, I was in the Marines. You can't run from them bastards, man. They'll get you every time. I was in Nam."

That was a fat lie, but I sat there and listened. The cereal was sweet, good, like candy, and the milk was filling. I lapped it up. I had a desperate hungry craving. I kept pouring it in and feeding my face fast as I could. He hardly noticed. He was off into his own mind.

"*BINH*," he popped his lips. "*BINH, BINH.*"

That was the sound of incoming fire exploding next to his head.

"Apple, Apple?"

"What Banana?"

"Over here, Apple!"

That was what he and his buddy, who King said was a Kentucky Boy, used to call each other, in code.

"How come you didn't just use names?" I asked between gulps. "What difference?"

"The enemy." He glared at me. He was getting into the fantasy. "They're a small people." He put his hand out at Howard's height. "Hard to see."

I sat back. My whole middle was comfortably soaked in milk.

"That's all right," he said, waving my imaginary pleading off. "Some other time. I don't really like to talk about it."

"All right," I said. "I understand. Let's play cards."

Anything to get his mind off all that fun he had missed in Vietnam. Anything not to think what might happen if the army caught up with me. What they did with the Lipsha Morrissey type I didn't want to ask. I just knew I didn't want to be a member of some fruit bowl in the jungle, not to mention of how they crazed your mind in training camp. Not for me.

There was a pack of cards on the windowsill, that window looking down into the sad gray patch of space. I thought perhaps they should have closed it off. That shaft went through all the way to the ground floor. You could hear ghostly doors slamming, voices in the entryway. It was supposed to be elegant once, but now the soft and threatful dusk of it gave me the creeps.

"Poker?"

"Yeah," I said.

"Five-card stud."

"Deuces wild."

I like the deuce wild. I like that puny little card becoming strategy.

We started playing. The dark came sifting gently down, so we put the lights on. The place seemed almost cozy when there wasn't any reason to have windows anyway. I was all full of milk and cereal like a good child. The meal had perked me up; Lynette made coffee, and although it tasted like dishwater run through a car battery, I sipped it gratefully. If this evening around the table, with King in a state of rare normality, was the most brotherly we'd ever get, I decided it was enough. One thing you'll notice. I did not let on I knew that both our backgrounds were sprung from the same source. And I hadn't asked about Gerry yet. I felt better keeping it to myself. For the moment, I didn't even care to flaunt that I belonged. Belonging was a matter of deciding to. Through many trials I had seen this to be true. I decided I belonged, whether or not King thought I did. I was a real kid now, or halfway real. I crimped myself an ace.

I'd had to learn the knack of cheating at cards when I worked as an attendant at the Senior Citizens. Otherwise they'd beat your hide. It wasn't cheating to them, anyway, just second nature. The games were cheerfully cutthroat vicious, and the meanest player of them all was Lulu. She'd learned to crimp, that is, to mark your cards with little scratches and folds as you play, when she started losing her eyesight. It was just supposed to keep her even in the game, she said. I learned to crimp from her before I ever knew she was my grandmother, which might explain why I took to it with such enormous ease. The blood tells. I suppose there is a gene for crimping in your strings of cells.

At any rate, I was getting to know the cards pretty good. I always like to keep my eye on where my jacks are going in the deck, because other people like to call the one-eyed jacks wild. I got a soft spot for the jack. The jack of hearts is me—who doesn't hold a sword in his hand, but a banana peel.

I raised King a moon. We wasn't playing for change but bits of cereal. There wasn't any change around and he was short on matches, so we used the marshmallow bits that came in the box. Stars were a hundred dollars, hearts fifty, moons were twenty, and the diamond was ten. The pieces of cereal themselves was all worth one. That's how it went. Every so often we would munch a little from the pot, to keep us going.

He took me with a full, swept the marshmallows to his side,

and threw them one by one in his mouth. We started over again. In the next room there was some show on with lots of guns burping. I wondered how to bring up Gerry.

Again, I decided to take the bull by the teeth. King was dealing.

"So you knew Gerry Nanapush when you was both in Stillwater," I said.

The cards spurted evenly from his hands. He didn't miss one.

"Oh *Ger*," he said with an awkward boasting laugh. "We were like this."

He put the last of his cards down, and held up his first two fingers, clenched together.

"That is, we were buddies until those asshole Winnebagos started spreading rumors about me."

"Oh?" I tried leading him. I was out of stars and betting hearts.

But he wasn't going to get no further into that. I waited a little while before I tried anything else.

"Well is it true," I said, "they have him in maximum security with the real big-time criminals?"

"Not that I heard," King said, for sure now uncomfortable. "I heard he's back in Mandan. It's . . . not all that secure."

King pouted his cheeks and pushed his moons over.

I asked him if he thought Gerry had really killed that smokey or was it pinned on him the way so many people said after the trial.

"I really wouldn't know," was all King muttered.

I wished he would have told me, because that's one thing I really wondered now that Gerry was my father. Had he really cut a living man down? I wanted to know what kind of seed I had sprung from. The television guns were chattering. We played in silence, and it came to me after a while that something was definitely wrong and agitating King. A couple of times he blurted bits of a tuneless song as though he was keeping his mind from touching a sore subject. He lit his Marlboros one off the other's end, and sometimes left two burning in an ashtray. He couldn't have been so deeply absorbed in a game where the stakes was a bowl of cereal, so I had to wonder what was wrong. I had a clue it was related to my questioning him on Gerry. After that, I'd had trouble letting him win a single game.

Long about nine he got to really looking jumpy. He was wiping beads of sweat off his upper lip, biting on his thumb. Finally he got it out he wanted to go in the next room, catch the news. So we quit playing. Lynette was curled up on the couch underneath an old coat, and the boy Howard was sitting rigid in the chair. Newsbreak came on, sure enough, and that's when I had my inkling of what was bothering King, what was strange here all along, maybe even why he was on the wagon.

He had to keep his wits about him.

The newscaster was talking. "Federal criminal Gerry Nanapush escaped while being transferred to the North Dakota State Penitentiary. He is believed to be at large in the tri-state region. Nanapush is six feet, four inches and weighs three hundred and twenty pounds. He was last seen wearing a ripped black nylon jacket, jeans, and a pair of white leather running shoes with red stripes. Nanapush may be armed and should be considered dangerous."

I whooped. "Treat with caution! Handle with care! Armed and dangerous Chippewa!"

I looked at King. "Can't keep an Indian down!" I said. "Right on brother!"

That was when I noticed King and Lynette weren't laughing or excited in the least. They said, "Shut up," in unison and turned back to the television. I was hardly bothered though. I couldn't have cared less. I only cared that I'd known that this was happening and now it was happening. All signs pointed to it.

For hours we sat as if paralyzed, there in the blue smoke

wreaths and fissures of drifting dust. I was happy in the television radiance. They were not. All four of us were waiting, though, for what happened next.

I was listening past the shows, past the noise and jingles, as hard as I could. That is why I heard. I was not surprised. I heard it clear with my extra special sense. Down on the first floor a door shut softly. Steps paused at the bottom of the skylight shaft. There was a delicate scrabbling of mice beneath the stars, and a foothold was suddenly gained. In my mind's eye I saw him spring into the close air. The copper pipes bowed outward in his hand. The hot ones, wrapped in asbestos, ringed or joined every three feet, led up the inside of the dusk-filled hollow shaft. I didn't have to look down the fake window in order to know he was climbing. I thought the whole building must have heard.

I thought so, but when I glanced over at King and Lynette they were still gazing slack-jawed into the ions like their futures was prefigured in the flashing shapes. They didn't blink when he knocked an ashtray off the windowsill in the kitchen. They didn't start when his tender footsteps slid along the warped floor. Only when he stood, enormous, gentle, completely blocking the silvery rays, only when he pointed his hand at them like a gun, did they stop drifting and bunch themselves in sense. Their shapes detached from the couch even as the boy's shape flattened into the chair. I looked down at the man's feet. They glowed, mushroom pale in the dark. The cushioned jogging soles were so radiant and spongy he seemed to float softly toward us.

3.

The famous Chippewa who had songs wrote for him, whose face was on protest buttons, whose fate was argued over in courts of law, who sent press releases to the world, sat down at the dirtiest kitchen table in Minnesota with his son and his cellmate, and picked up a deck of cards.

A marked deck.

For the marked men, which was all of us.

I was marked for pursuit by authority as was my father, but King was marked in another entire way. As Gerry explained in a quiet voice that had no business to issue from a bulk that could scarcely squeeze between the table and the wall, King was a squealer, an informer. He'd got Gerry's confidence and then betrayed it.

"I'm trusting," Gerry said to me, shaking his head, blinking his mild eyes, "especially of all my Indian relations. I confided to him all my plans to escape once, never knowing he was an apple."

That is: red on the outside, white on the inside.

"Your friend here, this King Kashpaw, was the King of Stoolies."

I looked at King. Here was a man you could call sick with one quick glance. His face was gray as lead, his eyes was darting side to side, his lips looked numb. He kept on licking them with dry clucking sounds. Gerry had maneuvered things so King sat between us, hedged in, at the back of the wall behind the little pile of Lucky Charms.

"Why don't you eat them," he said to King. "You'll need it."

"Luck of the Irish. See where it got them," I said.

Gerry looked at me and raised his eyebrows.

"What's your name?" he asked.

"I'm Lipsha Morrissey."

His slant black brows stayed up. His long hair was pulled back in a tail, and his thin black moustache hung down his lip, so that his teeth flashed out only when he grinned very broad. His grin flashed now, wolf white and sharp, in his big placid face. Until he grinned like that he looked asleep. Suddenly he tossed his hair back and bust out laughing. He laughed a good long time. It was a loud joyful comforting sound to Lipsha Morrissey, but to King and Lynette it must have been harrowing. The way he laughed, and then the slow method his eyes took me in by notches, when he was back to himself again, gave me reason to believe that he knew whose son he looked at. I was certain, at any rate, that he was my dad. His nose was even bigger than mine, but squashed in the same places. It was his hands that had really tipped me off.

All the time he'd been talking, grinning, even laughing, they had the cards playing in and out of their fingers. They had a life all unto themselves that was spent in knowledge of the cards, and I knew just what gave them that knowledge. He had a form of the touch. Behind the bars, though, he hadn't much chance to use it on humans. So his hands had poured their talents into understanding the decks. He cast his eyes down every once in a while, briefly, to see the face that his hands were memorizing. His fingers moved around the paper edges, found the nail nicks. His wolf smile glinted. There was a system to the crimping that he recognized. Those crimps were like a signature—his mother's. I'd only learned Lulu's system, not restyled it.

"She taught me," I said.

He only nodded, and his teeth showed again.

He looked at King, who was staring across the room. King's eyes were locked with Lynette's, and hers were paralyzed. She was squeezing Howard on the points of her bosom. The boy was saying over and over with monotonous grit, "Let me down. Let me down. Let me down."

"Let him down," said Gerry.

Instantly she dropped her arms. The boy landed in a pile of flop hair and poking limbs. He got up, brushed his T-shirt off, and went back to sit by the television. Lynette moved backward slowly until her rear end met the edge of the sink. She simply parked herself there. Her mouth formed a little bruised O. Her eyes were wild and wary as a rat's. It was the first time I'd ever seen her with no words for what was going on.

"I'm interrupting here," said Gerry. "Please excuse my butting in without knocking." He knocked on the table now. "Deal me in?"

"We were playing five-card stud."

"Stud. That's not quite appropriate for this one here," he said smoothly, indicating King. "Five-card punk's more like it." King smiled a sick, tight grin and took up his hand of cards.

"Tell your wife to take her knuckles off that dirty frypan which she means to sling at my head," Gerry calmly continued.

Lynette took her hand out of the sink with a little squeak and rushed past us. We heard her pick up the phone in the next room then slam it down again. Presumably the lines was no longer properly connected.

"We must decide," said Gerry seriously, taking a ragged toothpick from his breast pocket and sticking it in his mouth, "what we are playing for."

King felt much better, or seemed to, when he glanced at his cards.

"I got money," he said. "I got money in my account."

"We're not playing for your rubber check," Gerry said. "You probably used your payoff up by now. We won't play for money. But we got to play for something, otherwise there's no game."

King sat there bracing up his shoulders. He was coming back to his own.

"Aw c'mon," he said. "Who told you I turned evidence. I never did."

"I heard the tapes," said Gerry, with a pursed smile full of snake's milk. "Tapes of things I told nobody but you, my friend. Yes, we got to play for something. We got to have high stakes, otherwise there is no game."

"What did you come here for?" blurted King. He tried to laugh but he had to put his cards down to hide his shaking hands. "Whaddyou want?"

"I want to play," said Gerry very clearly and slowly, as if to a person who spoke a different language. "I came to play."

I had been sitting there, just listening.

"Let's play for the car," I said to King. "Let's play for the Firebird you bought with June's insurance."

At the mention of my mom, Gerry's face got stiff around the edges.

"June's insurance," he said wonderingly. I could see how his mind leapt back, making connections, jumping at the intersection points of our lives: his romance with June. The baby given to Grandma Kashpaw. June's son by Gordie. King. Her running off. Me growing up. And then at last June walking toward home in the Easter snow that, I saw now, had resumed falling softly in this room.

I could tell Gerry had not come here with precise notions on revenge, even though the testimony King gave had cost him years. Gerry Nanapush was curious and plagued by memory. He'd come here out of these. Only the urge to see the rat's life with his own eyes could have caused him to scale copper pipes four stories up and squeeze through that small kitchen window. Only that curiosity and the urge to see someone again, or the hint of someone, the resemblance of June, could have brought him.

Now, however, dream and curiosity had found their reason.

There was the car, June's car, which was a route of clean escape. If Gerry won the car, I knew I'd stay there and keep King strict company until my father managed to cross the border into Canada.

"Let's play for the car," Gerry agreed. "June's car."

But King didn't want to play for the car.

"It's mine," he said.

"No, it's really June's," explained Gerry. "Any one of us could be keeping it for June."

"You don't get it," said King. There was a struggle going on inside him, the sense of what her car meant to him rising through a deep unwilling fog. But in the end he couldn't voice what he felt.

"It's not fair," he muttered. "Just ain't fair."

"What is fair?" Gerry picked up the cards, shuffled, dealt them out again. "Society? Society is like this card game here, cousin. We got dealt our hand before we were even born, and as we grow we have to play as best as we can."

We picked our cards up.

"Well this really ain't fair," said King. "This is ridiculous." His neck was swelling up slightly, showing big veins. "By God," he said, "this ain't no way to treat an American vet! I never dodged it like you." He nearly spat in vexation. But Gerry's teeth just showed, crooked and gleaming white.

"Glad I didn't have to go," he said. "They couldn't pay me enough to commit their murders."

He sighed and raked the cards back into his palms.

"If it helps," he said to King, "don't think of it as losing a car but as saving your own snitching neck."

King went all rigid. Gerry was already serving two consecutive life sentences. He'd have to die and be resurrected twice before he'd quit the joint.

"Deal and call," King said in a choked voice. "Deal five and show."

Gerry shoved the deck across the table to me and nodded that it was my deal. His face was cool and serene, like the pictures of those Chinese gods. So I shuffled carefully. I saw the patterns of it happen in my mind. I dealt the patterns out with perfect ease, keeping strict to Lulu's form.

I dealt a pair to King.

Gerry got a straight.

And myself? I dealt myself a perfect family. A royal flush.

We turned our hands over, showing them, and then there was a long strained pause.

"I'll take the keys," I said.

Gerry was rubbing his chin, a silent study.

King took a long time working the keys off the ring. As he did so I took a deep breath and glanced up at my father.

"I'll drive," I said, "wherever you want to go."

King threw the keys down, but I never heard them hit the table. I never heard them because between the throwing and the landing there was a thud on the door.

"Open up! Police!"

Now it was me paralyzed. The room went whirling. Awful fear of being trapped squeezed my middle. It was even worse than I ever imagined. I heard them tramping in the entryway and their voices echoing in the air shaft. I heard their booming voices, gravel clicking in their holsters, the champing at the door of the steel harnesses at their belts, and in my mind I saw their raw red hands forming in fists.

For what seemed the longest time, we sat there stiff as bricks.

Then someone moved. It was Howard. He came running from the next room on his toothpick legs.

"Hold on! I'm coming," he yelled. "He's here!"

The boy ran to the door, fumbled with the catch that was placed too high for him, screaming all the time, "He's here! He's here!"

And how the boy had changed—gone from being a playground of flickering shadows to old age. He was suddenly a tiny, lined, gray grown-up who threw himself in concentration up to the latch, screaming the name of his father.

And you know, that was what scared me most. Him screaming his own dad's name.

"King's here! King's here!"

I sat there like a lump on a log. This was it, I thought, this was the wages of everything we done. This was the wages of the father meeting up with the son and the ghost of a woman caught in the dark space between them. This was the wages. This was the sad fact.

I couldn't linger too long on sad facts though, for Howard finally got them in. He stood there wheezing and crying and pointing at King. I thought the police would leap across the table and collar Gerry, then tie me up, and I had just mustered up the courage to get arrested with a decent struggle when I noticed that the state police were still standing in the door. It hadn't taken more than a quick look-see through that apartment for them to ascertain that Gerry wasn't there.

I whirled around.

He was gone. Vanished. He'd been hoisted from his chair into thin space. There was nothing but air where my dad had been. My lips formed his name, but I never said it aloud. To this day I think he laid a finger beside his nose and went flying up the air shaft. That's the only thing possible.

The police were mumbling. King was answering.

"Sorry for bothering you, sir," they said. "Have a good evening."

And then they shut the door and we were left there. It all happened so fast we felt stunned flat. I didn't even have time for relief that they never asked about me. Howard was laying on the floor, stretched out, still as death. I knew he was playing dead. I would have in his shoes. I picked him up and I put him under the coat on the couch. It was a woman's coat, an old plaid thing with one sleeve ripped loose and the lining split. It still held a sweet, fresh whiff of perfume. I smelled the woman's comfort as I tucked the collar up around his neck.

"It's okay," I said. "You lost your head a minute. Go on and cry."

But there was no tears. He lay there stiff and watchful, ready for the hurt. The sense in his black eyes already had retreated to an unknown depth.

"The registration," I said to King. "The fucking registration."

Lynette lurched to the bread box; her teeth were chattering. She messed around among some crumpled papers and dried bread heels, and finally came up with the form. She put it on the table and made him sign it. I grabbed the keys. I folded the paper, put it in my pocket, and then I quit them without a word.

4.

The car was stove-in on the right bumper so that one headlight flared off to the side. I had seen there was nicks and dents in the beautiful finished skin. I ran my hand up the racy invert line of the hood as I drove the tangled highways in a general homeward direction. I had the windows open, needing good fresh air. I was free as a bird, as the blue wings burning on the hood. Night was gentle and flowing swiftly to either side. The buzzing yellow arc lamps of the city were soon left behind, and the air began turning bold and sweet with the smells of melting earth. I thought I'd drive straight through the night, cleaving the soft wet silence with my peacefulness. I thought I would never quit driving, it felt so good. I had a full tank and I was buzzed up with Lynette's coffee and the power of events. I knew my dad would get away. He could fly. He could strip and flee and change into shapes of swift release. Owls and bees, two-toned Ramblers, buzzards, cottontails, and motes of dust. These forms was interchangeable with his. He was the clouds scudding over the moon, the wings of ducks banging in the slough, he was . . .

I was waxing eloquent in my mind when all of a sudden the back end started knocking. I slowed down and it got louder, so I speeded up again and it got quiet. I thought it must be the jack not properly secured in the trunk. What else would I think? I started waxing off again. But then the knocking would start up, so I'd have to bear down and speed. It finally got me to the point where it was disrupting my concentration to make a sense of things. I didn't want to stop, but I thought I'd have to just pull over and tie the jack in tight. So I stopped, and soon as I did I knew there was something strange going on, because the knocking started up fast and furious.

I jumped out, not knowing what on earth to think. I thought there was some animal trapped inside there. I wouldn't put it past King to throw a dog or something in his back trunk. The night was so dark. I didn't know that it might not spring for my throat, so I held the key out very ginger when I put it in the trunk latch. I turned the key and jumped back. The hood sprang up.

I couldn't tell what was in there, but it was sure big, and loud—gulping, sighing, half gagging. I finally figured out that it was human, and rushed to drag the body out. As soon as he could speak, of course, I knew it was by a miracle none other than Gerry Nanapush. He was curled up tight as a baby in its mother's stomach, wedged so thoroughly inside it took a struggle to get him loose.

"I just about bought it there," he gasped when he was free, sitting on the side of the ditch. "I never realized I'd get so low on air."

I just couldn't completely register what was happening. After a while he straightened out and took a little brush from his pocket and put his hair back smooth and sleek in its tail. There was a sharp sweat on him. I realized how scared he had been, and when I opened the car door, I put a hand on his shoulder to guide him in. These things had took their toll. He couldn't talk for a long time, so we let the road take us along.

It was miles and miles before he roused himself to ask if I would take the next right-hand turn I came to and drive until I hit

Canada. He said he'd be obliged if I could let him off near the border.

"I got a wife and little girl up there," he said. "I'm going to visit them."

"You're gonna make it this time," I said. "Home free."

"No," he said, stretching his arms out, evidently feeling better, "I won't ever really have what you'd call a home."

He was right about that, of course. I'd never seen. He could not go back to a place where he was known and belonged. No matter where he settled down he would always be looking behind his shoulders. No matter what, he would always be on the run. We talked a good long time about the reservation then. I caught him up on all the little blacklistings and scandals that had happened. He wanted to know everything about Lulu, his mom, so I told him how she'd started running things along with Grandma Kashpaw. I told him how she'd even testified for Chippewa claims and that people were starting to talk, now, about her knowledge as an old-time traditional.

"Times do change," Gerry laughed. "She was always damn good in front of an audience."

"She had her picture in the paper in Washington," I said.

"I saw it." He was silent. I guess he missed her pretty bad.

After miles of driving I asked.

"Did you know June?"

That question took him altogether by surprise. We were driving the small roads, the less traveled and less well kept. The dark was vast and thick. I had to drive slower and more careful than before.

After a moment Gerry said he knew June, way back when. A little while after that he blurted out, "Hell on wheels! She was really something . . . so beautiful."

"You sound like you was in love with her," I promptly said.

"In love with her like everybody else," he told me. "I know she burned out young. I heard that. But I always keep seeing her the way she was at the time of my first incarceration."

"Slim."

"But not *too* slim. Long legged. Always with a nice, a really nice laugh, but she was a shy one. So far away sometimes you couldn't touch her."

"She had a streak maybe, an odd streak."

"I don't know about that. She liked order. We'd live in motels. She would always arrange the room real neat, put everything away, make the bed every morning even though they'd strip it that afternoon."

"Something I can't remember," I said; "did she have nice fingers?"

"Nice!" he said. "She had the prettiest damn fingers in the world!"

"I was wondering," I said, "if you killed that trooper."

If I tell you he said *no*, you will think he was lying. You will think a man don't get two consecutive life sentences for nothing beneath the U.S. judicial system. You'll keep thinking that, too, unless you happen to rub against that system on your own. Then things will astonish you. I promise they will.

If I tell you he said *yes*, and relate to you how it all happened, it might get used against him. I'm sorry but I just don't trust to write down what he answered, yes or no. We have entered an area of too deep water.

Let's just say he answered: "That's the penetrating mystery of it. Nobody knows."

I could feel him looking over at me a long time after speaking. I concentrated on steering us very straight and put the heater on. Up until then, I hadn't really noticed how cold it was.

"Enough about me anyhows," he said. "What's your story?"

I told him all the things about me which I owned up to: how I had quit school for the betterment of my mental powers, and learned on my own; how I was took on early by the Kashpaws and remained on the rez to look after the elder ones. I believe that my home is the only place I belong and was never interested to leave it, but circumstances forced my hand. I mentioned the one girl I ever trusted, Albertine. I told how she was a sister to me.

"I knew her too," said Gerry. "Kind of quiet."

"She was?" I never thought of her like that.

"You're one hell of a card player," Gerry complimented.

"Oh." I got shy that I had outdealt him. "You must have played a lot in prison."

"There's nothing else to fool with."

Suddenly I blurted out, "I'm running from the army police."

"Oh, that's your problem! That's your problem! I knew you had a problem!" He started smacking his big knee and shifted around in the bucket seat. He seemed excited.

"Then we're both as good as cons."

"That's the damn truth," I agreed.

But somehow, since we were splitting up, that did not give me a whole lot of consolation. He slapped his fist a couple of times in his palm and laughed, shaking his head. Suddenly he caught his breath and halted.

"You couldn't have took your physical yet."

I said I hadn't.

"You don't need to worry about the army," he said, dropping his hands in his lap. "I'm glad."

I glanced over at him. But he wasn't looking at me and he wasn't moving at all. His head was turned. Evidently he was watching the same dark scenery that unrolled about us endlessly—spring's empty fields, standing water, and the signs of human life, the yard lamps, so modest and few and far between.

"Look here," he said. "I didn't have to go in the army because my heart is slightly fucked. It goes something like *ti-rum-ti-ti* instead of *ta-dum*."

"Oh," I said. "Lucky for you."

"Lucky for you too."

I kept on steering.

"You're a Nanapush man," he said. I could feel him looking at me. I could feel the soft, broad, serious weight of all his features. "We all have this odd thing with our hearts."

He put a hand out and touched my shoulder.

There was a moment when the car and road stood still, and then I felt it. I felt my own heart give this little burping skip.

So many things in the world have happened before. But it's like they never did. Every new thing that happens to a person, it's a first. To be a son of a father was like that. In that night I felt expansion, as if the world was branching out in shoots and growing faster than the eye could see. I felt smallness, how the earth divided into bits and kept dividing. I felt the stars. I felt them roosting on my shoulders with his hand. The moon came up red and warm. We held each other's arms, tight and manly, when we got to the border. A windbreak swallowed him up. I didn't want my lights to show, so I cruised for miles and miles in the soft clear moonlight, slow, feeling the comfortable dark behind me and before.

I didn't turn the headlights on until I hit the highways. Near dawn, I came to the bridge over the boundary river. I was getting pretty close to home now, so I stopped the car in the middle of the bridge, got out to stretch, and for some reason I remembered how the old ones used to offer tobacco to the water. I looked down over the rail.

It's a dark, thick, twisting river. The bed is deep and narrow. I thought of June. The water played in whorls beneath me or flexed over sunken cars. How weakly I remembered her. If it made any sense at all, she was part of the great loneliness being carried up the driving current. I tell you, there was good in what she did for me, I know now. The son that she acknowledged suffered more than Lipsha Morrissey did. The thought of June grabbed my heart so, but I was lucky she turned me over to Grandma Kashpaw.

I still had Grandma's hankie in my pocket. The sun flared. I'd heard that this river was the last of an ancient ocean, miles deep, that once had covered the Dakotas and solved all our problems. It was easy to still imagine us beneath them vast unreasonable waves, but the truth is we live on dry land. I got inside. The morning was clear. A good road led on. So there was nothing to do but cross the water, and bring her home.

LOUISE ERDRICH grew up in North Dakota and is of Chippewa and German-American descent. She is the author of a book of poetry, *Jacklight*, and three internationally bestselling novels: *Love Medicine*, *The Beet Queen*, and *Tracks*. Her work has been honored by prizes from the National Book Critics Circle, the American Academy of Arts and Sciences, and the *Los Angeles Times*, and has been translated into more than a dozen foreign languages. She lives in New Hampshire with her husband/collaborator, Michael Dorris, and their children.